Praise for
The Farwalker's Quest

2011-2012 Missouri Truman Award Nominee
2010 Bank Street Best Book
2010 Crystal Kite Finalist
2009 Cybils Award Finalist

"Joni Sensel writes like a dream—her language, her settings, and her humor make a great read. Ariel's world—part dystopia and part Eden—could be the future or it could be the past, but it is still all unique and compelling."
—Karen Cushman, Newbery Award winner

"Absorbing fantasy... Crisp dialogue, an exciting plot, and strong secondary characters."
—*Kirkus Reviews*

"This is a solid and well-paced fantasy in which the journey is more important than the conclusion... The theme of finding and accepting one's true calling resonates."
—*School Library Journal*

"At once elegant and lyrical, while also offering an intensely paced and action-driven plot."
—*Bulletin for the Center for Children's Books*

Other books for young readers by Joni Sensel

The Farwalker's Quest
The Timekeeper's Moon

The Humming of Numbers
Reality Leak

www.jonisensel.com

THE SKELETON'S KNIFE

JONI SENSEL

Published by Dream Factory Books
Enumclaw, Washington, USA

Editor: Margaret Miller
Cover Art & Design: Kirsten Carlson

Summary: When 14-year-old Ariel Farwalker sets out to return a dead
enemy's knife to its source, she lends strength to an evil that seeks
her attention. Aided by a new friend with a smuggler's savvy and
a talent for charming the wind, she must travel to the land of the
dead to save someone she loves and bury both the knife and the
past. If she fails, neither she nor her most beloved friends will survive.

ISBN-13: 978-0-9701195-4-4 • ISBN-10: 0-9701195-4-2

For all who imagine—or remember—
the far side of the bridge

The wind plucked at a hat lying among snow-dusted stones. A coyote, drawn by the scent of decay, had dragged it away from the dead man who'd worn it. Rodents had chewed what the coyote left, and rain and the passage of time had sped rot. Yet the hat held its shape, so the wind recognized it and understood how this hat might be used.

The leather fluttered and rose. Like a misshapen kite, the hat sailed down the mountainside, over the meadows toward Tree-Singer Abbey.

CHAPTER

1

Ariel Farwalker did not want to find another
squashed bug in her boot. When her toes struck a
lump as they slid past the laces, she jerked her foot back out
with a squeak. The invader was probably only a pebble, but
she couldn't forget the crushed spider on her sock a few
days ago.

Nace Kincaller, sitting beside her on the hearth bench,
looked up with concern from the crow perched on his wrist.
He'd been feeding it scraps of fried egg from his breakfast,
but now his green eyes and the bird's tarry black ones
focused on Ariel's face.

"It's nothing. I'm just jumpy." Ariel checked her wool
sock—no dead spider. "But tell your crawling friends to stay
in the woodpile. I put my boots on the hearth overnight to
dry them, not to give bugs somewhere cozy to sleep."

With a flick of his forearm, Nace tossed the crow to a
rafter. He tipped Ariel's boot cautiously over the floor. An
almond-sized bone tumbled out, pale on the flagstone.

Ariel groaned. "I should have known."

Nace fought a grin, but he raised his face to the bird and shook his head sternly.

The crow mimicked him, shaking its head in response.

"Don't bother. It's hopeless." Stuffing her foot into her boot, Ariel picked up the bone.

"Another one, huh?" Zeke Stone-Singer stood in the Great Room's doorway, still munching a leftover biscuit. No matter how much he ate, the long lines of his body never rounded. "What's this, nine or ten?"

"Twelve." Ariel was waiting for a thirteenth bone, but she didn't want to admit it, at least not to Zeke. He would scoff at her plan for these bones.

This latest was yellowed and knobbed on both ends. It had lain in her boot like a toe lost from its foot. That notion was startling. Most of the bones were the length of fir or pine needles, and she'd assumed they'd belonged to some weasel or rabbit before being delivered to her by the crow. Now she realized her growing collection might have come from a much larger creature.

As she fingered the bone, Nace touched her cheek. Ariel turned her face to his hand with a smile. Although he was mute, silence never pushed them apart, and often their skin served them better than words.

"Go ahead," she told him. "We'll catch up outside."

He nodded and rose for the doorway. The crow dropped to ride on his shoulder, feathers blending with the dark hair that fell past his jaw. As Nace crossed the room, Zeke stepped inside, and Ariel noticed the careful space between the young men as they passed. She sighed.

Zeke offered a bite of his biscuit.

"No, thanks." She waggled the bone. "If I get hungry, I'll have this to gnaw on."

"Ha! Looks to me like it's already picked clean."

"Yeah, so why does that dumb bird keep bringing them to me? It's not like a squirrel hoarding nuts to eat later."

Zeke's grin slipped and his pale eyes drifted from hers. "Are you sure Nace isn't telling it to?"

Fighting a flare of impatience, Ariel shook her head. "He didn't make friends with the crow until after it brought five or six. And he's tried to convince it to leave me alone. It just won't obey him like some creatures do."

Doubt remained on Zeke's narrow face, but he shrugged. "Then it likes you, I guess. Can't blame it for that. My mother's cat used to bring her dead snakes, remember? It's a gift. Enjoy it."

Frowning, Ariel stuffed the bone in her pocket. Later she'd drop it into the jar where she kept the others. "I'm not so sure it's a gift. Crows are bad omens."

Zeke snorted. "Winter's getting to you—you're not usually superstitious. I'm surprised you haven't strung the bones into a bracelet."

"I've been too busy dodging black cats. Never mind." She rose. "Where's Ash?"

"Meeting us in the woodshed."

Ariel had lived within the abbey's stone walls for weeks before she'd realized the Tree-Singers had to burn trees. Her friends had to cook and warm the abbey somehow, and peat was uncommon so high in the mountains. One of their most important spring chores was gathering branches and trees that had blown down during winter.

Yet unless winter's storms had been especially rough,

deadfall wasn't enough. Each autumn, the Tree-Singers reaped several large trees in a solemn event they called The Falling. First they sang to their favorite trees to identify others that were willing to leave the world and thus to help the Tree-Singers survive one more year. For three days, the people regaled those trees, thanking them for their selfless gift. Then came the saws. Tears fell when the appointed trees dropped.

The sacrifice of those hallowed trees made the woodshed sacred. The lintel was decorated, the wood stacked with reverence, and the floor swept each morning. The axes and saws that hung on one wall were treated much as Ariel's mother, a healer, had treated her best knives and needles. Though old, they were kept razor sharp so their work was quick and humane. The grizzled master of Tree-Singer Abbey was sharpening a blade on a whetstone when Ariel and Zeke entered.

"Thank you for helping us, Ash," Ariel said. "I know some of the others don't think we should do this."

"I have reservations myself." Ash Tree-Singer's green robe swished as he turned. Above it his face was as wrinkled as the bark of a cedar. "But when you found the Vault here, hidden under our floor, I knew our lives would change, and I rejoiced nonetheless. We cannot hold the past, but only grow from it, like seedlings taking root in a decaying log. This is one of those sprouts, is it not?"

"Yes." Ariel had discovered a store of lost knowledge there at the abbey almost two years before. Wisdom and drawings for clever devices had been painted on the undersides of flagstones and then hidden from sight to protect the knowledge from people who would rather wipe

it away. The hiding spot was forgotten, but the rumor of
those secrets turned into a legend. Though many people
had searched for a lode of lost riches, buried away in some
kind of Vault, it had taken a Farwalker—Ariel—to find it.

Since then, she'd been guiding Storians and Allcrafts to
see it, and they'd begun working to decipher the symbols
and to build the mysterious tools drawn on the stones. Ariel
didn't usually pay much attention except to pitch in when
more hands were needed, but she had a special interest this
time.

"We're trying to make paper," she told Ash. "Like vellum,
but from plants instead of animal skins."

"I'm sure the goats will be happy to keep their skins on,"
said Ash. "But it seems to me that boiling wood will only
give you wood soup."

"It sounds strange to me, too," Zeke said. "But I checked
with the stone that bore this set of marks, and I'm sure
we're understanding them right. If it works, we could copy
all the stones in the Vault and people elsewhere could learn
from them, too."

"I could carry more of them on my farwalking trips,"
added Ariel. "I've used cloth, but it's bulky and we need it
for clothes."

Ash waved a gnarled hand. "You needn't convince me.
The cherry tree approves, if you'll proceed with respect. I
just hope paper works better than the steam wheel did."

"That flopped," Zeke admitted. "But the new water
system works good. Unless you *liked* breaking ice to draw
from the well."

Ash's white eyebrows jumped and his laughter displayed
a few missing teeth. "Great sap, I can't say so. Running

water is sweeter. Even if we did have to reap saplings to use as molds for the pipes." He frowned at the ax in his hand. "You won't harm any trees today, will you? Take only branches downed or broken by snow."

"Of course," Ariel said. "We just need chunks and shavings. We would have whacked up fire logs, if the supply wasn't so low." Winter had lingered, so the woodshed was practically empty. "We'll bring back everything in the goat cart, so not even needles or twigs are wasted."

"Very well." Ash handed Zeke the ax and two chisels. "Not that leaving the world is a terrible thing, for a tree or a person, when the timing is right. Life and death are not so far apart as they seem. That's one of the lessons of wintertime trees."

"Like stones," agreed Zeke, although he was the only one who could hear the voices of rocks.

Ariel felt the bone in her pocket and wondered if it, too, was less dead than it seemed. Uneasy, she thanked Ash again before they hurried outside.

The March sky was clear for the first time in weeks, and Ariel greeted it with her face upturned and glowing. She felt she'd been swaddled and cooped up for years. The snow, which had been almost endless that winter, had slid off the roof into mounds that were so tall they'd blocked the light from the windows, shrinking the days into drab shades of grey. The orange fire in the hearth and the yellow flames on candles had sometimes seemed the only color left in the world. Now, at last, the thawing sky had turned blue!

Nace and the goat cart waited near the front door, with two goats in harness. The rest of the herd had spread into the meadow, where they pawed through patches of snow to brown grass. The only other sounds were the trickling of snowmelt and a tentative chickadee's song.

Nace flashed his wide smile and looked to Ariel for direction. With cold biting her round cheeks, she led him and Zeke up the meadow, skirting patches of snow, toward a dark line of trees. They passed the new mill that used the wind to grind oats. Ariel hoped her paper would turn out as fine.

Zeke eyed the vanes turning in the breeze. "I bet we could use the mill to grind the wood smaller before we boil it."

"Good idea," Ariel said. "You're smart." Though she'd known him the whole fourteen years of their lives, he still sometimes amazed her.

A few paces later, Nace caught her hand as it swung at her side. His fingers tangled with hers, squeezed, and let go as if passing a secret. A warm weakness rushed through Ariel, followed by an ache to be in his embrace. That yearning felt wrong, though, with Zeke there beside her. She'd loved Zeke for longer, and she was all too aware she walked between the two boys.

Frozen moss and dead leaves crunched under their feet. Ragged caws drifted down from the scattered crows overhead, and Ariel's mind drifted back to the bones. She could find the thirteenth today. It might be waiting in her room even now, left by the crow in a pocket or corner.

"What's that?" asked Zeke.

Jarred from her thoughts, Ariel looked up. A dark circle rolled down the hillside, bouncing and lofting on the breeze. If it'd been below them, she might have mistaken it for a wheel lost from their cart.

"It looks like... leather?" said Zeke as it tumbled straight toward them.

Nace raced to meet it and leapt to snatch the brown shape from the air. He inspected it briefly, clapped it on his head, and hurried back to Ariel and Zeke with a grin.

Ariel's body recognized the hat before her mind did. A tremor went through her, and she gripped the edge of the cart. There was something wrong with that hat, worse than split seams and mold, and she found herself gasping for breath.

Nace pranced up, the tattered hat canted over one eye. Memory slapped Ariel.

"Take it off, Nace." She tried to keep her voice steady. When he tipped the hat to her and set it back into place, she cried, "Get it off!"

Zeke didn't wait. He grabbed the hat and flung it to the ground.

Nace stiffened but looked to Ariel. Clutching both hands to her chest, she tried not to feel as though someone she loved had been tainted by someone she'd hated.

"That was Elbert's hat," Zeke said. They stared at its dented, warped leather.

Ariel had told Nace where she'd gotten the scars on her cheek and forearm. She'd described being kidnapped from her home by the sea, how Zeke had helped her escape, and what had become of her worst enemy. But she'd never shown Nace just where Elbert had died, in another high meadow some miles above, nor mentioned the hat he had worn.

Nace winced and moved to console her.

Zeke was closer. He wrapped an arm around Ariel and drew her away. "It's rotting cow skin," he told her. "Nothing more."

She leaned into his side. Zeke had struggled beside her. He'd shared her pain. He'd also heard the voices of ghosts in their past, and he'd tell her if he heard one now.

"No ghost wearing it?" she asked, to be sure.

"No," he said firmly. "Just blown on the wind."

"All this way?"

"Even stones, which are heavy, can tumble a long way downhill."

Ariel nodded numbly and took a deep breath. Zeke was right. It was only a half-rotted hat. It had blown miles down the mountainside, but it wasn't alive, and Elbert Finder had left the world two years ago.

Nace trampled the hat into mud thawed by the sun. The vigor of his stomp gave her strength.

Ariel straightened out from under Zeke's arm. "Sorry. I didn't mean to crack like an egg. Let's get working. My hands are cold."

Nace grabbed her fists and cupped them in his palms, blowing warm breath through his fingers to hers. His eyes begged forgiveness. She managed a smile.

"It's nothing," she told him, convincing herself.

Then she remembered the bone in her pocket and the others she'd trapped in a jar. Small bones, they probably belonged to a marmot. Still, Elbert's hat had not fallen to bits. It lay near her feet, the crown crumpled but humped as if trying to lift itself from the mud. Elbert's skeleton might be intact, too, free for the picking by crows.

Forgetting the comfort of Nace's warm touch, Ariel tilted her face up the slope toward where Elbert had met his violent end. A person had more than two hundred bones—but even a big man had a few dozen small ones.

CHAPTER 2

Six blisters later, Ariel returned with her friends to the
abbey. All day they'd gathered wood and chopped
it to bits. Whittling sticks into shavings, Ariel also had
whittled at the foolish idea that Elbert's hat, like the bones,
had come on purpose to find her. Surrounded by things
that murmured of the past, it was hard not to tangle in
gloom.

Zeke's offer to grind wood like oats went untried. By
late afternoon, there wasn't enough wind blowing to turn
the mill's vanes. Nace shoveled twigs and bark into the
woodshed while Zeke and Ariel put their chips into the
abbey's largest cauldron and hauled it inside. She stirred
in water and ashes that she'd swept from a cold hearth
yesterday. The dust stung her nose. Zeke wrangled the pot to
the side of the fire, out of the way of anyone cooking. The
mess had to simmer until it smelled sweet and turned into
mush, which might take a couple of days.

"Have you still got that bone in your pocket?" Zeke asked.
"Remember a story called Bone Soup?"

"It's about making something from nothing. Everyone tosses in some worthless scrap and together they made a good soup." She wrinkled her nose. "I'm not throwing the bone in, if that's what you're thinking!"

"It might add some magic."

Ariel tipped her head. Zeke usually believed in more practical things.

His grin faded. "But I suppose it could ruin the paper."

"No, thanks," she said. "Ash might not let us try twice." Besides, Ariel had her own plans for the bone.

Sure enough, when she returned to her room after supper, a new bone awaited: number thirteen. The size of a twig, it sat on her pillow like a promise of nightmares. This time, no crow perched nearby to watch her reaction.

Ariel stared at the bone. Dread had replaced any anticipation. Still, fear had never deterred her. It wouldn't now.

She opened the worn trunk she used as a dresser and retrieved the clay jar that contained her collection. Settling on her straw mattress, she unlatched the lid. She dropped in the bone she'd discovered that morning and plucked the bone from her pillow, adding it, too. Then she flipped her pillow so her face wouldn't touch where the bone had rested.

Thirteen bones jumbled inside the jar. Ariel covered its mouth with one palm and shook it. The dry rattle gave her a shiver.

As a much younger girl, Ariel had watched Fishers cast albatross bones to foretell a catch or ill sailing. Her mother had scoffed, pointing out that the most ardent casters had been the least talented Fishers. Still, other Fishers whom

Ariel respected would not set to sea without checking the
bones. Now she had to wonder if these crow-given bones
might hold a portent for her. She wasn't sure she'd be
able to interpret their spill, but in the past two years, she'd
learned many symbols. Maybe the cast bones would form
one she knew.

Holding her breath, Ariel upended the jar. The bones
dumped onto the flagstone. They didn't tangle as she'd
expected. They fell evenly spaced and arranged themselves
neatly. Ariel's breath caught and hardened to a knot in her
chest. The shape could not be mistaken. Although gaps
spoke for a few that were missing, the bones had once
formed a hand, and now they did so again. She imagined it
rising and clutching her throat.

No! Ariel swept her own hand through the bones to
destroy their arrangement—to stop them from reaching
or curling into a fist. Unable to breathe, she scooped the
bones into the jar, shut it tight, and stuffed it into the
trunk, under her farwalking pack.

The sight of her pack cooled her panic. It reminded her
that she had faced worse threats than bones. Although not
yet fifteen, she'd defied evil men to become a Farwalker,
reviving a trade that had been completely wiped out. She'd
traveled to places that shouldn't exist and outwitted those
who had wanted to hurt her. She refused to let a crow's
garbage frighten her senseless.

Yet she couldn't sit still, given what she'd just seen.
Ariel jumped to her feet. Nace had gone to bed down the
chickens and goats, but he'd back soon. He'd toss the
whole jar in the privy for her, if she asked. She needn't tell
him she'd cast the bones or how they had fallen. Saying it

out loud would make it too real. She'd simply make sure they couldn't come back, and then she'd let Nace's eyes dash away other thoughts. Or perhaps it would not be his eyes that soothed her. Sometimes he spoke to her with his lips, without words but in a truer language they were learning together.

Boots scuffed in the hall. Eagerly Ariel swung her door open.

"Ariel?"

She tried to hide her disappointment. She should have known by the sound, since Nace always moved with a cat's silence and grace. Zeke shuffled his big feet at her doorway.

"Can I come in?"

A year ago, he would have barged in without asking, full of confidence in the knowledge that they were best friends. But things had changed since Nace had joined them at the abbey.

"Uh, sure." Her legs jittered.

"Is something wrong?"

She squirmed. "No. I... was about to go check our boiled wood. Want to come?" Nace would wait.

Zeke whisked his straw-colored hair from his eyes. "No. I wanted to make sure you were all right. You've been kind of... serious lately. Used to be, you would have laughed at the crow. And then today—I hope it won't give you nightmares."

Ariel shivered.

"You've already had nightmares?"

"Some." They'd been murky and vague, terrors felt more than seen, hands reaching from darkness to— Hands.

Her neck stiff, Ariel fought to keep her eyes off the trunk and the ghoulish thing hidden inside.

"Why didn't you tell anyone?" Zeke asked.

"I did." Hoping he'd drop it, she shrugged. Finally she had to add, "Nace."

Zeke's gaze fell to the floor. "Oh."

"I'm all right," Ariel said quickly. "Or I will be, if winter will end. Thanks for asking, though. I'm glad you were with us today."

Zeke nodded, but he didn't look up.

"I'm... going now," she said, easing past him.

Softly he said, "You don't talk to me anymore. Why not?"

"I talk to you all the time! We're talking now, if you haven't noticed." But she knew what he meant.

"Not real talking. What did I do?"

"Nothing," Ariel said. Defensive thoughts rose, though. Zeke had been cool to Nace from the start, and Ariel had felt forced to choose.

"Nothing." Zeke nodded sourly. "All I need for bone soup." He turned to leave.

Ariel couldn't bear his hurt tone. "Wait, Zeke. I'm sorry, I just..." She swallowed hard. If she cast the bones with him watching, would they fall in a meaningless pile? But if the hand formed again, she'd have more reason to fear. Besides, shouldn't Nace be the first to share her secrets? Except Nace had no understanding of Elbert, a threat from the past that only Zeke knew.

Zeke's scowl softened and he took an awkward step forward. "Come on, you got something to spice up my soup? You know the story. An old turnip? A beet?"

His humor won her. Ariel wanted to joke, too, but her voice wouldn't do it. "The bones the crow has been bringing—I think they're Elbert's."

Taken aback, Zeke asked, "Why?"

"They're bones from a hand, Zeke! Not some weasel or squirrel. A big hand. Look, I'll show you." She bent to fumble with her trunk, but her fingers wouldn't work right, and the words tumbling from her mouth seemed to get in the way. "It can't be chance. Can't be. He's coming after me somehow." She spun back to Zeke. "I don't know what to do!"

Zeke moved closer, his awkwardness gone. "No. They're probably from a bear or raccoon. Their paws are like hands, too. But that doesn't matter. Bones are the same as fallen tree branches—empty. *That's* nothing, Ariel. Throw them away. Elbert Finder is gone. He's been gone for almost two years."

"I know," she moaned. "But the crow keeps bringing them to me and not anyone else, like it's hauling the whole skeleton one bone at a time. And his hat today, too, finding its way down the mountain as if seeking a head—"

Zeke took her by both shoulders, halting the rush of her words. "Stop. He can't hurt you."

The firmness in his voice surprised her almost as much as his grip. As Zeke had carved out his unusual trade, he'd been growing more like the stones: solid and wise.

"Are you sure?" she asked. "Would the stones warn you about anything bad going on?"

A shadow passed over his face, and his fingers slid down her arms before he released her. "The stones tell me plenty I don't want to hear. But not about Elbert." He turned away.

"What's that mean?" She reached after him. "Zeke!"

He spun back to her, and they nearly collided. Off-balance, Ariel flung a hand to his chest. They ended so close she could smell his boy scent and feel the warmth of his breath. Silently Zeke gazed down at her, for he was nearly a foot taller now. The grey depths of his eyes made her dizzy.

"I miss you," he said softly.

"I— I'm right here."

He shook his head slowly. "Not like you used to be. Not like before. That's the trouble, not winter or Elbert. Things should be more like they used to be. Or, I don't know, maybe... maybe more..." His face tipped closer.

Her heart thumping, Ariel held still while confusion roiled in her. He felt so familiar. If his arms wrapped around her, he could steady them both. She ached for that comfort. Her other hand rose to his shoulder, but whether to bridge the space between them or fend him off, she didn't know.

Her hands knew. They circled his neck. She leaned closer and a plea floated out on her breath. "Zeke?"

But his name clunked in her ears, the wrong name for these feelings. Avoiding the brush of his lips, Ariel jerked away. Her arms yanked her hands back where they belonged.

Zeke winced and exhaled hard. "Right."

"What are you doing?" Ariel whispered, but the question was meant for them both.

"You let *him* kiss you, Ariel."

Embarrassment rose through her, followed by a spurt of anger. "How do you know? Is that what the stones tell you? And how is it any of your business, Zeke?"

He exploded into motion, his arms flapping, his feet stomping. "Why shouldn't it be mine? *You're* m— I mean..." He spun to pace left and right. "I thought... aw, I don't—"

Ariel made a choked sound. Nace stood at the open doorway. His approach had been soundless, and Zeke's body had blocked her view until now. She stood frozen. Then panic flowed through her, threaded with guilt—and more anger, this time at herself.

"Nace!" Her greeting came out too shrill, and she wondered how long he'd been there.

Long enough. Dismay and confusion clouded his features. He spread his hands in a gesture she knew meant *What do you want me to do?*

She scrambled toward him, but she couldn't resist a glance back. The bitterness on Zeke's face whisked away. The hope that replaced it was worse.

"Thank you for trying to make me feel better, Zeke." Ariel kept her voice low, hoping it wouldn't carry to Nace, although the Kincaller would likely hear her thought anyway. "And... I'm sorry. But I don't 'let' him do anything. I kiss *him.*"

At that, Nace strode in to her side, his hands clenched into fists. He ignored her tentative smile, glaring at Zeke. Although taller, Zeke was a year younger, and without the Kincaller's athletic strength.

"You've always been like my brother, Zeke," Ariel said quickly.

The tension in Nace did not ease. He gave Zeke a curt jerk of one thumb: *Get out.*

"She can speak for herself, if that's what she wants," Zeke retorted. "Unlike a Kincaller I know."

"Zeke!"

Nace lunged.

"Nace, no!" Ariel reached to stop him. Too late. Nace grabbed Zeke and shoved him hard toward the doorway. Zeke struck the doorframe and stumbled.

Ariel moaned. Zeke righted himself and stepped forward again.

"Hit me all you want," he told Nace. "We both know how she'll like that. And you wouldn't have to do it if you weren't worried about me."

Nace quivered. Not sure which conflicting impulse would win, Ariel clutched his arm. "Stop!"

He yanked from her grasp and spun to her, his hair flying. Ariel tried desperately to open her heart to him, because she knew he would trust what he sensed of her emotions more than anything she might say.

"He didn't mean to say what he did!" she cried. "Please don't fight. Zeke's my best friend! And yours, too."

Zeke snorted.

Ariel reached to soothe Nace. But whatever he heard of her thoughts didn't reassure him. He threw up his hands, shouldered past Zeke, and stalked out.

"Nace, wait!" Her words went unheeded.

"I shouldn't have made that crack about speaking," Zeke murmured.

"No, you shouldn't." Empathy ruined Ariel's anger. "Are you all right? That looked like it hurt."

"Not much." He shook his head, his denial soon turning to disbelief. "You kiss him."

Ariel sighed. "You don't get it, Zeke."

"No, I don't! But if you ever talked to me any more, you could tell me. Tell me! I'll listen. I'll even try to understand."

A longing hit Ariel so hard she could taste it, metallic and slick. Zeke could talk to her effortlessly in a way that Nace couldn't, and months had passed since they'd shared more than mealtime chatter. She imagined curling next to him on a bench and describing the shivery feeling that Nace stirred in her like a breeze.

Her heart balked. Such words seemed better saved for Nace and too cruel to hand Zeke. Besides, she no longer trusted Zeke—or herself—to just talk.

"No, I can't, Zeke," she whispered. "Not that." And even one subject they couldn't broach put a high wall between them.

He turned and slouched out in the opposite direction from the way Nace had gone.

Ariel stared at the empty hallway and wondered if she should go after Nace. A mutual apology took only one look. She could hold his hand and try to explain, and he would hush her lips with his fingers and nod. He was probably in the courtyard, staring up at the stars.

She lifted her winter cloak from its peg near the door. A bone tumbled out.

Ariel flinched. Replacing the cloak, she steeled herself and picked up the bone. It felt frail, dry and cool. She could almost hear Elbert's laugh vibrate through it. The evening's events would have pleased him.

Two winters had passed since he'd left the world, but his skeleton still must be sprawled in the rocks. One hand, or perhaps parts of two, would be gone. When she closed her eyes, Ariel could see the gleaming remains, the ribcage sprung like a half-woven basket, the empty skull grinning— grinning toward her. Grinning and plotting revenge.

Ariel snapped the bone, flung the halves into the hall, and slammed her door on the broken bone and both boys. She had no idea how to fix their jealous strife. But she did know a way to fix her problem with bones.

CHAPTER 3

Ariel did not light a candle. Dawn was still at least an hour away, and she didn't want to risk waking anyone with the glow. She hadn't slept—not with a dead hand in her room—but the abbey was silent. So she threw off her nightshirt and pulled on her clothes and her cloak by feel.

After grabbing her boots, she tiptoed from her room. The flagstones chilled her toes through her socks. The cold didn't numb her Farwalker instincts, though. Her feet led her toward the front door of the abbey without bumping her into any walls or corners.

A sense of being observed made her shiver as she crept through the dark halls. It must have been because she was sneaking, that's all. The empty eye sockets in Elbert's bare skull couldn't see for miles through walls in the dark. By the time the sun hit the high meadows, where the snow must be receding from his winter-bleached bones, Ariel hoped to be well up the hillside, climbing purposefully in the birdsong and breeze.

The only noise now was the faint buzzing of snores. Longing swept her as she passed the rooms where Nace and Zeke slept. She might have asked either to accompany her, but after the quarrel last night, a solo journey seemed best.

When she reached the great wooden door, Ariel bent to slip on her boots and tie them. Straightening, she lifted the latch. It clanked and the door swung agape. Cold air sliced inside as if awaiting the chance.

An arm thrust over Ariel's shoulder from behind her. A hand slapped the wood, shutting the door with a thump. Ariel cringed, sure the rest of Elbert's bones had already come.

"Where are you going at this hour, alone?"

"Oh!" She spun. Scarl Finder stood over her, little more than a tall shadow. She hadn't heard him glide up behind. Although his brown curls had been mussed by his pillow, his voice had no sleep about it. His arm remained firm alongside her head.

Ariel released a limp breath. "You scared me."

No smile lit Scarl's dark eyes or softened the angles of his face. "You ought to be scared, not of me, but of lions. They hunt in the half-light, and we've talked about that. Why are you ignoring my warning?"

Ariel opened her mouth, hoping an answer would fill it. The hungry yowling of mountain lions had disturbed several evenings of late, but she hadn't thought of earthly dangers at all. "I... I thought you meant sunset. I forgot about dawn. I don't want to be anyone's breakfast."

Her guardian relaxed slightly. Perhaps he'd expected an argument from her; she gave him one often enough. "You're not usually even awake before breakfast."

"You're not usually guarding the door." She'd been as silent as she knew how to be. "Did you hear me?"

"No. But I'd like an answer, so I'll ask again: Where were you going? Nace is still in his bed, so it must not have been to a tryst." His voice teetered between annoyed and amused.

Ariel shifted her weight. "My feet are restless, that's all. It's been too long since we traveled. I'm anxious to farwalk again."

"It has been a stifling winter," he agreed. "But I know you better than that. Either tell me what's roused you before sunup or go back to bed."

Ariel fought a habitual resistance to orders. Unlike most apprentices, she had no Farwalker master to teach her, so she'd grown used to figuring things out for herself. Besides, she wasn't certain how Scarl would react.

"You'll think it's silly," she said.

"Try me."

She looked at her hands, her fingers knotting together. "I need to see Elbert's bones. Make sure they're still there. And scatter them. Or bury them. Or something." Crushing them with a rock sounded more vengeful than she cared to admit.

"Not to honor them, surely. Are they giving you nightmares?"

She nodded. "And you know how that crow has been pestering me? Watch." She reached into her pocket. Last night, she'd knotted the bones into a sock to be lighter to carry. Untying the sock, she spilled them once more. The bones landed neatly in the shape of a thumb and spread fingers.

"I haven't seen any ghost," she murmured, staring at

the hand on the floor, "but it feels like he's grabbing at me from out of the world." Hearing her own quavering voice, Ariel made a face and prepared to return to her room. Scarl wouldn't scoff, not after prying the reason from her, but he'd probably assure her the bones' shape could somehow be explained, or at least that a long trip up the mountain was foolish. She'd have to slip out later, unseen.

"Let me get my coat." Scarl's expression was somber. He crouched to sweep the bones into his fist. "And something to fend off sharp teeth. I don't think a lion would try two together, but we'd better be ready, in case."

"You'll climb up there with me?" She was torn between relief and dismay. By accepting her fears, Scarl had validated them.

"I killed him, didn't I?" He took the sock from her. "The least I can do is help you put him to rest, however you need to do it."

Although grateful for his answer, Ariel looked away. They rarely spoke of the day Scarl had saved her life by finishing Elbert's. It reminded them both of a time when she hadn't considered Scarl a friend, let alone the closest thing she had to a father.

"It'll take us all day," she said. "That's why I got up so early."

"I haven't forgotten the place any more than you have."

Something in his tone caught Ariel's ear. "Have you had nightmares, too?"

His expression remained neutral as he chose how to answer. That alone told her.

"Not for the same reasons, I expect. I'll be right back." He turned toward the heart of the abbey and glanced over his shoulder. "You know I'll catch up if you head off without me, don't you? Except then I'll be angry."

She tried to smile. "You, angry? Never." But she added, "I won't." She wanted his companionship, but she would have been helpless to stop it regardless. As a Finder, he could track her unerringly. And though he suffered a limp from an old injury, Scarl's long strides still moved faster than hers.

Ariel stepped outside while she waited. The dawn breeze, crisp with the smell of snow, riffled her bangs and nipped at her ears. The sky had gone grey while she and Scarl had talked, so the nearby peaks stood out against it. Clumps of snow shone in the hollows, defying spring's efforts to melt them. Ariel pulled her cloak tighter and hoped ice wouldn't hamper her search for white bones. Out here in the awakening world, though, her fears held less weight. Even if much larger bones appeared next, no skeleton could stand up to stalk her. It wouldn't need the crow if it could.

When Scarl joined her, he brought the walking stick that helped him offset his limp, but also a metal poker from the hearth.

"What's that for?" she asked.

"I've got my staff and my knife." The latter hung at his hip. He gave her the poker. "You carry this. In case I'm feeling too lazy to battle any lion that jumps us."

She scowled. "It's heavy." She'd rather complain than imagine its use as a weapon—especially if Scarl's were already defeated.

"Don't carry it. Lean on it like a cane." At her expression, he added, "Unless you want to wait for the safety of daylight."

Ariel grumbled and shifted her grip. Feeling like an old woman, she set off.

Once they got moving, she enjoyed swinging her weapon, stabbing dried leaves and beheading seed stalks. She imagined splintering bones with it, too. Scarl wisely stayed out of range.

The sun rose over their shoulders as they climbed, warming the miles. By the time it had slipped west to glare in their eyes, Ariel's legs were tiring and she leaned on the poker, glad their return trip would all be downhill.

She recognized her destination with a half-mile to go. A large slab of the peak had fallen and come to rest aslant on the slope. It made a cave-like shelter beneath, but Ariel cared only about the slab's uphill edge—the last place she'd seen Elbert alive. His bones should lie somewhere in the rubble below.

"Odd to see it again, isn't it?" Scarl said.

Ariel nodded. "So much has changed. Not here, I mean. Us." The first time she'd been here, she'd been recently orphaned and running from Elbert and Scarl toward home. Since then she'd embarked on her trade, proven the truth of a legend by discovering the Vault, and made a new home at the abbey with Scarl and Zeke. She'd also met Nace. The loss of her mother at Elbert's hand would never be forgotten, but the pain had been soothed by new loves.

"There's a saying," Scarl said. "'You can never set foot on the same ground twice, for every step alters both the earth and the walker.'"

Ariel ran ahead to avoid thinking too much about Scarl's saying. If it was true, nothing could be trusted to stay the same. Good things and friendships would never last, and bad men, although dead, might come back.

As she turned the corner of the slab, her eyes darted. No skull stared at Ariel from the base of the stone. No bony arm reached from the litter of pinecones and leaves. She scrambled along the loose shale, searching.

After a moment, she spun to Scarl, behind her. "Oh, I'm a dolt—you can just find it! You brought your Finder's glass, right?"

Scarl eyed the top of the slab as he walked beneath it. "If I remember right, the body came to rest about... here." He bent, shoved aside clinking rocks, and withdrew what looked like one more bleached stick.

"Forearm, I think." He measured it against his own to confirm and then, after a moment of indecision, set the bone at the base of the slab.

Ariel used her poker to shove aside rocks and debris near his feet. She turned up only shreds of rotting clothing. "Where's the rest? You think an avalanche dragged it away or something?" Or had the crow already hauled it to a cache near the abbey?

Scarl grimaced. "Or something."

Ariel followed him as he circled the slab to its low side, where they could both scramble up onto the stone. A white jumble rested on its far edge, above the place where they'd stood moments before.

Scarl led her up the incline. Ariel tried to ignore memories of being forced up this stretch, Elbert's big paw around her neck. The knife-wound scars on her cheek and left forearm itched. She had thought her life would end that fateful morning. Fortunately Elbert had been so busy with her that he'd not heeded any knife but his own. Ariel wasn't sure if Scarl's stab or the fall from the height had stopped Elbert's heart, but the combination had. Scarl had made certain.

As they drew near the pile of bones now, he glanced at her. "You all right? Bad memories here."

"Yes." But the word trembled. The bones lay where Elbert had last stood alive. Ariel couldn't tell if fingers were among them or not. Although the ribcage had fallen to pieces, the skull sat grinning toward the abbey, much as Ariel had imagined. The bones seemed to vibrate against the rock, emitting a barely perceptible growl.

Ariel took a step back. "Do you hear that? Is it my imagination?"

"The buzz? I hear it. It puts me in mind of—"

Seized by a fury, Ariel swept one boot through the pile. She expected the bones to soar over the edge, but instead they all burst in a white puff of dust. Since her kick met almost no resistance, she tottered. Her arms flew wide for balance, and Scarl grabbed her. Bone dust swirled into their faces, accompanied by a cloud of black flies.

"Oh!" Buzzing wings tangled in Ariel's hair. She clenched her eyes shut and whisked her hands through her locks.

Slowly the awful swarm dissipated. Ariel shuddered. "Hideous things!"

"Too reminiscent of a riddle I know," Scarl replied.

"I hate riddles," Ariel said, still swatting at her clothes. "But tell me."

He obliged:

"I cannot move, though I may crawl.
I buzz, though not a bee.

Once I smelled, but now I smell.
I stare but never see.
What am I?"

"Yeah. A rotting corpse," she muttered. She studied the mound of dust. "But nothing was left *except* flies. What would they want with bare bones? Were they in the marrow? I didn't see—"

"We're talking about Elbert. I wouldn't be surprised if he tore wings off insects as a boy, and they're still gathering to celebrate his demise."

"They didn't carry him up here, though. Think the crow did?"

"Not likely. But there *is* something here besides flies." He dragged the end of his staff through the remaining fragments and dust to dislodge an object hidden beneath. As it emerged, Ariel recognized it: a large knife.

She stepped back from the blade that had given her scars. "That was still in his hand when he fell. Not in its sheath."

"That's my memory, too." Scarl didn't seem particularly troubled.

She voiced words that had been jabbering in her thoughts for hours. "There's a Hallow's Eve rhyme that goes, 'Restless spirit, move your bones. Rise from rot and mildew. Vengeance can be yours tonight. Find the one who killed y—'"

"Stop. There's no need to spook yourself further. It's odd to find these things here, but it need not be unnatural. Mountain lions sometimes drag prey up a tree. They also like high, rocky outlooks. One must have hauled the body up here to gnaw the bones clean."

"I thought they only ate fresh meat."

"I thought so, too, but who knows what they'll do when they're hungry?"

"But the knife—"

"It lay under a corpse a long while," he said firmly. "It may have smelled edible, too. Worth bringing up to lick clean, at least. Enough of this. Come." He kicked the knife toward the edge of the slab. It tumbled and stuck in the dust, not quite making it over the rim. Scarl frowned but turned his back on it and drew Ariel's sock of bones from his pocket. "Or do you want to get rid of this first?"

Ariel took the sock, dropped it, and stomped. She felt the bones inside crunch, but they didn't disintegrate like the others had. So she untied the sock to pour out the splinters. Glad to see they no longer fell in formation, she ground them into the rock with her heel. Then she flung the sock to the wind. She wouldn't want to wear it again.

"Are we done?" Scarl asked.

She forced her voice to be light. "I suppose the worst he could do now is make us sneeze."

"If that." He checked the height of the sun. "So we should try to get home before dark."

Ariel nudged the knife with her toe and bent to peer at the blade. It bore no trace of her blood. She pinched the hilt between two fingers and raised it. The wood felt gritty and gouged—perhaps damaged by teeth. An ivory triangle was inlaid in the handle.

At first Ariel assumed the inlay was bone, and sinister connections raced through her thoughts. Then a detail struck her. She swiped the triangle clean with one fingertip.

"Huh." She looked up at Scarl. "Did Elbert tell you where he came from?"

"Originally? No."

"There's a shark's tooth embedded in this." The vicious detail gave Ariel the strange sense that she shared more with Elbert than ever. Had they both been born near the sea? She tried to envision him young—blonde and boy-faced like Zeke, only burly instead. He may have been cruel then already, propped up by this knife. Or perhaps his jolly demeanor had once been authentic, and rather than tormenting flies, he'd cut bait with friends.

Scarl interrupted her musing. "Leave it, Ariel. Or throw it to break on the rocks, and forget it. He's gone. He can't trouble you again."

Ariel rubbed her thumb over the tooth, inlaid so expertly that she could barely feel where the wood stopped and the serrated tooth began. A tingle ran through her bones to her feet. They wanted to move. After hundreds of farwalking miles, she'd become highly attuned to that impulse. She turned to stare over the brink of the slab and northwest, where her feet itched to lead her. Rocky peaks rose in the distance, hindering any journey that way.

"Ariel!"

The concern in Scarl's voice made her move toward him, but her fingers wrapped firmly about the knife's hilt.

He eyed it with disapproval. "A trophy?"

"No. I just want it." She tried to understand why and fell back on an excuse. "When you gave me lessons with your knife, you said I should have my own weapon, remember?"

"What I remember is how adamantly you refused. Why this one now?"

"Because." To master a thing that had hurt her? To rob Elbert's power? "It might be handy against a lion."

Scarl grimaced. "It's more likely to worsen your nightmares. And mine."

His dismay pricked her heart, but it also focused her purpose.

"That's why I need it," she said.

CHAPTER

4

"This knife is too close to us here, like a thorn," Ariel said. Gripping the hilt, she let Scarl escort her down the sloped rock. "I want to take it back where it came from. I'll cast it into the sea. Or a river or lake or whatever they've got." She jumped to the ground and retrieved the poker she'd left there.

"If you do, Elbert will be in your thoughts the whole time."

"It'll be worth it."

He caught her arm. "Are you sure? If you allow his memory to haunt you this far past his death, you're letting him control you as much as he ever did when you were a prisoner. He forced you out of bed and all these miles today. Do you want to hand him that power? You certainly wouldn't give it to me."

She hadn't thought of it that way. To muffle a twinge of discomfort, she retorted, "You're bossy enough without it."

"I see. I'll remind you of that next time you want something of me."

"I take it back," Ariel said. "Because I want something now."

Scarl shook his head. "I won't carry that knife, if that's what you're thinking."

"No." She ignored the direction her feet wanted to take her—for now—and started downhill toward the abbey. "I want a walking stick. Like yours, only smaller. Would you find me one?"

He joined her. "That shouldn't be hard."

"And you'll go farwalking with me, won't you?"

"Have I ever let you go alone?"

"No, but you don't usually try to talk me out of it, either. My feet want to go, Scarl."

He accepted that justification in silence.

As they descended, he found her several possible staffs. Ariel settled on a length of aspen with a brown twist through the wood and a knot at the top. Scarl indulged her by taking the poker so she could begin breaking in the staff to her hand.

At last the abbey's roof came into view below. Goats grazed among puddles of snow in the yard, and Ariel spied the tiny figures of both Nace and Zeke. Zeke was bent at some task and struggling to discourage curious goats from sticking their snouts in his work. Nace hurried up to retrieve them, but he stopped and folded his arms at what must've been sharp words from Zeke. The distance was too great for Zeke's voice to be heard, but their gestures and postures spoke louder.

Ariel sighed. She didn't need a dead enemy to trouble her mind. She had enough heartache from friends.

"Why can't they get along?" she asked.

"You know the answer." Scarl smiled. "They say too much of a good thing makes the best curse. It's true for love as well, then?"

"Don't laugh. It hurts. I'll be glad to escape for a while. Can we leave tomorrow?"

His eyebrows shot up. "I didn't realize you meant to go farwalking so soon. The weather's too nipping yet, Ariel. It's barely half March."

"I don't care. I'll wear all my clothes at once and sleep with rocks warmed in the fire."

His silence tugged at her conscience. She'd forgotten that he'd be uncomfortable, too.

"I mean, if it's just you and me," she added, "we can curl up together under tree roots and ledges to be cozy enough. Can't we?"

"Your faith in my ability to find such shelter is touching," he said. "But if that blade weighs on you so much that we need to hurry, let's just destroy it."

"That would only work if I could cut out my memories and smash them along with it," she said. "I don't want to destroy it. I want to take it somewhere out of my life."

"That won't wipe away your bad memories," he said gently.

"I know. They'll be balanced by new memories, though—memories where *I'm* carrying the knife."

"Ah." At last Scarl nodded. "All right. Perhaps we can leave the nightmares behind. Give me a chance to gather some gear, though. I still need to mend Willow's tack. And you have paper to make."

"Oh! You're right. It might be cooked enough now. If I

can mold it this evening, we could still leave tomorrow." At his dubious look, she said, "The day after?"

"Thursday. No sooner."

She agreed. The two days between would give her time to craft her walking stick—and break the news that she'd be gone for a while to her friends.

By the time she and Scarl arrived at the abbey, both Nace and Zeke had long gone out of sight. As she returned her poker to the hearth, Ariel found her pot of wood soup off the fire, the brown mush inside cooling.

"Zeke has been fussing with it all day," explained Ash, who was there fixing supper. "I wouldn't be surprised if he'd tasted it, too."

"I hope not," Ariel said. The stuff smelled like molasses but looked more like cheese curds in whey. It was hard to imagine how anyone could write symbols on it. Doubtful, she left Elbert's knife by the hearth and headed to her room to free her tired feet from her boots.

She got only as far as her threshold. In the middle of her floor lay a rib.

Another bone! Or... no. Her breath left in a rush. It was only a peeled stick. Approaching, she could make out a few symbols carved on its surface. In the summertime, Nace shaped messages for her from flowers or feathers, but when those couldn't be found, he resorted to marks on fabric or pieces of wood. She bent to retrieve it and read his message.

Meet me? Nace.

Ariel pressed the symbols to her chest as if her heart could answer in beats to his own. She tossed the stick on her blanket and turned, sore feet forgotten.

Scarl, still unlacing his boots, saw her pass by his doorway. "You're not going out again, are you?"

"Not for long." Ariel walked backward so she could reply without stopping. "I just want to find Nace. He's probably penning the goats."

"If you see Zeke, remind him not to dally."

"I will." She turned and ran out.

Unlike the goats, Nace was not at their pen. Ariel scanned the hillside, which was gilded with the slanted light of late day. She finally found him near the edge of the woods, perched in the fork of a horse chestnut tree and chewing on the end of a porcupine quill. When he saw her, he tossed it away and swung down immediately. His hand plunged into his pocket for the small slate and charred stick he carried. Ariel waited while he scratched quick marks on the slate: *Last night—I'm sorry.*

"I'm sorry, too. I should have followed you. But I hate it when you two go after each other."

Nace grimaced. He brushed his slate with the heel of his hand and wrote, *Where today?*

"Out with Scarl." She'd tell him later about the bones and their strange host of flies. Right now, she just wanted to earn Nace's smile. She reached toward him.

He dodged, his charcoal poised over the slate. He got as far as Zeke's name. But he couldn't find the words he wanted—or he realized Ariel wouldn't know the marks for them, because he understood far more symbols than she did. In a flash of frustration, he flung the slate and charred stick on the moss. Then he took both her hands.

His touch sent a thrill through her and put a hitch in her thoughts. Ariel found herself leaning against him without being sure when or how she'd moved there. Her cheek nestled into the hollow of his shoulder. Like the birdsong overhead, the pulse of his heart reassured her that all things were well.

"Remember when you first came here?" she murmured. "I had so hoped you'd be friends." Nace had shared Zeke's room briefly, and they'd studied symbols together until Zeke had realized that Nace had come to the abbey not just to learn but to be with Ariel.

Nace released her fingers to wrap his arms around her. One of his hands strayed to trace down her arm, scribing symbols that spoke to her heart. Ariel closed her eyes to better feel them inside. Graced with more than the usual Kincaller's skill, Nace could listen and speak with his mind, and though she could rarely pinpoint when it happened, or how, she trusted her instincts about what he told her that way.

What she heard now in silence was the passage of time: yesterday giving way to tomorrow, winter to spring, children growing up and maybe growing apart. She understood what he meant about change and how useless it was to struggle against it. Yet surely old friends should not be cast aside. The problem was how to hold onto one love while embracing a love that was new.

When at last she looked into Nace's face, dim with shadows, she realized that, indeed, time had passed. Dusk had fallen.

She squeezed him and drew back. "We should head for the abbey. It's practically dark, and you know how Scarl gets."

He wagged his head in reluctant agreement and clasped

her fingers to walk hand in hand. Before they'd gone far, though, he stiffened and stopped. He inhaled, not just breathing but testing the air. The birds had fallen silent.

"What—?"

Nace leapt forward, towing her through the trees toward the abbey. Understanding only his urgency, Ariel ran as fast as she could, but she was built more for walking than running, and her legs were already tired. He dragged her, stumbling, around briars and boulders. With his free hand, he snatched a thick stick from the ground, rapping it against trees they passed. The battering echoed like the hammering of a frenzied woodpecker.

They burst onto a narrow, goat-worn track beneath a stone ledge. Candlelight glowed from the abbey below, and Zeke was walking midway down the slope. His white linen shirt floated over his legs, which were lost in the twilight.

"Oh, Zeke, were you spying on us?" Ariel demanded, before she realized he was not skulking away.

Zeke turned, peering toward them. "Uh! Do you really think—"

Wham. Nace slapped his branch on the stone alongside them. Ariel took the whack as a threat.

So did Zeke. He groaned. "No! Just leave me alone, Nace. And stop rubbing it in! Or do I have to make you? Don't forget the stones are my friends, and I'll use them." As Nace pulled Ariel farther downslope, Zeke cursed and marched back up to meet them.

Nace ignored Zeke's approach. He veered wide to the outer ridge of the track and pointed his stick at the ledge. Ariel followed his gaze. A low, gliding shadow slid over the rock above Zeke. Her heart skipped. The shape tensed to pounce.

"Zeke, stop! It's a lion!" She could smell it now, too, a pungent musk on the breeze. All she could remember was never to run. Running would trigger a chase they would lose.

Nace thrust his stick at Ariel and stuck his fingers in his mouth. His whistle sliced through the air. She cringed from the blast. The mountain lion hunkered, but a growl floated down. It was hungry enough for a fight.

Nace threw Ariel an urgent gesture that she took as advice to make noise. As she opened her mouth, he bent, grabbed her thighs, and lifted her on his shoulders. He'd done it before, playing, but never so abruptly. The shout on her tongue came out as a squeal.

Zeke was no Kincaller, but he seemed to remember every lesson he learned, so by the time Ariel regained her balance, he was facing the cat with his legs and arms splayed to look larger. He eased away from the ledge, singing loud nonsense sounds to the stones.

"Go away!" Ariel yelled. Her voice bounced as Nace jogged with her to Zeke. "Eat somebody else! You can't have him! Or any of us!"

The shadow wiggled, still tempted, still primed to leap. Its growl rose to a hiss. Ariel brandished her stick. Her other hand clenched on Zeke's collar to unite them. She held her breath, searching the ledge. From this angle the lion was lost in shadow. If it still chose to attack them together, they'd feel its claws before seeing it move. And with a choice of prey, it would strike at the weakest one—her.

"Nace," she wailed, "tell it we taste bad or something!"

His fingers squeezed tight on her legs. Then he, too, grabbed Zeke's shirt and pulled.

They backed as one down the slope. Ariel cocked her stick to throw it but thought better of casting away their only weapon. Instead, she kept shouting.

Zeke's singing had greater effect. The stony ledge answered with an echoing *crack*.

In the subsequent hush, Ariel felt blind and helpless. But the stone popping beneath it must have startled the lion. Through her legs she felt the tension drain out of Nace.

"It's gone?"

He nodded, exhaling hard. He didn't lower her, but he let go of Zeke's shirt.

After more backward paces, they turned toward the abbey. Nace whistled a note of relief and amazement that made Ariel's heart lurch, because it told her he'd expected the lion to pounce. Only Zeke's rapport with the stone had saved them.

"Wait, Nace. Stop." She couldn't tell how much of the mottling in her vision was the night and how much was a threatening faint. "I need to breathe."

He obeyed, one hand stroking her shin.

"Did you hear it stalking Zeke?" She knew how well he could sense the moods of wild creatures, but her question helped stave off that encroaching blackness.

He nodded and gestured. From above and in the dark, Ariel felt his movements more than she saw them, but she was familiar enough with his signs that she still understood: *I heard excitement. Hunger. And I heard Zeke too close.*

In an unsteady voice, Zeke said to his feet, "Thank you.

The stones might have tried to warn me, but I... wasn't really paying attention." He had trouble doing it, but at last he raised his face to direct his thanks to Nace.

Nace shrugged awkwardly beneath Ariel's weight, no more eager to lock eyes than Zeke was.

"Let me down," she whispered. Nace lowered her. She grabbed his hand and threw her other arm around Zeke in a hug.

"That was awful," she said into Zeke's shirt. "I'd die without either of you. Let's get home."

"Good idea."

She released Zeke. But before her feet moved, she wrapped an even more fervent hug around Nace.

As they hurried the short way to the abbey, Ariel told them about Elbert's bones on the slab. Nace frowned and shook his head but didn't try to elaborate. Ariel remembered he'd left his slate in the trees. In moments like these, she hated his muteness.

Once she'd finished her story, Zeke said, "That explains this." He pulled a rumpled sock from his pocket. "Sorry. I found it in the meadow and thought it looked like one of yours. I wondered how you lost only one."

Growling, Ariel snatched it. "It beat me home! Stupid crow. I'll have to burn it." To Nace, she added, "The sock, not the bird. But don't tempt me."

Silence fell until Zeke said, "Tonight's lion might be the same one who gnawed the bones clean. I'm glad he didn't get a fresh set from me."

"Don't even say that." But Ariel couldn't help wondering if Zeke might be right, and her imagination honed the idea. Some Fishers believed shark meat gave them the shark's knowledge, and Reapers had similar hopes about stags. If the lion had swallowed Elbert's memories, too, Zeke's stalking may have been no random hunt, but a grudge. And anything could happen here while she was gone. It might be harder than she'd thought to leave him and Nace.

CHAPTER
5

"**Y**ou're going farwalking," Zeke said when Ariel walked into the Great Room before bedtime. "Already."

She stopped, her tainted sock in her hand. She'd come to throw it into the fire, hoping to avoid awkward questions. The hearth benches were usually empty this late. At least Zeke was alone. "Did the stones tell you that?"

"Scarl did," he answered. "But why didn't you?"

She squirmed. "I just decided. I was going to announce it at breakfast." So much for her plan to make sure both young men heard it at once.

"Can I come?"

She stared in dismay. Zeke joined her trips only rarely, and this would not be a good time to change that habit. Her mouth flapped as she sought a reply less harsh than "no."

"Ariel, how often do I ask you for a favor?"

She had to admit the answer was never. "But you've said farwalking is boring."

"Sometimes it is, but I want to go with you this time."

"Why? Did Scarl tell you where I mean to go?"

"No. Where?"

"My question first. Why?" She wondered how much he'd admit.

Zeke's eyes slid from hers. "I just feel like getting away from the abbey. And... the lion."

"You're a terrible liar."

"Fine." Emotions battled on his face. "I asked the stones about Elbert."

So that's why he'd been on the hillside that evening. A chill ran through her. "What did they say?"

"I only wanted to make you feel better! I didn't expect any answer except that he'd passed into dust, which is how they speak of something that dies. The stones don't bother about people much. We're here and gone too fast—"

"I got it, Zeke! What did they say?"

His voice fell so she had to move closer. "They started muttering to each other about rocks rolling uphill. When I asked what that meant, they fell silent. And they wouldn't explain."

Ariel wondered if Zeke might be making it up. "How is that about Elbert?"

"I don't know. It might not be, which is why I didn't tell Scarl. It just makes me nervous. Rocks rolling uphill would be *wrong*. And now you're being secretive, too. Are you going back to Nace's village or something?"

"No." She told him her plans.

He blanched but did not try to dissuade her. "Please, let me come. Please. Don't forget I was there the day Elbert died. I can help you avoid rockfalls, too. They happen a lot in spring thaws, and I can hear any big stones that are thinking of moving."

His desperation was hard to resist. At last she replied, "Let me think about it." What she really meant to do was seek Scarl's help. Maybe he'd deny Zeke's request so she wouldn't have to disappoint him herself.

She turned to leave.

"Um... sock?" Zeke said.

"Oh." Ariel flung the sock to the fire, where the wool twisted and charred. The trembling black ashes made her think of the crow. "Maybe Scarl and I were the rocks rolling uphill as we climbed up there today."

Zeke took up the poker to stir the ashes. "Maybe."

When she left him, she paced the halls for a while, despite tired feet, before stopping at Scarl's half-open door. Candlelight beckoned from behind it. She peeked in.

"I was wondering if you would come in," he said, without glancing up from the timepiece he'd acquired on their travels. He'd been tinkering with it all winter, trying to understand if not actually revive it, and now he probed at its works with a needle in the candle's thin light. "What's got you so restless?"

Ariel flopped onto the floor beside him and drew a deep breath. "Boys."

"Ah." His voice hardened. "Any particular boy I need to speak with?"

"Maybe, but not for the reason you think." She told him about Zeke's request.

"You know I leave farwalking decisions like this to your instincts," he said. "Follow them."

"I want your advice, though. Or... your help in telling him no."

Scarl set aside his timepiece with care so the tiny parts did not spill. "I'll enforce your decision, if that's what it is. But I won't take the blame for a message you're reluctant to give."

Ariel wrinkled her nose. He saw too much sometimes.

"And if you truly want my advice," he added, "if I were you, Ariel, I might let Zeke come."

"Why? I was hoping to escape from all that. Their competition is driving me crazy."

"Well... I don't think it's my place to meddle in this," Scarl said. "But I have eyes in my head. Have you heard the old saying, 'Absence floods the heart with fondness'? I think the more you shut Zeke out of your life, the more he will pine to be in it."

Ariel scowled. "And I'm so unpleasant that traveling with me will put him off me for good?"

Scarl laughed. "Now you're putting words in my mouth. You asked for my thoughts. I gave them. You're the one who has to decide." He took up his timepiece again.

"You're on his side, though." She sounded like a petulant child, and she knew it, but childish arguments held an odd comfort.

"I didn't know there were sides to be chosen," he said. "I see the sparks dancing between you and Nace, and I know what that's like. But I also feel for Zeke. He loves you, too."

Ariel picked at a fray in the hem of her shirt. "If Zeke comes, maybe Nace should also."

"As you will. I can put up with both if you can."

She snorted. "You mean you'll hammer peace between them, if you have to."

"Or tie and gag them, perhaps."

Ariel's grin soured. "I'll let you know how much rope to bring with us."

When she returned to her room, a crow's feather lay on the doorsill. Glad it wasn't a bone, Ariel picked it up and carried it to her walking stick.

She'd already lashed Elbert's knife to the staff. The blade was well swaddled; she wouldn't give it the slightest chance to draw blood again. It had pleased her to bind it, retribution for once having been tied up herself. She'd made sure the shark's tooth on the handle still showed. When she took up her stick, the heel of her hand rested comfortably on the butt of the knife. Now she tied on the feather so it would flutter around the knife in a breeze. Finished, she laid the staff in the hall. Even with it bound, she didn't trust the knife enough to sleep in the same room with it.

Still, she was shocked to find the staff gone in the morning. Her search had just started when she ran into Zeke.

"I don't have it," he said. "But I know who does. Nace."

"Thanks." She shoved past.

"He was down by the creek," Zeke called. "Can I come with you or not?"

For an instant, she thought he meant then. She turned back, a curt response ready. Then his meaning struck her—along with the recognition that he'd never done anything except try to help her. Her heart and her instincts both gave the same answer.

"Yes."

His huge smile shone. She did her best to match it.

She found Nace hunched at the stream, rubbing her staff with wet sand to smooth it. His movements were forceful, as though strong emotion went into his work. Ariel wondered if he knew of her plans. She could never tell how much he overheard in people's thoughts and how much he depended on words. Prepared to mend damage, she bid him a good morning.

He looked up and smiled. After rinsing the staff, he offered her the grip to test it.

Relieved, she took his arm instead. "I'm going farwalking soon. You figured that out, huh?"

He shrugged and waggled the staff.

"I want you to come."

He set down the staff and pulled her to sit on a stone with him, close. Cupping her face with both hands, he looked in through her eyes. Ariel's whole body ached to press up against him, and his lips parted, so although he held her at bay, she thought he might answer her with a kiss. But then he clamped his lips tight. He took out his charcoal and slate, which he must have retrieved early that morning, yet he didn't write. He shook his head slowly: *No.*

"No?" Disbelief twisted her voice. "You won't come? Zeke's coming! I want you with me, too."

He shook his head again, closed his eyes, and then opened them to scratch on his slate. He wrote more slowly than usual, with the slate held so Ariel could not see the symbols until he was done. Which was just fine with her. She didn't want to read any marks that explained his refusal.

When at last he turned the slate to her, she read with

reluctance. "You're a butterfly, Ariel," she read aloud. Her heart swelled and admitted some hope. But there were many more marks on the slate.

She read on. "I'm not stupid—" With a grunt of outrage, she stopped. "Nobody said you were!"

He shook the slate at her to finish.

"I'm not stupid," she repeated. "If I close my hand on you, it will either crush you or send you flitting away. I can only keep still and hope you alight." She looked up. "But I've already lit, Nace! On you!"

He ripped a dead frond from a fern and slowly wiped clean his marks, shaking his head.

Jealous of the attention he was giving the slate, she snatched it. "Forget this! Look at me!"

He did better than that. His fingertip traced a sign on her cheek that she knew by feel: love.

"Then why won't you come?" she whispered. "Is it..." She bit her lip. "Is it because I couldn't tell Zeke no?"

He dropped his gaze to consider, and she saw that her words held some truth. Gently he took back the slate to scratch out more symbols. Dread weighted her heart as he wrote.

If I go with you and Zeke, the marks said, *he will make me close my hand. I know myself well enough to realize that. And I think Zeke knows it, too.*

She didn't know what to say. He'd expressed her own fear that the young men's competition might quench her love for them both.

He set the slate aside, smiled weakly, and offered his hand. She took it, but she felt more like she was drowning and grasping for a lifeline than holding hands with the young man she loved.

"Oh, Nace. Maybe I shouldn't go after all."

He wrapped his arms around her as if to keep her. Then he let go and reached again for his slate—which, just at the moment, Ariel hated.

Go, Farwalker, he wrote. *My fingers will be here outstretched.*

Before they went into the abbey, Nace kissed her at last. Her lips throbbed with a kissing she would not soon forget. She was terrified it might linger in her heart as the last, not just for a few weeks but for the rest of her life.

Trying not to think of the future, she spent most of the day fussing with wood mush. Yesterday Zeke had lashed linen to sticks as if making a needlepoint frame. Now they dunked his frame into their cooking pot and raised it to drain out the water, leaving a layer of mush on the cloth like sand on high ground after a flood. Unlike sand, though, once the wood mush had dried they could peel it up in a sheet. It was stiffer than cloth, but light and much faster to make. Ariel used a charred stick to draw her Farwalker's mark on one corner.

"It works!" She jumped up to hug Zeke and then froze. So many hugs might not be wise.

Pretending not to notice her halt, he raised the paper to the light. "Thinner would be better. Let me try another."

Ariel backed away. "I'll get sticks for making more frames."

Even working indoors in the evenings, with their paper drying by the fire, they barely used up the wood mush before Thursday arrived.

Nace did not see them off. He'd released the goats

early and must have wandered away with them. Though
his absence from the abbey yard stung, Ariel had expected
as much. Their parting before bedtime last night had been
somber.

"Don't let him tempt the lions," she asked Ash, who'd
come out for goodbyes. "Please make sure he's inside dawn
and dusk."

"I'd sooner convince the birds not to sing than to pen
up your Nace," Ash said kindly. "But I'll try to advise him
when he comes in for meals, and I'll ask the trees to watch
over him. Don't worry. Nace is a wildling himself. He's not
likely to lose sight of their ways."

"Good days until we return, Ash," said Scarl, their
packhorse's reins in his hand.

Zeke nudged Ariel. "Which way?"

She shifted her hand on her staff and rubbed her
thumb over the shark's tooth. They had limited choices for
leaving the mountains, particularly this early in spring, but
Ariel trusted her feet to find the shortest safe route. The
impulse to walk came immediately.

"Somewhere rocks roll downhill, and not up," Zeke
added, low.

"Where we can be friends and that's all," Ariel thought.
The tug on her boots did not waver. She could feel its pull
like a tide.

"To a sea that's missing a shark." She opened her eyes
and stepped forward.

Their first days of travel were rough. Ariel's feet led them
north, which meant threading between peaks without relief
from the cold. To sleep without shivering, the three had to
pile together like puppies, and the days weren't much better.

No one complained, but Zeke warmed his cheeks against Willow's broad flanks, and Scarl kept his hands stuffed in the opposite armpits.

"Do the stones think the weather will turn nicer soon, Zeke?" Ariel asked.

He shook his head. "They're not good to ask. Snow, rain, clouds—they like it all." He pointed ahead to a dark, buzzing knot. "But speaking of clouds... have you noticed those flies?"

Ariel had been trying to ignore them.

CHAPTER 6

For several days now, a black, roiling fog had hung in the air just behind them or, sometimes, ahead. It reminded Ariel of the flies that had risen from Elbert's remains. Whenever she spotted the swarm in her path, she had to concentrate to prevent herself from swerving away. She didn't want to feel as though she were following them. Yet she liked being shadowed by them even less.

"Awful cold yet for bugs," Zeke observed.

"Maybe that's why they're staying so close," Ariel said. "They smell the horse and they're drawn to his warmth."

"They're not landing on him, though," Zeke replied. "Or anything else. They just float."

Ariel scowled. "Like a ghost." She turned to Scarl. "Will you tell us a story? It'll help me forget those nasty things. And how cold my nose is."

"I think you've heard all I know. How about a riddle instead?"

"I like riddles," said Zeke.

"I don't," Ariel said. "They make me feel stupid."

"You'll have an edge for this one," Scarl said.

That intrigued her. A farwalking riddle?

"Cross once and meet smiles. Cross twice and leave tears," Scarl said. "Cross thrice and expect to earn screams. Why?"

Ariel's brow puckered. What could be crossed? Arms and legs, thresholds, streams, land. She'd met smiles on her first arrival in several villages—although surprise and disbelief were more common—but she'd never left tears, and the screams didn't fit, either. Still, if it wasn't a Farwalker riddle, why would she guess it any sooner than Zeke?

She glanced sideways at Scarl. The look in his eyes told her the answer. The flies must have given them similar thoughts.

"Oh! I know!" she said.

"Already?" Zeke protested. "Don't say it, let me—"

But Ariel was already talking. "It's the bridge out of the world. Crossed once to come in as a baby, the second time leaving the world when you die, and sneaking back in the third time as a ghost."

"You remember that story," Scarl said.

"How could I forget?" He'd told her last summer about the bridge out of the world. "All I can think of is Elbert finding his way back over somehow." She glared at the flies not far over their heads.

"If a knot of flies is the best he can do," Scarl said, "I wouldn't worry. They're not even biting."

"Tell me that story, Scarl," Zeke said.

"Why don't you tell him, Ariel?" the Finder suggested. "Sometimes telling a story can give you power over it and stop it from troubling your thoughts. And storytelling would be a fine skill for a Farwalker to have."

"You'll tell it better."

But Zeke encouraged her, too, so she huffed air into her bangs and launched into a description of the shadowy bridge. Long ago, she told him, it had been easier to cross. Frightened by the dead, those living nearby had tried to stop ghouls from coming back to the world. When the living and the dead had a fight on the bridge, flames flared from beneath it to burn a great hole. Since then, the bridge couldn't be crossed by the living. Only unborn spirits coming into the world and the dead ones leaving again could get past that hole. Other barriers were added to help keep the dead where they belonged.

Ariel held Zeke's interest so well that he stumbled. When she finished, he asked, "What kind of barriers can stop a ghost?"

Ariel appealed to Scarl.

He shook his head. "The story doesn't say. But I'm sure you've heard of methods for warding off spirits. Running water, powerful symbols—that kind of thing."

"Holly branches, I guess," Zeke said. "Horseshoes. And silver."

"You think those would stop Elbert?" Ariel asked.

"You're assuming he'd want to come back," Scarl said. "Most who leave the world are content to move on."

"And good riddance," declared Zeke.

"Sometimes." A note in Scarl's voice caught Ariel's attention, and they swapped a rueful look. Ariel thought of her mother. Softly, Scarl added, "Regardless, we also must move on without them."

Zeke saw their sad glance. "Uh... it's not always good riddance. I only meant Elbert."

"It's all right, Zeke. We know." Ariel felt worse for Scarl than herself. It had been nearly two years, and he could mention Mirayna Allcraft without wincing now, but clearly he still mourned the woman he'd hoped to marry.

For a few weeks that winter, he'd shown a flicker of interest in a delicate Tree-Singer at the abbey, and Ariel had plotted ways to throw them together. She'd encouraged Scarl's admiration of Madrona's paintings and helped him gather feathers to give her for applying the paints. If anything passed between the two beyond the kindness Madrona showed everyone, however, Ariel caught no murmur of it. Perhaps Madrona's heart belonged too firmly to trees. Scarl's gaze soon stopped lingering on her, and his attention returned to chores and to fixing his timepiece.

Still, Ariel sometimes felt the weight of his loneliness when they traveled, and she noticed again that evening, too. Scarl sat up late at the fire after she and Zeke snuggled into their blankets. Pretending to sleep, Ariel watched Scarl through slit eyelids. He stared into the coals for more than an hour, massaging his lame ankle or rubbing his knuckles in an unconscious attempt to knead away some other ache.

She'd seen the same thing before. If she fought sleep long enough, before he lay down he always bent close, tucked her blanket more firmly around her, and stroked her hair with a touch as light as a leaf's fall. That secret tenderness sparked her tears, making it hard to maintain her fake sleep. Ariel wished she knew how to plug the hole in Scarl's heart, but she could only ache for him, and her feelings for Nace had helped her understand why the company of other loved ones wasn't enough. She missed the Kincaller's strong hands and quick smile already.

Over the next week, Zeke solved every riddle Scarl knew while Ariel led them farther north. The foothills they traversed never flattened to plains. Instead the folds in the land grew steep-sided again, the heights rocky and rippling with windswept grasses. Cascades spilled into gorges, and cliffs rose from the rivers below. Not even the heavy mists off the water dissuaded their escort of flies.

One night Ariel awoke when she felt Scarl bolt upright. Moonlight glinted on the blade of his knife.

"What?" Her head still buzzing with sleep, she sat up to scan for her staff. She feared Elbert's knife had cut itself free and now posed some threat. But her walking stick, with the blade, lay inert on the ground.

Scarl blinked at her. After peering toward their drowsy horse, he re-sheathed his weapon and hunkered at the banked coals of their fire.

"Nothing. Forgive me," he whispered, since Zeke snored on beside her. "Nightmare."

"Geez, what about?"

He stirred up the coals. "You needn't trouble yourself with my bad dreams."

"You'd trouble yourself with mine."

When he didn't answer, she said, "I'm sorry. It's my fault for wanting this trip. You were right. This knife makes me think of Elbert too much. But I can't just smash it and forget. I have to... I have to put it away. I know that doesn't make sense."

"Yes, it does. You have to conquer it. And you fight

with your feet." He fed the fire until flames licked at the darkness.

A subtle motion to the side caught Ariel's notice. "Build it up more. Zeke's shivering."

Scarl turned. His eyes narrowed. "No, he isn't." He lifted a flaming stick as a torch.

Zeke's blanket was crawling with flies. More settled each second.

Scarl waved the brand over the blanket. The flies lifted off, some sizzling through the flame and then burning like sparks. Others buzzed through the dark to land on Ariel instead.

"Ugh!" She scrambled to her feet, leaving the flies writhing on her blanket. "You think they've been roosting on us every night?"

"I hope not," Scarl said.

Zeke rolled over, muttering about the noise they were making. He spotted the flies and sat up, his eyes wide. "Yuck."

Ariel snatched a bare corner of her blanket and snapped it. The flies scattered. Scarl ignited more with his torch, filling the air with makeshift fireflies. They stunk. Ariel gathered her blanket into her arms and huddled with Zeke, afraid of embers dropping into her hair.

A soft beating sound joined their sizzle and buzz. A set of dark wings, too large for a bat, swooped back and forth, snatching two and three sparks at a time.

"Oh, don't tell me!" As Ariel spoke, the crow landed to gobble a few settling flies that had not caught on fire.

"It can't be the same bird," Scarl said. "Another, perhaps. Though I didn't think they flew in the dark."

"Crows don't eat flies, either," she replied. It snapped its beak here and there, defying her words.

"This one must like them toasted." Zeke grinned.

The crow hopped and pecked as flies began to escape. When none were left in the circle of light, the bird cawed and leapt into the dark.

"Talk about nightmares," Ariel moaned.

"Look on the bright side," Zeke said. "We're not dead meat."

"Yet," she retorted. "But you shouldn't be so cheerful. All the flies were on you to begin with."

"Really?" Zeke looked more intrigued than repulsed.

"More likely on me," Scarl said. "I awoke sensing motion."

Although the night calmed around them, they remained wary, nestling slowly back into their blankets.

"Sleep," Scarl said. "I'll keep them off if they return."

"We could take turns," Zeke offered. "So you could sleep, too."

"I've slept enough for one night."

"There weren't flies in your nightmare, were there?" Ariel asked.

Scarl shook his head. The look on his face made her wish he would tell her about it, but she knew it was useless to plead—and for the sake of her own nightmares, she did not need to know.

She didn't expect it, but sleep visited Ariel again before morning. When she awoke to thin sunshine and birdsong, the midnight fright could have been a bad dream—except that by noon, a mass of flies was following them once more.

The dark cloud seemed smaller, but that may have been wishful thinking.

"Where's that crow during the day?" Ariel grumbled.

"What we need is a big flock of swallows," Zeke said. "But we're more likely to start spotting seagulls, I think."

He was right. The breeze had begun whispering of seaweed and salt, and the rivers in the gorges below became fjords. They'd reached a rugged seacoast. As they approached what appeared to be land's end, however, the earth did not slope but sliced into the sea, too steep to descend. They turned to follow the dramatic coastline.

Later that day, Scarl asked, "Where are you taking us, Farwalker?" They were traipsing a barren headland with a broad view but no hint of humans. "This seems an inhospitable place for a village."

"I'm not sure. My feet want to go this way, though." Perhaps she'd made a mistake by focusing on the shark's tooth, not a village, but she wanted to follow her instincts as far as she could. Above them, the black veil of flies swooped and shifted. Even here, where sea winds scoured the land and stunted the trees, the flies had not been discouraged. "Maybe Elbert was born on an island, and the flies will lift us to carry us there."

Scarl didn't smile at her joke. "Into the sea to feed fish seems more likely. Unless we're about to meet people who cling like cliff-dwelling birds."

Not much later, Ariel said, "Maybe Elbert's people are trolls." She'd come to the top of a stair that descended into the earth. Hands had carved the stone steps, but the stairwell itself was earthen and crumbling. "Shall we find out?"

"I hope you're not serious." Scarl peered in as Zeke
tapped the first step with one foot. "Caves and tunnels cut
by nature are risky enough. Those cut by men are too old to
be trusted. It's more likely to collapse on us than to take us
anywhere we want to go."

"I know." Ariel had bad memories of caves. But she
couldn't ignore the will of her feet.

"I don't think we should go this way, either," Zeke said.
"Even if we could bring the horse."

Ariel couldn't remember him ever questioning her route.
"You don't usually have an opinion," she told him. "Why
this time?"

Zeke squirmed.

"You know what I like about Nace?" Ariel said. "He
may not talk, but he's utterly honest. You don't speak your
mind—and it shows on your face."

"It's not my fault," Zeke protested. "These stones are...
taunting is the best word, I guess. Inviting us to bring our
bones in. They know too much about dead things. But I
didn't think you'd want to hear more about bones."

"Oh. You're right," she said. "Sorry."

Scarl told her, "Find some other path."

Ariel turned from the stair and denied her feet what
they wanted. After an uncertain moment, they stepped
forward and past it. Relieved, she marched onward.

Soon water surrounded them on three sides, beyond
tumbles of brown bracken fern and green vines. Adjoining
cliffs loomed, torn and eroded as though clawed by giants,
and the sea boomed in pockets below. Ariel skirted fresh
sinkholes and seeps. Boggy soil kept sliding from under her

boots, and mud stained her trousers where she'd repeatedly slipped to one knee.

"I don't like the feel of this earth," Scarl said. "And there can't be anything out on the point, or we'd see it by now."

"That stairwell went somewhere." Ariel didn't stop. "Let me try a bit farther." If she could find a route down from the narrow ridge they were on, they'd be able to cross the tamer slopes nearer the water. There were coves below, too, littered with tree trunks and branches that'd been tossed in by waves. From above, the driftwood looked like jumbled bones. At least these were too big to be human.

"Willow's balking," Scarl said a few moments later. He stopped with the horse. "Are you ready to backtrack?"

"I guess we'll have to." Reluctant, she took several more steps alone to see if they gave her any new view ahead. "My feet want to go down, but except for those stairs, they can't find a w—aagh!"

The soil turned to slurry beneath her. Scrabbling for footing only flung it away harder. She screeched, flailed her arms, and dropped to her seat, but a chute opened underneath her. Even digging in her heels and grabbing handfuls of earth didn't slow her. The earth slid fast, and Ariel skidded down with it.

CHAPTER 7

The crest of the mudslide overtook Ariel from behind, pushing at her and threatening to engulf her head. She gulped air and applied instincts she'd shaped in the sea, swimming with the slide instead of trying to fight.

The mud slowed when it reached a gentler slope and stopped, clogged by a scatter of blackthorn and boulders. Ariel lay limp and panting, afraid any motion might start the ground churning again. After a few solid moments, she plucked her limbs from the ooze and rose unsteadily to her knees. The smell of wet clay crowded into her nose.

"Well, that was one way to get down," she said to her feet. "Thanks a lot."

Her companions shouted from above. Their voices sounded small. When she turned, she was amazed how high above her their silhouettes perched—like birds on the rim of a cliff.

"I'm all right!" Mud dripped out of her hair. Her palms had been scraped and the blackthorn jabbed at her shins, but nothing else hurt. Spying her staff, she dragged it from the mud and leaned on it. She took tentative steps up the path of the slide. It was like trying to climb a waterfall. Her feet slid back to where they had started.

"I don't think I can climb up to you, though," she called.

"Hang on, Scarl's getting his rope," Zeke yelled.

Unfurled down the chute, the rope was laughably short.

"I think you might have to come down to me," she shouted.

"How?" Scarl demanded.

"Well... the way I did it worked."

They thought she was joking and clearly did not find it funny.

"I'm serious! It doesn't hurt if you think of riding a wave. Just keep your feet downhill and watch for big rocks. And you'd better sit down first."

After a brief consultation with Zeke, Scarl stowed his rope and reached into the pocket where he kept his Finder's glass.

"Just stay there," he called. "I'll find a better way down, perhaps back where more bushes anchor the soil."

Some half hour before, Ariel had peered down through the brambles Scarl meant. Those tangles of growth draped jagged razors of rock.

"Are you sure?" she yelled, as Zeke and Scarl led Willow back the way they'd come. "That seems even more—"

The horse leapt forward and sideways, teetered right on the edge, and then found his footing again. While he scrambled, Ariel's human friends vanished.

"Scarl? Zeke!" She peered all around Willow, but he was alone; his bulk hadn't merely knocked down or hidden Scarl and Zeke. The trembling packhorse showed Ariel his hindquarters and whinnied uncertainly down the far slope. Ariel could only imagine her friends sliding, like she had, down the opposite face of the ridge. Not being able to see their descent, to know they were riding the mud as safely as she had, was torture.

Swiveling his head toward Ariel, Willow blew in confusion. Then, more the Finder's horse than anyone's, he stepped gingerly away from her. His hindquarters bunched and he sank almost to sit on his haunches as his forelegs splayed from beneath him. Willow, too, disappeared from the ridge.

Ariel called her friends' names until her throat felt raw. No one answered.

"They're all right." She talked aloud to drown out the fear of disaster. "They're fine. We just need to meet up." But she struggled with a rush of panic. Scarl could find her, and Zeke probably could, too, if the stones would help him—but only if they hadn't been hurt. And with Willow descending behind them, they may have slid to a safe halt simply to be crushed by a tumbling horse.

"So what do I do?" she murmured. She did not mean to ask her feet, but they answered, so she obeyed, clambering on down the slope toward the point. Her heart balked, reluctant to go even farther from her friends, and twice Ariel stopped to scan the ridge and reconsider. But rounding the headland seemed more possible than climbing back up. Her feet grew more insistent. She didn't dare doubt them.

Only when she reached the waterline did her fear really mount. Now she could see what looked like the headland's farthest point. White spray scattered around it. A hollow knocking kept time as the waves beat on carved rock. Both told her the headland was impassable on foot. She couldn't even wait for an ebb tide. The high water mark fell above where she stood; the tide must be nearly as low as it got.

Ariel scrambled over rocks toward the point anyway, her breath coming in sobs. Unless the ground ahead was drier and less slick than it looked, she'd have to swim in that chill, rugged sea. The hard part would be stroking out far enough to round the headland without being dashed against rocks or swept away by a current.

Just before she kicked off her boots to dive in, an unexpected shape caught her eye. Tucked in a cleft alongside her was a sagging stone house.

Sitting ruined and not far over the high water line, it looked almost as if it had washed up as flotsam. The house was no larger than a sheepfold, and its slate roof had caved in on one side. From where she stood, she could see no windows or doors, but as Ariel went toward it, she spied a low arch. Though the place looked abandoned, perhaps it contained something useful—like dry wood that could keep her afloat in the turbulent waters off the point. Her staff was too thin.

"Hello, is anyone here?"

She ducked through the arch. She had to stop for her eyes to adjust to the darkness, because the ground was littered with stones and debris. As the gloom receded, she tried to lift a downed timber. The roof beam was even too heavy to drag.

"Who are you?"

"Oh!" Ariel whirled. Movement fluttered from the

darkest corner of the room. A hand snatched her wrist and towed her toward the doorway.

"You sure aren't a ghost, so you don't belong here. Where'd you come from?"

Once outside, Ariel's first thought was that she'd met an elf. Small-boned and fair, the creature stood half a head shorter than she did. A boy, Ariel decided, when he spit and repeated his questions with grit in his voice. For all his gruffness, however, he was no older than she was. His hair was the color of winter butter, even lighter than Zeke's, and chopped raggedly over his ears. Those were so delicate as to be almost translucent. His eyes were close-set but sky blue under scowling brows as bleached as his hair. A whorled seashell hung on a lanyard around his thin neck. When her gaze fell on it, he stuffed the shell into the collar of his jerkin as though afraid she might take it.

"I'm Ariel Farwalker," she said. "I'm so glad I found you. I need someone's help. My friends and I were walking above, and we all slid down in mudslides—"

"Aye, treacherous earth, this." The blue eyes flicked to the slope and the muddy blot Ariel had climbed out of. "You're lucky you're breathing."

"I know. And my friends slid down the other side of the ridge. I was trying to get there. Do you know a way? I'm worried about them."

The boy squinted at Ariel, at the hut, at the hillside. "Didn't know any Farwalkers were still in the world. If you're one of 'em, can't you find the way?"

"My feet led me to you! What's your name? Won't you help me?"

"I'm Dain." The boy spit again. "And there's no easy way t'other side of the ridge."

"I'll take a hard way! Will you show me? Oh, please!"

He gauged her. "I don't suppose it'd hurt. But nothing's free, Farwalker. What can you trade?"

Ariel bounced with impatience. "I can take you anywhere you want to go. I have gifts from other places for your village, too. Or one of my friends is a Finder. He'll find for you. But first I've got to find *him.*"

Dain's face lit with an idea.

"Please," Ariel begged, "if one of them's hurt..."

"Trade to come on the tide, then?"

"What's that mean?" Ariel had grown up on the seaside, but she'd never heard this expression.

"It means I'll do for you now, if you'll do later for me, when I ask, knowing only that the asking will come. Like the tide."

Ariel's throat tightened around such a broad promise, but she nodded. "Yes, fine, if it's fair. Can we hurry?"

"Anything?"

"Anything I have the skills for. Or the Finder does." She thought of Zeke, too, but explaining his skills would take far too much time.

Dain nodded. "Done. Come with, then." He turned back into the ruin.

Ariel nearly burst with frustration. "Wait, did you not understand? They're around—"

"No, *you* don't understand, Farwalker girl." Dain grabbed her arm once more. "Stop talking so much and follow."

CHAPTER

8

Dain yanked Ariel into the same dark corner of the hut he'd emerged from. He seemed to drop to his knees. From her waist height, he hissed, "Are you coming or not?"

Ariel's eyes pierced the shadows. Dain was standing in a pit on rough steps leading farther down into the dark. It could be a passage, but it might be a cell.

"I am," she replied with a gulp. "But what is it?"

"The tunnels. Jump down." Dain descended a few steps to make room. He steadied her when she stumbled and shifted his grip to her hand. "Don't let go," he added. "Might never find you again."

He led Ariel down into clammy darkness. By the tenth step, her world shrank to the tight squeeze of Dain's fingers and the slick, uneven stairs underfoot. She clamped her staff under her armpit so she'd have a free hand to reach to the wall. Hewn from the rock, the passage was barely as wide as most doorways. Dank smells rose about her, and she instinctively ducked to keep from banging her head.

She stumbled at the end of the stairs, unprepared for the flat.

"Two skips left and one right." Dain hurried forward. Ariel didn't understand what he meant until the wall fell away from her hand and then smacked back into place. There were passages branching off this one. Ariel's respect for Dain's guidance—and her fear of being left—grew.

Needing to hear more than the echo of footsteps and the distant slap of water on rock, she asked, "Did somebody dig this?" It was not much like sea caverns she'd known back home.

Dain pulled her into a left turn. "Some's been dug, some's natural, some's an old— ah." A gleam shone ahead, where an oil lamp made from a hollow kelp bulb rested in a niche in the wall. Dain reached for it. After so much darkness, the tiny flame glowed like the sun. It lit a junction of five passages, counting the one they'd emerged from.

"You did good, Farwalker girl," Dain said. "I had to have fire the first time I came in. And it's a devil's task to get through this fork without sight."

All five gaping mouths looked alike to Ariel, but Dain towed her into one without hesitation. The floor slanted up, and soon daylight pricked overhead as if they were walking a very deep canyon. Before their way became enclosed again, the angle of the slope above them let Ariel know they'd crossed to the opposite side of the ridge.

Breathless from their pace, she asked Dain, "Aren't you scared of a cave-in?"

He shrugged. "I find new dead-ends and places to swim all the time. Water's higher than it was in the old days." He turned a corner and stopped short at a blank wall.

"Uh-oh. Wrong turn?" Ariel asked.

"Nah. Just haven't come this way in a while. Forgot." He thrust the lamp at her, backtracked a few paces, and pulled a long boathook from a crack in the tunnel. With it, he fished in the darkness at the top of the wall. A knotted rope dropped with a thump. Hanging from above, it helped Ariel to see that the wall didn't reach quite to the ceiling.

Dain replaced the hook. "You climb rope?"

"Guess I'll have to." Desperation propelled her, and the knots gave Ariel's hands and feet purchase. After clambering onto the shelf at the top, she looked back down at Dain. He tossed her walking stick up. The third time, she nabbed it.

"What about your lamp?" she asked. That would not suffer a missed catch.

Dain blew it out. Crouched on the brink, Ariel didn't dare move. She followed the sound as he climbed and joined her on the ledge.

His whisper came through the dark. "Hands-and-knees is all there's room for up here."

"How do I hold onto you?"

"Don't. Just follow. Nowhere else to get lost."

Emptiness bloomed alongside her as Dain moved away.

"Wait! Which way?" she cried, afraid of tumbling over the face she'd just climbed or, for that matter, other drops in the dark. She swept ahead with her staff.

"This way. This way, Farwalker girl. Far-crawling girl now, maybe, huh?"

She followed Dain's voice and only bumped her head once. They emerged into the side of a curved tunnel of brick that allowed them to stand and had a light at the end. Ariel had to shield her eyes from its glare.

When they stepped into that daylight, Dain pointed. "There?"

Ariel squinted through her fingers. "Oh! Yes!" She hurried a short way downhill and east toward spilled earth. "Scarl! Zeke!" The mud on this side had flowed all the way into the water. Willow stood beyond. He was matted with clay and his pack had slipped around to his belly, but he cropped the sparse grass as though nothing more than a lunch stop had happened.

Neither Scarl nor Zeke stood beside him. Ariel whirled to search the ochre-stained waves, dreading the sight of drowned friends.

A head popped up from the far side of a muddy heap. "Ariel!" Scarl stood and began clambering toward her.

Feeling like she could breathe for the first time in an hour, she ran to meet him. "I'm so glad you're— careful!" He slipped nearly the rest of the way to the sea. At least now she could help him out if need be. "Where's Zeke?"

"He's here, too." Scarl eyed Dain, who came behind Ariel. "But he's struggling to breathe."

"What's wrong?" Ariel crawled through the mud toward him, not bothering to try to remain on her feet.

"Mud in his lungs, broken ribs, I don't know." Scarl looked at Dain. "Can you get a Healtouch from your village?"

"Don't got one."

Scarl's mouth tightened.

Zeke lay propped on the clean slope near the far edge of the mud. As Ariel approached, he gave her a weak smile.

"You know I don't... swim as well as you," he wheezed. "Goes double, swimming in... mud."

She knelt beside him. "Oh, Zeke, does it hurt?"

"Yeah, but mostly it's... like Willow's... sitting on me. Can't..." He coughed and grimaced with pain. "Catch m' breath."

Ariel laid her hand on his muddy shoulder and threw a wild look at Scarl. "What do we do?"

Dain stepped up behind them, nimbly picking through the mud. "It's his windbox that's broken? I might can help, then."

"Oh, please, Dain!" said Ariel. "How?"

Dain replied, "I'm a Windmaster's apprentice. Move. Let me listen."

The Windmaster Ariel had known growing up could predict and sometimes influence the weather, but his success depended largely on the mood of the wind. Leed Windmaster would have laughed at someone who said wind and breath had anything in common but air. Nonetheless, Ariel moved out of the way.

Dain bent his ear close to Zeke's face and told him, "Breathe best you can." Briefly he listened, and then he pressed on Zeke's chest. Zeke winced.

Scarl reached to stop Dain. "Hold on. We don't want to—"

Dain jerked his head up and whistled through his teeth, the sound not loud but shrill.

Ariel would not have believed what happened next if she hadn't felt it herself. A gust of wind swept downslope to buffet both her and Scarl. She steadied herself with both hands on the ground while her hair whipped and her clothes fluttered. Above her, Scarl stumbled backward under the wind and slid in the mud nearly to the water before he could stop.

"I said let me listen," Dain muttered.

Ariel didn't dare comment. She only gripped Zeke's arm as Scarl, looking stunned, recovered his ground.

"You're gurgling and sticking," Dain told Zeke. "Close your eyes and open your mouth. Wide."

"What are you going to do?" Ariel asked.

"Fix him," Dain said. "Or you want he should catch the 'monia and die? 'Cause he will."

Zeke shot Ariel a desperate look, which she relayed to Scarl.

"I have no knowledge of this," he growled. "I'd turn your companion over my knee, but I doubt I could get close enough."

"You can't," Dain said. "You want I should help him or not? He's your friend, not mine."

Zeke choked, "I'll... decide. But let *me*... listen first." One of his hands scuttled sideways to exposed stone, which he stroked. His eyes closed and his lips moved.

When Zeke opened his eyes again, he said, "Do it."

Throwing Scarl a smug look, Dain tipped back Zeke's head and drew his jaw open wide.

"Probably hurt some," he said.

Zeke flapped one hand in submission. Without releasing Zeke's chin, Dain reached with his other hand to the shell on his lanyard. Ariel had forgotten about it. The holes in the shell made her guess it must be a wind pipe, though it didn't look much like the only one she'd ever seen. Dain raised it to his lips, tipped his face to the sky, and began to play.

The tones that emerged were part whistle, part hiss, and part screech. They rose and fell, sounding first like the howl in a storm and then like a whisper in grass. The air stirred and churned, amplifying the sounds until the noise became painful. Ariel cringed, ducking her head. Scarl gripped her shoulder to reassure her—or maybe just to stay on his feet.

With a final hollow note, Dain bent and blew his pipe straight into Zeke's open mouth. Air rushed past to follow that puff. Zeke's back arched and his body inflated visibly. Ariel gasped.

Dain scrambled out of the way, dropping his pipe from his lips. Zeke convulsed and rolled to one side, clots of mud flying from his open mouth. A watery, spewing cough followed. The air stilled.

In the sudden silence, Zeke vomited violently, heaving and spitting until tears leaked from his eyes. Dain moved farther uphill. Ariel cringed at the smell, her own innards uneasy, but she stroked Zeke's back to comfort him. As he grew limp, helpless in his retching, Scarl edged past her to support Zeke's chest and head.

The convulsions finally eased. Zeke lay panting in Scarl's lap, wiping his mouth.

"Oh," he gasped, "that hurt *a lot*, Dain. A lot. I can breathe better now, though. I think I could sit up, Scarl. Maybe."

As Scarl propped Zeke up, Dain kicked mud over Zeke's mess. "Did that once to a drownt Fisher. He puked real good, too. He'd been windless too long, though. Wasn't quite right in the head after that. But you weren't out cold, so your head should still work."

Ariel wiped Zeke's face with her sleeve. "Are you truly all right?" she whispered.

Zeke took a tentative breath, drew it deeper, and nodded. "My ribs ache, but the weight's gone. Easier to inhale."

Scarl left Zeke to Ariel's tending. He rose and approached Dain.

"Forgive my suspicion," he said. "I'm not sure what you are, Dain, but you're no apprentice."

Dain shrugged and turned away. "The wind likes me." But Ariel caught the pleased glow in his face.

"Well, I'm grateful," Scarl added. "I doubt we can trade you anything to equal what Zeke means to us, but we'll try."

Dain's eyes darkened. "Oh, aye," he said, his voice soft. "You do owe me."

CHAPTER

9

Before long, Zeke felt able to stand, with some help. "Suppose you'll want to see the others who live here now, hey?" Dain said. "It's not far."

"Do we have to go back into the tunnels?" Ariel feared Zeke might not manage the hard parts.

But Dain shook his head and waved them down the grassy strip clinging between the waterline and the steeper cliffs above. "Just down 'round the corner, that's all."

Ariel braced Zeke while Scarl removed their packs from the horse, carrying his and Zeke's both. They left Willow to graze, since the horse could not wander far. Dain led them along shore toward the point.

Ariel found herself not merely following Dain but studying him as he picked his way among the wrack tossed ashore by the sea. Now that she had time to compare him to Zeke, she wondered if she'd been wrong about his gender. Dain might be a wisp of a fellow who moved with uncommon grace. The name sounded to her like a boy's, and Dain's coarse jerkin and trousers seemed mannish enough. But the creature dressed in them could be a fierce girl, one who'd challenged Ariel's courage with irony by calling her "Farwalker girl."

It would be rude to ask, and she couldn't ask for opinions from Scarl or Zeke with Dain right there to hear.

As Ariel tried to think of a question that would reveal the truth indirectly, Dain brought them to a tiny cove hidden just shy of the point. A spring gushed from broken rock to cascade into the sea, and a dozen stone houses clung impossibly, like limpets, to the steep-sided cliffs on both sides. Their gables jutted in all directions, and some were so crooked that Ariel wondered if their furniture rested in piles in the lowest corner of each house. The one person she saw looked crooked, too—a bent old man packing mud between the stones of his house. He stared, not returning Dain's wave.

Dain led on between the houses, where a few mostly derelict boats bobbed at the end of a cobbled slipway. The boats were tethered to rings embedded in the slip or the cliffs. They tugged against their slimy green bowlines with every back-surge of the sea. Ariel could see swaying kelp and pale shingle through the water, but it was too deep to wade, and she wondered if the Fishers swam out to their boats.

"What do you call this place?" she asked.

"Dead Man's Cove."

Thinking of Elbert, Ariel shivered. But the village couldn't possibly have been named for someone a mere two years dead. "Were ships wrecked on the point?" she asked. "And dead sailors washed up?"

Dain narrowed his eyes at her. "No. If anyone who

doesn't belong here sets foot ashore, he's soon to be dead and adrift in the cove."

Ariel swallowed hard.

"And my mama's a one-legged pirate," Dain added, amused by the effect of his words. "Cassalie! Hey, Cassalie!"

Dain waved toward someone who'd just surged from the sea and was now treading water. The dripping head belonged to a woman. She had stronger, browner features than Dain's but hair of the same empty color, even wet. It ran in a tight plait over one ear like a creamy sea snake. Whisking water from her face with long fingers, the woman blinked at the new arrivals.

"Strangers!" Dain added. He looked askance at Ariel. "Might need to run a marlinspike through 'em."

As smooth as an eel, the woman swam toward them. "From over land?"

"We're afoot, not aboat, aren't we?"

"Well, it looks like they might have crawled from a hole!"

Ruefully Ariel glanced down at her clothes. In her worry for Zeke, she'd almost forgotten how mud-caked they were.

"We're not usually this dirty," she called. "We got caught—"

"In a mud bath, I see," said the woman. "No matter. We've water aplenty, that's certain."

When she reached shallows, she stood, and Ariel saw two things at once: Cassalie was long-limbed and lithe, and she wore nothing at all in the water, at least not from the waist up. As she waded nearer, a mesh bag appeared, tied around her waist and bulging with shellfish, along with a stubby knife in one hand.

Alongside Ariel, Zeke made a small, strangled sound.

The rapt look on his face hinted that he never noticed the woman's gathering bag or her knife.

Scarl cleared his throat. "Zeke." He'd averted his eyes, and with a tiny shake of his head, he nudged Zeke to follow suit. But surprise and a certain intrigue were also stamped on his face.

Cassalie laughed, a splashing sound that harmonized with the swish of water around her. "Oh, have I shocked you?" she called. "So sorry. None left here cares, and I've grown mindless to it. It's such a waste to get clothes wet. Here." She sank in the water to hide her breasts. "Toss me my wrap, Dain. Keep it dry, now."

Dain grabbed a bundle from near the water's edge and flipped it over the waves with a slight, singsong whistle. Cassalie caught it.

"There now," she called. "All furred, as if I hadn't got any shy parts." She'd stood again and waded closer, now wrapped by a spotted skin that had once belonged to a seal. It didn't hide much of her legs, neither of which was a carved wooden peg. Her feet were not finned like a mermaid's, either—Ariel checked as the woman came over the cobblestones toward them.

"Welcome, I think," Cassalie said. "You don't look cruel enough to be pirates, though you're dirty enough. Or if you are, you'll be disappointed. We have nothing to steal. I'm Cassalie Reaper. Clearly you've met Dain, who doesn't usually bring home such interesting flotsam." She extended one hand in a fist, knuckles toward them.

Ariel had figured out many unfamiliar greetings, but she wasn't sure what to do with a fist.

Scarl ventured his own fist, reaching it near but not touching Cassalie's. "Scarl Finder," he said. "Well met."

With a smile, Cassalie knocked her knuckles on his.

"And I'm—" Ariel began.

"Hold off with the nice-ies," Dain said. "The boy's had a lick o' drowning in that mud."

Cassalie's eyes widened. "Oh! You put the wind in him, then? Is he all right?"

"Think so," Dain replied. "But best he should lie down and rest, Cass."

Cassalie hurried to Zeke and swept an arm around him. "Why didn't you say so to start, Dain?"

"Well, it's not desperate, clearly. He's standing."

"No thanks to the dawdling." To Zeke she added, "Come this way. We'll get you soothed. What's his name?"

Zeke answered for himself.

"Ah!" Cassalie replied. "If you're speaking, you must be half right."

"Told you," Dain said. "But don't any of you have regular trades? I mean, Finders I know, but Farwalkers marched away into the sea, and what good's it do singing to stones?"

"Dain!" Cassalie scolded. "Run ahead and put on the kettle. Before I fillet you." Dain obeyed, trotting toward a nearby cottage.

"Perhaps we should clean up first," Scarl said. "We can't go in like this."

Cassalie laughed. "You're right! And I'll guess you'll feel a mite too shy to strip. We'll give Zeke a warm bath in a basin, but you two had best dunk. Use the creek-fall so you don't itch from salt. But help me get him to the door first.

I'll send Dain back with warm things to wrap up in while your clothes dry."

"Is Dain your... child?" Scarl asked as he helped Zeke up the uneven slope.

Cassalie snorted. "A child of mine would have more manners." She sobered. "Suppose it comes to the same, though. Lost her parents at ten. I took her in, you might say."

"Her." Ariel couldn't help but repeat it.

Cassalie turned her seawater gaze on Ariel. "Did Dain tell you different?"

Ariel reddened. "Uh, no, I just—"

A line in Cassalie's brow smoothed and she waved off Ariel's answer. "No, no, I don't blame you, and that's a long tale. But never mind us. I haven't heard tell of strangers coming in from the land side. Are you lost?"

"Not a bit. But I'm sorry, we got off wrong with our greetings." Ariel introduced herself.

"Farwalker? You must be an albatross to get here through the mountains." They reached Cassalie's doorstep. "You don't bring bad luck like an albatross, do you?"

"No! I hope not, at least." Ariel glanced about for the flies. They hadn't followed this far. Perhaps they'd been confused by the landslides and tunnels. "I mostly bring news and gifts to share with your village." Besides the old man, she'd spied only one pinched face peeping from behind a curtain; the few other houses might have been deserted. Usually their arrivals created more stir. "If there's anyone else here to share with?"

Scarl had noticed, too. "Surely you and Dain aren't as alone as you seem?"

"Oh, no." Cassalie chuckled. "Well, depends how you count it, I guess. We've a couple of old 'uns still clinging on, but most won't come out until I reassure them. The rest, just a handful, live out on their boats. They only come in for water or to hide from bad weather." She gestured to a few specks on the horizon.

Scarl said, "I'd expect they have plenty of warning for storms. With an apprentice like Dain, your Windmaster must be quite skilled."

Cassalie reached her hand to the latch but did not open the door. "We have none but Dain, though she's only fourteen. The wind snatched her master one day from the point." She dropped her voice. "Don't tell Dain I said so, but the master begrudged her talent and tried to do more than his own skills could manage. The wind either failed him or punished his cheek. Dain thinks the wind took the master aloft, but I've seen his sorry bones under the sea." She swung the door open, adding brightly, "Go drown the mud, then, and we'll get Zeke bathed, too. Dain! Is that kettle a-boil yet? We need to soak Zeke!"

Although Zeke looked daunted about being left alone in Cassalie's care, Scarl and Ariel dropped their gear and hurried back to the tumbling creek. Its icy water stole their breath. Even more impressed by Cassalie's nude work in the sea, Ariel scrubbed off the mud as fast as she could and hauled herself out.

"Rather unlike your old home in Canberra Docks," Scarl said, as they wrung out their clothes as best they could while standing in them.

"I'll say," she replied. "But in some ways, Cassalie's like Fishers I've known. A lot prettier, though."

"I'd say she's a splash of the wild sea itself," Scarl said. "But I'll be content if she tends Zeke as fast as she talks."

Cassalie welcomed them back to her house with an armful of seal fur robes.

"Already? You're quick, and Dain's slow. But come in." She thrust the skins into their arms as they entered, keeping only the one that barely clad her. "Step behind a sail and change if you like, or wrap up and dry in your clothes, if you'd rather. Wet dribbles can't hurt a thing here."

A striped sail hung between the entry and the rest of the house to hold warmth that otherwise might've leaked out the door. Cassalie drew it aside for her guests to duck past. Beyond, Dain knelt feeding the fire. Zeke, clean and bundled, lay propped beside it. The stone walls were draped with more tattered sailcloth, which softened the main room and veiled others beyond narrow doorways. The furnishings consisted mostly of short stools and a table. The floor indeed was uneven, but the stools did not slide, and the fire gave the place rustic charm.

"Two more for your tea, Dain." Cassalie turned to Ariel as she began to strip the plait from her hair. It fell in damp waves around her. "Prod her a bit, would you? And I'll put on my land skin so your fellows won't keep blushing each time I move. That's no way to treat guests, is it? Shocking them. Blimey."

She laughed and ducked out of sight behind a drape. Looking downright disappointed, Zeke turned to peek as her legs disappeared, but Scarl was careful not to watch Cassalie go.

Still, Ariel could tell from the taut lines of his neck that his disinterest took effort.

CHAPTER

10

Scarl steamed in his clothes near the fire, but Ariel stepped behind a sail to strip off her wet things and snuggle into a robe before sitting beside Zeke at the hearth. Cassalie returned carrying her collection bag and wearing a supple, grey leather dress that nearly brushed the stone floor. Her hair, all loose waves now, shone golden against it.

"What is that leather?" Ariel asked. She'd also noticed it in the shirt under Dain's rougher jerkin. The dress was pieced of sizable strips, and she hadn't seen so much as a deer track on the ridge.

Cassalie smoothed her skirt. "Shark, I'm afraid. They're so clever that I hate to reap them, but shellfish and sea slugs won't do for all things. Speaking of which, are you hungry?"

"You've killed a shark?" Ariel exclaimed. "By yourself?"

Zeke's jaw dropped, too.

"It's not so hard when they're sleeping." Cassalie emptied her bag into a basin and began rinsing the shellfish with water from a bucket. "A mite unfair, but not hard. The hard part is raising them to the surface before they're ripped to shreds by their mates. The blood calls them."

"I don't know sharks," Scarl said. "What are they like?"

"Like a lion in the water, with fifty more teeth," Zeke told him. "They eat Fishers for snacks when they get bored with seals."

"Oh, no," Cassalie said. "They bite the wrong thing sometimes, that's all. Mistakes."

Duly impressed, Scarl said, "I wondered how a Reaper managed on such unstable land."

Cassalie flashed him a smile. "I climb the cliffs after bird eggs, but I do most of my reaping from the sea. Mussels, crab, the odd flatfish, sea lettuce, and such."

"Isn't it cold to dive naked, though?" Ariel asked.

"I suppose," Cassalie said. "But wet clothes wouldn't warm me, only slow me and drag. I've got to dive slick and fast to get what we need before my breath gives out. I rub on seal fat when the weather's too chill."

"How deep do you go?" Zeke asked.

"Oh, when I'm feeling strong and the sun's bright, ten fathoms."

"Wow."

Cassalie giggled. "You make it sound so exotic. I do what I can to feed us, that's all."

"That's all," Scarl said wryly.

She flipped a scallop shell at him. Startled, he caught it.

Cassalie bustled to the fire. "Now you're all making *me* blush. Stop. Where's that tea?"

Their tea was steeped over dried kelp. Ariel had to get used to the taste, but the warmth was soothing. They sat around the fire, sipping from cups made of moonsnail shells.

"Tell me now, if I'm not being rude," Cassalie said, "whatever above the sea or below it brought you to us?"

Ariel hesitated, unsure how frank she should be about Elbert. She'd been prepared for a rough or violent place—not kindness or people who might mourn him.

"Two things," she began carefully. "First, I'm a Farwalker, so I travel to faraway places." As she described her usual tasks, Cassalie stopped her.

"I think I understand, and how lovely," she said. "I can rouse the old'uns and hang the flag in the morning for the Fishers to see. They can sail in to meet you on the incoming tide."

A knock rattled the door. Dain jumped up to answer, but the door didn't wait. It flew open, and a boat hook shoved the sailcloth drape aside. Next came the old man they'd noticed outside patching mortar. He stopped short to see them all sipping tea.

"All well, Cass?" His rheumy gaze settled with suspicion on Scarl.

"Oh, yes, Isaiah! Look—visitors!"

"I seen 'em," he said. "Strangers. You sure you're all right, then?"

Cassalie assured him she was. She began introductions, but Isaiah waved off her words and Scarl's greeting.

"Time for sugar-talk later. I'll let Tilda know you're not being murdered. Pardon t'interruption, Cassalie."

"Bring Tilda back, if you like," Cassalie told him. "Or you'll get another chance to meet our new friends tomorrow. We'll gather at flood tide."

Grumbling about sea-snakes and strangers, the old man ducked out.

Cassalie covered a laugh. "Please forgive his poor welcome!"

Scarl shook his head. "He's looking out for you, that's all. It wouldn't be the first time we were taken for thieves."

"Or worse," Ariel said.

"Then you nearly belong here, since it's a smuggler's cove," Cassalie replied. "But we can talk of that later. I'd like to hear more about the Vault you spoke of, if you won't mind repeating it tomorrow. I could listen while I fry scallops for you. Would that be a fair trade?"

"Scallops, mmm." Dain licked her lips. Ariel smiled, too.

While Cassalie shucked scallops with her stubby knife, Ariel told her about the treasure she'd unveiled in the abbey. She mentioned that Allcrafts she'd led there had begun to build forgotten devices, and Scarl showed the timepiece that didn't yet work. Cassalie and Dain admired it anyway.

"Like a metal sand dollar," Cass said. "But it must work a little, because it reminds me that I'm using up all of your time, and you said two things brought you here. What's the second? I must be keeping you from it."

Ariel glanced at Scarl, no longer sure she should say. He offered no help.

"There's a shark's tooth," she said. "In a knife tied onto my walking stick."

"I noticed the stick, not the knife or the tooth," Cassalie said. "May I see it?"

"I'll get it." Dain ran to the entry to fetch it. "Ugh!"

Ariel frowned. "Do you recognize it?"

Dain pushed through the drape, holding the staff at arm's length. "It's bloody."

"What?" Ariel had rinsed it with her clothes in the creek. "It must just be mud that I missed."

"Don't reckon." Dain held up her hand to show a damp red streak too bright to be mud. With a cry, Cassalie jumped up.

Ariel said, "It cut you! I thought the wrappings—"

"Nah." Dain wiped her hand on her clothes and displayed unbroken skin.

"It must be yours," Scarl told Ariel. "It probably nicked you during the mudslide. You didn't feel it?"

"No, I..." Ariel searched herself for a wound and found only old scars. Besides, when she took the staff from Dain, the bindings around Elbert's blade were snugger than ever, since the leather was shrinking as it dried. Yet more blood oozed from between them.

"Creepy. But it figures, knowing where that knife came from," Zeke muttered.

"Where might that be, a nightmare?" Cassalie's nose wrinkled. "Chumbuckets, Ariel. Does your trade make you bear such an unpleasant thing?"

"It's not mine!" Ariel said. The last blood drawn by that blade had been hers, though. Perhaps some had dried at the handle to be wetted and drip out when she rinsed it. That seemed unlikely, but eerier explanations made her breath too hard to catch.

More blood dribbled onto the floor.

Cassalie grabbed a sea sponge and scrubbed at the puddle. "Please take that out of my house."

"I'm sorry." Ariel stumbled outside with the staff.

She'd planned to cast the knife into the waves, but not yet. Ariel wanted to find the right spot to drown it forever—somewhere Elbert had known, or somewhere he'd stood. She had work to do before she'd know where.

So she scurried to the creek and plunged the knife into the flow, cramming the end of the staff between rocks. Fresh water spilled over the blade. The runoff turned pink before it finally cleared. She could leave the staff wedged there and get rid of the knife later. Ariel hoped the wood wouldn't become too waterlogged. Since Nace had smoothed it for her, she liked to think she could touch his hand through the grip.

It struck her that if clasping her staff could bring her closer to Nace, touching the knife pulled her nearer to Elbert.

A stench of rot swirled around her. Ariel's gorge rose. She jumped back, leaving the staff sticking out at an angle. Now she smelled only saltwater and kelp.

Yet her stomach still trembled. She hadn't imagined the stink. Elbert's blade had some power here that it hadn't before, or an evil flushed out by the fresh, running water.

Ariel backed away, leaving the knife for later, when she'd have help from her friends. By then, there shouldn't be any more blood.

CHAPTER

11

By the time Ariel returned to the house, Scarl had taken the sponge from Cassalie and was wiping up the last of the drips.

"I'll take that out to clean, too," Ariel told him.

"Never mind. We've a whole sea of sponges. Here—" Cassalie plucked it from Scarl and flung it into the fire. The flames squealed and leapt in a putrid green blaze.

"Whew! Do sponges always burn like that?" Zeke asked.

"Never," whispered Cassalie. They stared while the flames ebbed around the charred lump.

Returning to her stool, Cassalie ran her hands over her knees, visibly trying to calm herself. "A shark's tooth, you said. I won't blame the shark. How did this thing bring you to us?"

"It's a long story," Ariel told her. "And not a nice one. But I wanted to see where that knife came from."

Cassalie's pale eyebrows jumped. "Here?"

Ariel didn't want to be rude, but she was certain. The urge to walk had left her feet.

"I'd like to deny it," Cassalie said, "but the cove has harbored its share of both shark's teeth and evil." She shook her head. "Not recently, though. And not in a way so uncanny!"

Dain asked, "Is the knife cursed?"

"You might say so," Zeke said. "It belonged to someone named Elbert."

Dain's eyes widened. "I had an uncle named Elbert."

"Oops," said Zeke in a small voice. Ariel could see no resemblance except that Elbert had also been blond.

"Went off long ago, though," Dain added. "Don't hardly remember."

Cassalie shifted uneasily. "Eight years or so gone. He was a Finder, too, and decided to find somewhere better. There aren't many treasures here to be found, nor much at all for anyone not fond of the sea."

"Plus Cass wouldn't have him," Dain said. "That's why he left, you ask me. I remember that much."

"Dain! I'll thank you not to share such things with guests!" Cassalie added more softly, "That's done and gone. As is Elbert from here."

Ariel decided to stick with the truth. "From the world. Elbert died two years back."

"Oh." Cassalie studied her. "Not to your sorrow, I see."

"Nor yours," Scarl observed.

Cassalie looked into her lap. "It's wicked of me. But no, this news brings me no grief."

Dain's face, although solemn, held more curiosity than sadness. Unspoken stories hung low in the room, but nobody offered to tell them, or asked.

Cassalie broke the silence. "What will you do with his weapon?"

"I was going to throw it into the sea," Ariel told her. "But I wouldn't want blood to attract sharks where you dive."

Cassalie shivered. "Perhaps Dain can lead you to somewhere I don't."

"Oh, aye," Dain said, her voice melancholy. "I know places to lose stuff forever."

"Let's talk of something sweeter, before we spoil the taste of our scallops." The Reaper reached for a fry-stone. "Please tell me more about your abbey. And trees. I mostly know them from driftwood."

While Cassalie cooked, she plied them with questions until Ariel's throat grew scratchy. Then Ariel and her friends listened as Cassalie told of a time when those who lived here did little but smuggle by boat. The tunnels had helped them whisk away stolen goods and evade pursuit.

"And sent more than one robbed sailor to his death," Cass added. "Knives other than yours have dripped red, I expect. Dain and I are descended from scoundrels and thieves." She laughed. "So watch us carefully with your things! Though Dain's probably the only one who still knows the tunnels. It's dangerous, and I worry. Our people hid there during the Blind War, they say, but to me they seem stifling and much worse than death."

"That shelter may be why you're here at all, though," Scarl said.

"I suppose. I know little of war tales or how others survived. Our last Storian left the world before I came in. Can you tell me more from your travels?"

He could and did.

After they ate, Zeke and Dain nodded off at the fire. Ariel curled between them, wondering what evil clung to Elbert's knife. She'd not seen his shape, heard his voice, or met anything in her nightmares but grasping hands, and for that, she was grateful. But *something* was haunting the knife. Surely the glimmers she knew as the Essence, sparks of the life force itself, would not render blood, flies, or stenches... though she supposed even those had a purpose and place. Perhaps the Essence could be bent astray or had an opposite force.

Ariel shivered. In becoming a Farwalker, she'd once ventured into a dark, unpleasant void. If sparks of the Essence could appear in the world, perhaps splinters of that Nothing, that unformed-ness, could, too.

Afraid to ponder it too much near bedtime, Ariel was glad Cassalie kept coaxing stories from Scarl. The low, even rumble of his voice soothed her, fitting well with the murmur of the waves in the cove. Cassalie was more like a tide. She would chatter at high speed for long minutes, barely giving Scarl time to answer her questions. Then, as if catching her breath, she would ebb, only smiling whether Scarl filled the silence or not. Often he chose not to, but that didn't seem to disturb her. In those moments, they all listened to the waves striking outside, the crackling fire, and the sleepers' steady breathing, which harmonized well.

"It's a treat to have new friends to talk with," Cass murmured. "Dain and I are so worn to each other, we barely speak. And to think of all the villages the three of you see!"

"Few with a welcome quite like this, though," Scarl said.

Cass laughed, which seemed to be her response to most everything. "Or quite so much trauma, I hope!" But she smiled at her hands, and Scarl's eyes rested on her without comment. Ariel could feel invisible waves rippling and bouncing between the adults. It was odd, because it didn't make her feel left out, though she was. It made her feel the same way the fire did—warmed, though she was neither the wood nor the flame.

"Oh!" Cassalie rose to draw aside a curtain and peep at the darkening sky. "The day flew while I wore out your ears, and night's falling. Where will you sleep? Foolish me, here I stuffed you with scallops and questions without giving more important matters a thought!"

"We'll sleep under the sky," Scarl said. "We do all the time."

"No, no, I can't let you do that. Often at night, the sea brings in rain, and Dain hasn't mastered the weather so much as she sometimes thinks."

Half-awake, Dain mumbled a vague protest.

"The boathouse would work," added Cass. "It's not terribly cozy, but I can give you warm furs. Zeke, though—maybe I should keep him by the fire."

"Huh?" Zeke awakened at his name. "Where are we going?"

"To bed," Ariel told him. "In the boathouse. Want to come? Or stay here?"

"We don't bel— Oh. Yeah, I'll come with you." Groggy, he rose.

Her arms loaded with furs, Cassalie led them to a listing stone shack at the top of the slip. Behind its large wooden door, a boat was rotting inside. They arranged musty sails on the floor for a mattress. After Cass bid them good night, Scarl asked Ariel what she'd done with the knife.

She told him. "It stunk like a dead thing."

"We'll leave it there, then," he said. "Until daylight, at least. I've never put much truck in superstition, but I'll sleep more soundly when that blade is gone."

Shivering, Ariel tried not to think of how often she'd slept with it near. The boathouse felt hollow and chill after the hearth, and the walls' crumbling mortar wouldn't stop any flies, but perhaps they'd stay out with the knife. She imagined the blade flying through to stab them, but the chinks were too narrow for that.

They wrapped in their blankets and drew furs overtop, Ariel snuggling between Scarl and Zeke. Once wakeful, though, Zeke was restless. When Ariel asked if his chest hurt, he said, "I'm all right. I just... I heard the stones of the cove in my sleep. Saying something about going where we don't belong."

Ariel laughed. "The first thing Dain said was that I didn't belong here. Even the rocks think like smugglers, I guess. But Cassalie's friendly enough."

"Dain's not so bad, either. I probably was dreaming. Think we'll stay very long?"

Scarl's voice came through the dark. "We could, a short while. Our nights might be warmer if we wait here a week, or even two, and let spring catch up. I know you were anxious to be off from the abbey, Ariel, but with that done..." Waves slopped outside. "It's your decision, of course."

She smiled at the rafters and wondered how much of his desire to linger truly centered on weather. Perhaps she could ask Dain to send them off with a spring breeze regardless.

Then, with a discomfort that kept her awake long after her companions, she wondered exactly what Dain wanted in trade. Clearly the young Windmaster had something in mind, something almost too great to ask. She was biding, that's all. Ariel had occasionally caught the other girl watching her that evening with a curious mix of excitement and dread. And she'd known by Dain's bitten lip and quick glances away that she'd been thinking of the debt—and just how to collect.

CHAPTER

12

By the time Ariel rose the next morning, Cassalie had hung a bright flag on the cliff to signal boats to come into the cove. She'd also laid out a breakfast of hot lichen porridge, and she chattered brightly the whole time they ate. Afterward Ariel asked, "Would anyone mind if we stayed here a week?"

The Reaper's eyes sparkled. "Mind? Shall I beg you?"

"You needn't keep feeding us," Scarl assured her. "We have food of our own, and I can always find more. I should be doing that now." He reached for his coat.

Cassalie stopped him. "Don't go yet. Unless it's just an excuse to get away from my questions. If so, I can hush."

"No." Scarl's lips twitched. "The pain of your company is... tolerable."

And indeed, as the Reaper's smile grew flustered and she bustled after more tea, Ariel repeatedly caught Scarl... doing what? He wasn't watching Cassalie. It was more like he was listening to her with his skin—alert to her movement as if about to respond, but without ever tensing a muscle.

Ariel whispered to Zeke, "Have you noticed how much Scarl likes Cassalie?"

Zeke frowned. "Don't you like her?"

She rolled her eyes. "Forget it."

Before long, Scarl rose. "I've sat idle enough." He turned to Cassalie. "What do you need that I might find for you, in trade for our breakfast?" He ignored her protests. Reminded of Dain's evasions about what she wanted, Ariel wondered if everyone here was so hard to trade with.

Cassalie, however, soon laughed and gave in. "Aye, then. There is one thing— no, wait. That's not fair. Let me think of something else."

"Tell me."

"Well... it's not finding. It's naught but hard work. There's a seam of brimstone in the cliff. We chip it out and burn it when everything else is too wet."

"Brimstone?" Zeke asked. "I want to see!"

Cassalie wrung her hands. "If it's too much to ask, please say so."

Scarl waved off her concern. "Dain, can you show me?"

Dain jumped up. "Aye. I've another stone to show you, too, Zeke. It's not far."

Ariel saw her chance to talk with Cassalie alone. "I'll stay and help with our dishes."

"Those can wait," their hostess told her. "But I've got sea-grapes to pluck while the tide's out. I'll take help with that."

They all trooped outside, the brimstone hunters climbing the stones of the cove while Ariel and Cassalie knelt at tidepools below. Ariel shot a quick glance toward her staff, which remained lodged in the creek-fall. She'd deal with it later.

"That's blister work, prying out brimstone." Cassalie plunged her arm into the tidepool. "I hope your papa won't be sorry he offered."

"He won't." Unfamiliar with sea-grapes, Ariel watched closely as the Reaper's hand worked. "But we're heart-kin, not blood-kin. My father left the world when I was little."

"Oh! I guessed that Zeke was unrelated, but— ah." Cassalie sifted sand through her fingers until all that remained were three green marbles that she plucked from thin seaweed vines. She dropped two in her bowl and popped the other into Ariel's mouth.

Ariel expected a saltwater blast. Instead, the grape burst with a lemony crunch. Grinning, she, too, thrust her fingers into the sand.

"Did Dain tell you I owe her a trade?" she said as they worked. "Every time I ask what, though, she only gets this odd look on her face. Do you know what she'd like?"

Cassalie shook her head. "I can't imagine. Unless... she might hope to find some trace of her family."

"What happened to them?"

"It's a sad tale." Cassalie moved to the next tidepool. "They lived on the windward side of the ridge. One night she had a row with her father, who was rather severe. She ran outside to the wind."

Her eyes gained a faraway gleam. "As a toddler, she'd toss foam off the sea to the breeze, which would spin it for her into patterns. Such talent! She hadn't yet learned how to use it much, though, and when she got upset, the wind roiled, too. A squall blew in that night, and the rain set off mudslides. When Dain finally calmed and returned to her house, it was buried in mud, and help came too late. Her parents and brother were swept out of the world, and she blames herself." Cassalie shook her head. "What she most needs is forgiveness, but you can't trade her that. Perhaps she hopes for some keepsake buried that night."

Ariel nodded. "If it exists, Scarl can find it. And I'll dig it up."

Privately Ariel hoped Cassalie was wrong. A failed search would bring Dain only disappointment. Yet success might be worse, because the last thing Ariel wanted to dig up was bones.

Hammering sounds drifted down from above. Cassalie gazed up the slope to the bent figure there.

"Scarl's had someone reaped from him, too, hasn't he?" she asked.

"Yes."

"It shows." Cass glanced sidelong at Ariel. "Your mother?"

"No. Someone else."

"Ah." Sea-grapes rattled into the bowl. Cassalie's hands never stopped, but her neck kept twisting so she could look up.

Finally Ariel could resist it no longer. "He's interested in you, you know."

"He is?" Cassalie turned wide eyes on Ariel, fighting a smile. "He says so little about himself. How can you tell?"

"I know him."

The shy delight on Cassalie's face dulled. "He has a woman in every village you visit, then."

Offended, Ariel scowled. "No!"

Sand splashed and the Reaper faced Ariel squarely. "Tell me true, Ariel."

"Not even one. Although a few have been interested in him. You're way different, Cassalie."

"I doubt that," Cass murmured, but her hands dipped into the tidepool again.

Ariel wanted to say something more, but she wasn't sure if it should be encouragement, advice, or a warning. Instead, she asked, "Would you teach me to dive like you can?"

Cassalie flashed her a wink. "If it'll keep you here longer, we'll start your lessons today."

They returned to the house with a full bowl and cold arms. Dain and Zeke returned shortly, the latter gushing about what they'd seen.

"There's a stone with a hole the wind sings through," he told Ariel. "Dain says the wind's laughing. And the stone likes it, too. They're best friends. You should hear 'em! Oh— I guess you can't. Not like we can." He and Dain shared a look. A jealous twinge caught Ariel off guard.

"She can hear with her ears, though," Dain offered.

"Sure," Zeke said quickly. "That's almost as good."

Ariel managed a smile.

When Scarl appeared, he brought more than the brimstone. "I remembered a story about brimstone," he said. "So I thought to try finding before I came back." As they all crowded close, he brushed grit from a rock marked with swirls like a seashell.

Cassalie gasped. "A stone nautilus!" She traced the whorls with her fingertip.

"From a world before this," Scarl told them. "A sea creature so old that it's turned into stone. In the story I know, they remind us that all things leave the world, but our shapes here may linger to guide those who remain."

"I'd like to hear that story, Scarl," Cassalie said.

"Perhaps after Ariel talks with your neighbors," he said. "I just saw a boat being beached on the slip."

As Ariel ran to the window, Scarl set the fossil on a ledge over the hearth.

"Oh, you don't mean to leave it?" Cassalie asked Scarl.

"Please," he replied.

She bit her lip, clearly struggling to accept the gift.

"You'd better get used to it," Ariel said with a grin. "I've got farwalking gifts to give, too." She rushed to get her pack from the boathouse.

Maybe one of her treasures would appeal to Dain. That would lighten Ariel's heart, as well as her pack. It also might ease disappointment later if their mysterious trade didn't work out as Dain hoped.

CHAPTER

13

Two boats had sailed into the cove. They brought
a young family that included two children and a
pair of weathered Fishers who looked enough alike to be
sisters. Isaiah, his wrinkled wife, and a gaggle of silver-haired
widows also tottered from their homes to the slip.

"A bit shy on young folk and men," Scarl noted.

"The sea takes all our men, sooner or later, and it's hard
to make young folk without them." Cassalie shaded her eyes
to check for more incoming boats. "No one else is bound
for land, Ariel. Shall I introduce you?"

"I can." Ariel stepped forward, raising her voice. "Thank
you, and well met! I'm Ariel Farwalker, and—"

"I knew a Farwalker, though he wouldn't admit it,"
piped Isaiah. "Ol' Jack Healtouch couldn't cure a warm day
in spring. Wandered everywhere, though. You 'member Jack,
Tilda?"

Heads nodded. "Oh, aye, I knew Jack."

"Gone seventy years now!"

"'Zat right, Isaiah?"

"Know who else I remember? Oma Storian! You were too young, but—"

Conversations sprang up, but without Ariel. Not wanting to be rude, she shot a helpless look at Cassalie, who covered her mirth with her hand.

"Hold on," she whispered. "They'll ease in a moment and recall what got them started."

That turned out to be true, but Ariel never managed more than a couple of sentences before someone interrupted. While the elders buzzed about what should've been in the Vault, the father of the children approached Ariel.

"'Preciate your efforts here, Farwalker," he said. "These old coots haven't had such a grand time in years. Unless something in your Vault catches fish, though, you're wasted on us."

"There probably *are* things to help Fishers," she told him. "The Storians are still figuring it out."

He nodded. "You come back in a few years and let my younglings know, then. If it's not inconvenient. We'll make do, either way."

She began drawing gifts from her pack, thinking those, at least, would focus attention. They did. Medications, seeds, and trinkets were passed for inspection and drew *oohs* and *ahhs*. Yet somehow every one ended back in her bag.

"Them things is lovely, girl, make no mistake," one of the Fisher sisters told Ariel. "Thank ye kindly for hauling 'em here. No spare room on a boat, though, and seeds won't grow there, either. You take 'em to someone who needs those things more. We can get by without. We've had practice with that."

The elders drifted away, apologizing for how easily they tired. The boaters didn't want to miss the outgoing tide. Soon Ariel stood alone on the slip with her friends.

She kicked her pack. "That was the worst I've ever done!"

"Don't be silly," said Cassalie. "I'm not sure what you're used to, but we'll be talking about the Farwalker's visit until the octopus sings."

Scarl laid his hand on Ariel's shoulder. "You know what they need, don't you?"

"Everything! But they won't take anything!" Ariel dropped her voice so Cassalie couldn't hear. "This place is going to die, Scarl. They don't have enough people to even have children."

"Then you can bring them new blood, or you can help the youngest move somewhere new," he told her. "Nothing remains in the world forever."

Dain approached. "I was whisperin' with Lila, from the boat there." Lila, a bright-faced girl of ten or eleven, had been the only member of Ariel's audience who'd been rapt the whole time.

"Lila hates boats," Dain said. "Always has. And now she knows what she wants instead. When it's time, she's going to ask for a Farwalker test."

Ariel's breath caught. "Truly?"

Dain nodded. "Won't nobody know how to test her, I bet, but she's already learned the directions from stars. When they're near shore, she'll swim in to practice on land. That's what she says, anyhow."

"See?" Scarl told Ariel. "You might gain an apprentice from here. And that would be a stunning success—two Farwalkers in the world in five years."

Ariel blinked after Lila's boat. Responsibility for an apprentice was too much to imagine, but the idea eased her sense that she'd failed.

She turned back to Dain. "You saw my gifts, right? Are there any you'd like for our trade? The tree seeds? Trees like the wind." She bent to rummage. "Or I think I have a copy of the marks that tell how to make a windmill."

Dain spit. "My wind doesn't need things like that."

"What, then?"

"Later." Dain ran to splash in the waves. "Let's swim!"

As Ariel stared after Dain, stymied, Cassalie asked her, "Do you still want to learn how to dive?"

"Oh, yes! But..." Ariel's voice dropped. "Do I have to go naked?"

Cassalie grinned. "Dain won't, either. Wear your clothes and we'll dry you out later."

While Scarl climbed the rocks with Dain and Zeke, who jumped off to compete for the biggest splashes, Cassalie showed Ariel new ways to kick and how to hold her breath longer. Ariel went deeper than she'd ever gone, once deep enough to snatch a starfish from the seabed. She saw other creatures she'd like to show Nace, but having thought of the Kincaller, her concentration slipped. It seemed a very long time since she'd hugged him.

At last Cassalie said, "Enough for today. I'm bound in to get warm. Will you join Dain and Zeke?"

"I'll be fine by myself. I grew up on the sea."

"Not in our currents." Cass called to Dain as she retrieved her clothes. "Watch Ariel, too, Dain. I'll leave the door unlatched. Send the wind to bang it if someone's caught in the rip."

"Aye."

"I'll make tea, if you'd like some, Scarl," Cassalie added. The hope in her voice was rewarded. Scarl pushed Zeke, flailing, into the water and climbed down from the rocks.

"Come jump with us," Dain called to Ariel. "You'll get deeper than a dive from the surface." She plunged down herself.

Ariel watched for a few moments from where she floated. They had a rhythm of climbing and splashing together that was complete without her. She imagined the flips and somersaults Nace could have done. Zeke was neither as bold nor as strong, but his limbs sliced through the water, and on land he leapt effortlessly over the rocks.

Dain seemed to have noticed. Her eyes followed him, and grins flashed between them after every leap. When she took Zeke's hand so they could jump down united, Ariel felt a flutter inside. She kicked over for a share of the fun.

They saw her coming and waited on the ledge they'd been using to launch from. Dain and Zeke had worked their way up to this height, so to Ariel, the water rippled a dizzying distance below. Kelp and rocks shadowed the seabed.

"Push out from the shore," Dain advised her. "Like this." She swung her arms and leapt. The wind held her aloft like a bird on an updraft before she finally plunged downward. *Ker-splash!*

"We can go together the first time, if you're nervous." Zeke offered his hand.

Scoffing, Ariel jumped.

As she fell, a wild thought blew through her. She should've taken Zeke's hand just to see how it felt. She'd squeezed his hand plenty of times, but not in a long while. Not since she'd met Nace. Zeke's hands were longer and more delicate. She tried to recall how his fingers meshed with her own.

Water slurped her, making her eyelids pinch shut. By the time she bobbed out, she'd made a decision.

"Fun, aye?" asked Dain, treading water nearby.

"Yes." Ariel returned to the rocks, and Dain followed. Zeke awaited them both at the top.

"All three at once? That'll make a big splash." Standing in the middle, Zeke held out both hands.

Ariel grabbed one. "Too slow!" She jumped to pull him down without Dain. Clutching his hand didn't feel like she'd hoped, though. The rush of falling so overwhelmed their connection, she could hardly feel it at all, and her grip broke once they hit the water. It was too hard to swim with locked hands, anyway. As it was, they were so close they kept kicking each other.

"Why'd you do that?" Zeke asked, spitting water.

"Just playing," Ariel said. "I didn't mean anything."

Still above on the rocks, Dain gestured for them to move out of her way. As Zeke turned to swim, Ariel plastered herself onto his bare back, wrapping her arms and legs around his body so he was still free to swim.

"Dolphin ride?" she said. Years ago, they'd played this game often, though Ariel had always made a better dolphin. "Oh—maybe not, since your chest hurt yesterday. Sorry."

She released him, sliding off his skin, and only after she'd let go did she really feel his body beneath her embrace. The familiar, playful position had gained new sensations, a scalding awareness that stuck after they no longer touched.

Zeke searched her face. "I feel okay today. But you're different."

"No, I'm not." Embarrassed, she splashed him.

Dain hit the water not far away. The splatter showered them both. As soon as she surfaced, she said, "Let's try again—I won't be slow this time!"

Ariel pushed a smile to her lips, which were stiff from the cold. "You go," she told Zeke. "I think I'll dry off."

"Aw, not yet." Zeke cupped his hands to squirt her.

She spanked water at him again in exchange but turned to stroke toward the slip. The thought of holding his hand had knocked something loose and now their friendship wouldn't settle back into place.

Dain called Ariel back. "You've only jumped twice!"

"I'll jump more tomorrow," she said. "Right now I'm cold, and there's something else I want to do."

The sea pulled at her as she waded out. Halfway up the slip, still dragging her feet, she realized some of that weight couldn't be blamed on wet clothes. When she'd said she had something to do, she'd secretly hoped Zeke would follow. And help. Because she planned to pull her staff from the creek and find out from Cassalie where Elbert Finder had lived.

She turned, a request on her lips, as Zeke and Dain again hit the sea, elbows locked. Water showered, the biggest splash yet. She felt jealous of someone, but she wasn't sure who. Maybe anyone who could simply hold hands with a friend without being flooded by thoughts and confusions.

Ariel marched away without hailing them. She could finish with Elbert's knife by herself.

CHAPTER

14

As promised, Cassalie had left her door ajar. Ariel paused in the sheltered entry. Warmth and the smell of kelp tea drifted to her from beyond the sailcloth curtain. Should she call inside and ask for something to dry herself with, or simply walk to the hearth, dripping? She peeked in.

With his back partly to her, Scarl sat at the small table before the fire. His elbows rested near two cups. Light footsteps sounded, and then Cassalie, once more in her sharkskin dress, swished into view and paused alongside him. Ariel reached to push aside the drape, but something in the woman's posture stayed Ariel's hand.

"Can I get you more tea?" Cassalie asked Scarl. "Something to eat? A bit of dried fish?"

Scarl declined with thanks. "I'm content just to sit here with you, Cassalie. If I'm not in the way or keeping you from your work."

"No, no, I don't mean to chase you off." She did not move away, either, confirming Ariel's hunch. There was a tension in Cassalie, or the room, not unlike the snap of air before a storm. Ariel's finger drew the sail open half an inch farther.

"Quite the contrary." Cass nibbled her lips. "I'm very pleased you see fit to linger." She laid her fingertips lightly on Scarl's forearm where it rested on the table.

He glanced at her fingers. Blushing, she started to pull them away. With a flash of his hand, Scarl stopped her, trapping her fingers with his and drawing them back. His gaze lifted to Cassalie's face, which was startled but glowing.

No sound came from either of them. Ariel held her breath and wondered what Cassalie was seeing in Scarl's eyes.

"I fear I don't have time to be shy, Scarl Finder," Cassalie whispered at last. Or perhaps she was breathless.

"I have no particular liking for shy."

Ariel could not see enough of his face to read his expression, but she could hear his amusement—and something else in his voice, too, a throatiness unfamiliar to her. Whatever it was, Cass could not hold his gaze, but looked down at his hand grasping hers.

He brought it to his lips, which barely brushed her skin. Cassalie swayed as though she might faint.

"I hate to see you sleep in the boathouse again," she murmured, so low Ariel strained to hear. "It's drafty and damp. I would... offer you..." She gulped but couldn't go on.

Motionless, Scarl waited a very long moment before his cheek twitched around a sly smile. "A bed?"

Cass winced, but she peeked at his face, and this time she managed to hold his regard. "My bed," she whispered.

Scarl sobered. His thumb stroked the back of her hand.

That tiny caress filled the room. "I would very much like to accept."

Cass heard it, too. "But."

Scarl sighed and looked away. He didn't withdraw his hand from hers, but he lowered them both to the table. "I have my young one to think of."

Ariel had to wrap both arms over her mouth to keep herself from bursting in to contradict him. But Cassalie's face rekindled with hope.

"If that's all," she said, "I have plenty of space. I could make a pallet for Ariel and Zeke in my pantry. Unless... unless what you mean is you wouldn't want them to know."

"It's not that," Scarl said. "They're both nearly grown, and we have few secrets between us. But Ariel's too grown, in my mind, to sleep alone with a boy, even one as familiar as Zeke. Especially one so familiar, in fact."

"Ah." Cassalie's voice grew thoughtful. "What if she slept with Dain and we put Zeke in the pantry? Dain adores her, there's room, and— But I'm persuading you now. I don't want to do that." Flustered, she pulled her hand free, turned away, and busied herself gathering teacups. "I'm sorry."

Scarl studied her straight back for a moment filled with the rattle of dishes. He rose, took one stride to reach her, and slid his hands onto her waist. Her motion stilled, but her gaze remained forward.

Softly he said, "I would not have you sorry." He bent his face to her hair and inhaled. As if that breath pulled her, Cassalie left the dishes and melted against him. His arms wrapped more snugly around her.

"But are you certain, Cassalie?" he added. "I... We won't be here forever."

She spun sharply to face him. "And who is? I know exactly how quickly the sea or cliffs can reap me out of the world, Scarl. Me or anyone else. I'm quite sure." Her palms rose to his shoulders.

Scarl stroked the firm line of her jaw with one thumb. "Let me speak with her, then."

He shifted his weight toward the entry, reluctance in even that partial motion. Ariel knew she'd be discovered if she didn't flee. She backed off on tiptoe, slipped out the door, and sped as fast as she could to the water's edge. Skidding to a seat so her tailbone went numb, she scooped up a handful of pebbles and began chucking them at the water as if bored beyond measure. Zeke and Dain were still shuttling between the waves and the cliff. They didn't note her return.

Scarl's footsteps approached slowly—too slowly, she decided, for him to have seen her and given chase. She breathed more easily and tossed another rock with a *plop*.

He sank beside her on his haunches. Neither spoke for a dozen licks of the waves. Ariel supposed he was choosing words to explain why they might sleep somewhere different that night. This should be good, she thought. She hoped she could make him squirm just a bit.

When he finally spoke, he said only, "Well?"

Prepared for many things but startled by that, she asked, "Well, what?"

He squinted at the sea. "I'm a Finder, Ariel, and you matter to me. I know where you are most of the time without trying. As soon as I thought to speak with you, I felt you at the door. And you stood there dripping long enough to leave a puddle."

The stones Ariel sat upon seemed to grow sharper. She fidgeted. "I'm sorry. I didn't mean to listen at first, and then I just—"

His sharp gesture cut her off. "I only want an answer to my question."

"Wh-what is it?"

At last he looked over at her. Her confusion must have been plain, for his face softened slightly. "How upset will you be if I accept Cassalie's offer?"

Relieved by his eye contact, Ariel could not resist a smirk. She tapped her curved lips. "Well, hmm, I dunno—"

"I'm not asking your permission," he snapped. "I'm just trying to learn how large a price I will pay."

She gaped at him, stung by his tone. She'd been so pleased to see that bright splash of romance, but worrisome ripples now spread through her heart. Would it change him or weaken the bond they had forged?

And then she noticed how hard he was rubbing his knuckles. The edge in his voice was only partly for her. He was also trying to silence an old loyalty scratching at him from the past. Ariel respected that struggle, but it served no one now. It was an echo that needed to still.

Swiftly she leaned over and pecked his cheek. "I'm happy for you, you dolt. And you know *she* would approve. I'll sleep anywhere, with Dain or in the boathouse again by myself." She scrambled to her feet, afraid to feel the stab of a jealousy she knew hovered near.

She didn't move fast enough. A question slipped from her. "You'll still keep your promise, though, right?" He'd promised never to leave her until she no longer wanted him to accompany her.

"Without fail."

She got three paces away before his voice came again. "Ariel."

She turned. She could read Scarl's eyes well enough to recognize relief and perhaps even gratitude in them. Then they hardened, and he said, "I do *not* want to be spied on with Cassalie again."

She was tempted to tease him, but recalling moments with her own sweetheart helped her resist. "I promise."

Ariel hurried away before she could think more about it—and before vague, muddled fears of losing Scarl here could overcome what she knew to be right.

Finding herself among the stone houses, she recovered her bearings and slipped to the creek. Her walking stick was still jammed in the rocks. The shark's tooth in the knife hilt gleamed through the water.

Ariel checked Scarl's whereabouts. If he remained on the shore, he was hidden behind houses. Zeke and Dain bobbed in the waves, their backs turned to her.

Unseen by all, she took up the staff. She'd planned to ask Cassalie for guidance, but a Farwalker could find the way with her feet. No one else understood anyhow. And maybe she ought to get more used to walking alone.

Placing her palm on Elbert's knife, she asked her feet to lead her.

A shiver racked her. She blamed it on clothes still wet from her swim. They'd dry soon enough, and she'd be too busy to notice.

When the impulse to move arose in her feet, Ariel turned away from the water and ran.

CHAPTER 15

Willow whinnied in greeting. Hobbled, he grazed the sparse grass where they'd left him. Ariel paused to pluck green stems from between rocks to feed him. His whiskers tickled her hands.

"More on the way back," she promised, moving on with her staff.

When she reached the tunnel she'd emerged from with Dain yesterday and her feet urged her in, she stopped short. She'd need a light in the dark. She didn't want to waste time going back for one, though. Her feet pulled her firmly ahead, trying to lead her to where Elbert had lived. Since it hadn't been too far through the hill yesterday, Ariel plunged in. As the glow from the tunnel's opening waned, she used her staff to probe for barriers or drop-offs.

Slowing, she patted the wall, wanting to turn but unable to find the side passage she and Dain had crawled from yesterday. She backtracked, reaching higher — there! Yesterday she'd been so intent on reaching Zeke and Scarl that she hadn't noticed how high the crawlspace had been.

Sliding down from above had been easy. It proved more of a task to climb up. Ariel sprang toward the passage but fell back repeatedly until her scrambling toes caught a hold and she kicked herself up.

Collecting herself on her hands and knees, she thrust the staff before her, mindful of the long drop at the far end of the crawl. This passage was black, the stone suffocating. Wistfully she remembered the lamp Dain had left farther in. Nothing in her pockets would light it. She'd come too far, though, to retreat.

Ariel crawled more and more slowly as her staff failed to find the drop or the knotted rope she expected. She was certain Dain had led her up the rope to the crawl space and then on their knees for not too long before they'd emerged. This tight space stretched on and on.

Finally Ariel stopped. Her panting bounced off the rock, loud. Without the scrape of her staff and body on stone, the pressing dark felt like a grave. She tried not to think of how far she'd wormed in here or how much crushing rock loomed above. The crawl space must have branched somewhere she hadn't noticed. She wasn't retracing the way Dain had led her.

Yet her feet, trailing behind her bruised knees, urged her on. Nervously she obeyed, moving fast to snip a thread of panic unspooling inside her. Her feet had helped her avoid danger before; she hoped they understood about cave-ins. She should've brought Zeke.

The rock beneath her grew wet, with puddles in low spots. Then a wavelet swamped Ariel's hands to the wrist.

"Oh!" She pulled back too quickly, banging her head. The sighing water receded, and a deeper surge answered it

through the rock. The tide had been ebbing when she left
the cove, but it may since have turned, and the sea could
flood this passage before she got out.

Her feet still wanted her to go forward, and *now*.

Another wave reached her. While she pondered retreat,
a new sound rose above the distant crashing of breakers,
as close as the lapping at her sodden knees. She'd almost
mistaken it for own breath in the dark until the soft
brushing deepened to a buzz.

Her staff, on the ground before her, vibrated between
the stone and her hand.

Saltwater surged, splashing. The buzzing grew angry.
Ariel didn't dare let go or leave it; she needed the staff to
plumb her way out. She lifted it from the water. The noise
stopped, leaving only a gentle dripping.

Ariel slid her hand up the wood toward the knife. Her
fingers crossed the leather wraps and swept toward the hilt,
but then they plunged into a large, mushy lump that felt, for
an instant, like bubbling sea foam. *Bzzzzzt!* She'd grabbed a
thick knot of small, beating wings.

She shrieked.

Flies burst from under her fingers like bees from a hive.
In the tight space they swarmed her. She dropped the staff
and flailed to keep off the flies. Her elbows and shoulders
cracked hard on the stone as she batted at blackness and
tried not to inhale. Flies struck her skin, bouncing between
her and the walls, until Ariel curled tight and covered her
head with her arms.

More waves came, sloshing instead of receding. The
droning buzz faded. Over the rush of water, which kept

growing louder, Ariel became aware of someone calling her name.

She sat up, the air still black but mercifully free of insects. Wet lumps littered her clothes and her hair.

"Ariel!" The voice echoed far down the tunnel.

"Zeke?" Ariel's heart, eager to find help in the dark, took control, and she started toward the caller—she thought. Immediately she banged her cheek into a wall. In her panic, she'd spun, and now the sea swirled around her, elbow deep on all sides. Fear and cold water numbed her farwalking sense. She was no longer certain which direction she'd come.

A voice shouted again. Ariel splashed toward it, banging off the stone walls through a flood that deepened by the moment.

She spotted a glow, then Dain scampering toward her like a three-legged dog, one hand keeping an oil lamp dry near the ceiling. Zeke crawled behind.

Ariel barely heard his scolding. She rushed to meet them.

"No, turn!" Dain panted. "Turn! We're near to this end. We won't beat the tide going back!"

Ariel stopped, uncertain. Dain banged into her. "That way!" She shoved Ariel back.

Ariel spun. Seawater blasted her in the face. Spluttering, she wiped her eyes.

Dain pushed from behind. "I can't get past you! You gotta lead. Keep your face high and breathe when it ebbs. Then hold your breath and crawl against it—fast as you can!"

Another surge hit them. The oil lamp went out.

CHAPTER

16

The return to darkness drove Ariel into motion. She plowed into the merciless tide, catching breaths as each surge eased, which wasn't often enough. Her knees and head cracked more than once against stone, but she barely felt any pain. Fear drove her too hard. All she could do was breathe ragged gulps and shove herself forward. If she put a palm or her shins on the staff where she'd left it, she didn't notice as she passed. It may have floated off.

More water smashed in and stayed, getting deeper. Her thoughts flew to Zeke. She was the better swimmer, with more practice holding her breath—and she hadn't gotten mud in her lungs yesterday. Was he still behind Dain and still breathing? Without room in the dark, cramped tunnel to trade places, she had no way to know, and no way to help him except to go faster.

As she flung herself forward on her hands and knees, her arms struck a low barrier—a bit of driftwood, a rock? Her momentum spilled her face-first overtop of it. Water rushed over her head. Choking, she jerked her face out just as

Dain ran into her from behind. The collision knocked Ariel under again. A hard edge pressed into her belly.

Dain flailed and rolled off. They untangled themselves, and Dain's hands yanked Ariel up from behind. But water now slapped at the top of the tunnel, forcing Ariel to hold her breath anyway. She struggled with the thing in her path. It wasn't a rock. It was sturdy stick at an angle—not driftwood, but the staff. Her hands recognized its grip through the swirling water. It had drifted ahead of her to lodge in the tunnel, blocking the way as if intentionally. She bashed it loose with both fists and raced past, not sure how much longer she could go without a breath.

Glimpsing whitewater now, she wondered, crazily, how Dain had relit the lamp. Ariel slammed into the end of the tunnel before her brain told her the light was coming from her left. An arch opened there, filled with more sea than sky. They'd made it! Ariel pushed off the wall and burst out through a breaker flooding into the hole.

Spinning to help her friends, she found the rocks too steep and the surf too strong. She bounced against the cliff and thrust her arms back in through the arch, but Dain and then Zeke emerged on their own. She grabbed them. Dashed by waves, they all dragged themselves along many boulders until at last they reached secure footing and could climb out.

Ariel looked back. The sea had submerged their escape hole completely.

"Good thing... we chased you," Zeke said between gulps of air. "We saw you... take off and head... into the tunnel, and.... if we'd gone back then for Scarl's help like I wanted, some of us—maybe all of us—might've been drowned."

"I'm so sorry!" Ariel said. If she'd gone as fast as her feet had implored her and not stopped to wonder or battle with flies, she would've have been fine, but her friends might not have been. "But how did you find me? I didn't go the way I expected to go."

"Followed the tracks of your knees in the dust." Dain shook oily seawater out of her lamp, which she'd managed to keep. "The light helped us catch up. But why'd you come in by yourself, anyhow? You could've died lots of places if you'd gotten lost."

"I'm a Farwalker," Ariel said. "I don't get lost."

"That didn't answer the question." Zeke glared.

Ariel gazed up the hillside. They were far out on the point. The stone ruin where she'd met Dain squatted a short ways inland. Between, rows of squared stones and a crumbling wall suggested homes that were gone now. Landslides had left several scars on the hill.

"I wanted to return Elbert's knife where it came from," she admitted. "Where he'd slept."

Zeke clapped a hand to his head in dismay.

Dain rose. "Come, then. This way."

"No," said Zeke. "Let's just get back to the cove."

"The knife's gone anyway. In there." Ariel pointed. She felt as though Elbert's knife had escaped... but not before doing its best to drown her.

Dain shrugged. "Got to go past, anyhow. 'Cause we sure can't head back the same way we got here. Not for a few hours, at least."

They picked their way uphill and inland toward the stone rubble. The homes on this side had been dug into the hill like animal dens, with only small sections of stone protruding. Those were now remnants. Such homes may have been cozy and safer from winds, but they were also more easily buried.

Dain gestured to one hollow, mostly caved in. "Uncle Elbert's."

Ariel stopped to stare. What was left seemed crumbling and cramped for a man as big and loud as Elbert Finder had been.

Zeke tugged her along. Ariel let him, having no desire to step into the ruin. She might not even have done it to plunge the knife into the earthen floor. It would have felt too much like stepping into Elbert's grave.

Dain angled toward the ruin that hid the other entrance to the tunnels. Taking a slightly different path, Ariel wandered among several cut stones that probably had once belonged to a building but now were arranged, one by one, in a pattern. A few had been carved on. The first bore a design, but the next held a mossy likeness of a man.

Ariel's feet stopped. The stones were markers. She stood in a graveyard.

Dain was hurrying ahead without looking back. Ariel winced. Dain had lost her family on this side of the ridge, and being here obviously didn't soothe her. Ariel welcomed the breeze slicing through her soaked clothes, since she probably deserved the chill it gave her.

"Why are you stopping?" asked Zeke.

"Shh." Ariel showed him. "Graves. Memory markers, at least. Dain's family might have stones here somewh—"

Her feet tingled, and she turned to her right in response. Three stones in descending sizes, a little rock family, stood in for the human one that'd been lost. The largest bore the shape of a fish and the middle, a flower. They were more recently carved than most on the slope. But the freshest work showed on the smallest. No weeds grew around it, and the bright lines of a border had been scratched within days.

"Dain's family?" Zeke repeated.

"Cassalie told me," Ariel whispered. "They—"

"What'd you stop for? Come on!" Dain's voice sounded cross.

Zeke and Ariel moved forward. Glaring at the sea, Dain awaited them in the stone hut's doorway.

As they arrived, she grumbled, "I know you seen 'em. I like to keep the weeds off Dain's stone, that's all."

"That's—" *Sweet*, Ariel had started to say. Then the name she'd heard sunk in.

"Whose stone?" Zeke asked.

Dain flinched. "My brother's, I mean. His name— never mind! It's no business of yours! Are you coming or not?" She darted into the shadows.

At Zeke's bewildered expression, Ariel lifted her palms helplessly and followed Dain in.

Dain thrust her empty lamp into Ariel's hands. "Hold this." She rummaged in a corner and removed a lump of tallow, a fresh wick, and a firestick from a half-buried clay pot. Softening the tallow in her hands, she refilled the lamp and lit the wick without making eye contact.

Ariel couldn't forget the girl's flustered words. "I'm truly sorry you had to come over here after me," she said. "My mother left the world two years ago now—" Her throat closed, but she forced herself on. "It'd be hard for me to go back to our cottage. Without crying, at least. I tried once and couldn't do it. You're brave."

Dain didn't answer, except to lead the way into the tunnels. Zeke took some coaxing. Dain promised that nowhere on this route would be wet.

Once they'd left daylight, however, she said, "I already spilled it, so you might as well know. Dain was my brother. My name's really Neela."

The shadows thrown by the lamp flame wavered and lunged as Ariel tried to make sense of what she'd just heard.

"But don't call me that. I won't answer." The girl with the lamp hurried faster as if to get away from her name.

Ariel debated staying silent before asking, "Why not?"

Dain—Neela—pressed on her eyelids. "'Cause I killed Dain, that's why. *Neela* killed him. I can't give him my life. It's too late for that. But we can share it."

Ariel worked hard not to frown. Zeke just looked confused. To help him, Ariel said, "Cassalie told me about the mudslide that buried your house. But—"

"Cass wasn't there that night. What did she tell you?"

Ariel recounted the disastrous storm.

"You got some, but not all," said the girl posing as Dain. "Our papa wanted Dain to be Windmaster. Wanted it something fierce. But he wasn't good at it, and I was. Pa said it wasn't a fit trade for a girl. He'd cough fishhooks if he saw a Farwalker girl. But I couldn't help it! The wind likes me, is all, and it did tricks for me whether I asked it or not."

"He should've been proud," Zeke said softly.

Pain filled Dain's laugh. "Sometimes we made what the wind did for me seem like breezes and airs that my brother had called. But I took more'n one thrashing for mocking Pa's orders. Or for weather I had nothing to do with."

Zeke growled.

With the stink of burning tallow wafting around them, Ariel asked, "Did he beat you that night?"

Dain nodded. "And that was the last time."

"But none of that was your fault."

"Oh, aye, it was. Cass didn't tell you I brought the storm, did she? She thinks it was luck, but I asked for that rain. I just didn't mean for it to take everything. Not like that."

Ariel didn't know what to say.

But Zeke did. "You might not believe this, but I've killed people, too."

Dain stopped in her tracks. "You couldn't," she whispered.

"I didn't mean it, either, exactly," he said. "I was trying to stop some bad men. I stopped them, all right. More than I expected." He told her how pleading with stones overhead had caused a cave-in, crushing two killers who'd taken him and Ariel captive—and sending two friends from the world along with them. "It was awful," he finished. "So I know how you feel."

"I doubt it." Dain's voice was no longer harsh, though. "If they weren't your family." They reached the ledge with the knotted rope, where the lamplight gleamed wetly in her eyes.

"I guess you're right," Zeke admitted. "But I still have nightmares about it. So whatever makes you feel better is all right with me—Dain."

She looked at him hard, but Zeke only grabbed the rope and said, "Up?"

As they climbed to the ledge and then crawled toward freedom, Ariel admired Zeke's wise compassion. If he hadn't been there, she might've argued with Dain, or at least said the wrong thing to make matters worse. She wanted to reach through the dark and hug him. She resisted, afraid of repeating the awkward moment when she'd clung to him as they'd swum in the cove. She loved Zeke best when her feelings for him snuck up on her. It ruined everything when either of them got too self-conscious.

So Ariel forced herself to stop thinking about it. Her thoughts bounced back to Dain. Perhaps now she'd be able to finish their trade. It probably had something to do with her brother, and she hadn't known how to say it without revealing the truth.

Ariel didn't ask while they crept through the tunnel. It'd be wiser to have Scarl near when the request finally came, so she could call on his help if the trade were unfair. Besides, Ariel wasn't eager to dwell on the fate of anyone who'd been buried alive. Not while she was still in an underground passage that had too nearly become her own makeshift tomb. It would've pleased him no end if she'd found Elbert's home, only to die there as he'd died near hers.

He wasn't there to feel pleasure, of course. Ariel scolded herself for even thinking that way. She'd done more or less what she'd come here to do: return the knife to its home and the shark's tooth to the sea. It was over. She'd won. She could forget about it.

The prickling in the back of her neck wouldn't listen. It was probably just the cove's name, the ruins, and her memories, but in the clammy air of the tunnels, Elbert felt all too close.

CHAPTER
17

When Ariel, Zeke, and Dain emerged from the tunnel, the sun was sinking toward the sea. They hurried to reach Cassalie's house before dusk. On the way, Ariel convinced Zeke not to mention their misadventure to Scarl. They could let him think her staff had just washed from the creek into the sea. Since they'd escaped with no more than bruises, Zeke agreed—if she promised never to mention Elbert Finder again.

Dain sealed Ariel's vow with these words:

> "Though I'm nothing made of iron,
>   no sword or stone can shake me.
> But speak the wrong words only once,
>   and just like that, you break me."

Zeke crowed. "You like riddles, too?"

As he challenged Dain with several, Ariel sighed and studied the sun-gilded clouds. She wished she'd made a promise before leaving home by forging a sky pledge with Nace. A kiss blown to the moon every night could have bounced off and fallen to him, binding them over long days apart. She wondered if he might be watching this sunset. Then she hoped he wasn't, that he was safe in the abbey and not outdoors where predators prowled.

Once back at Cassalie's, the three friends clustered gratefully around the hearth. To Ariel's dismay, Dain and Zeke riddled on, silenced only when Scarl posed a hard one.

As night fell, Dain said, "I'd like to sleep in the boathouse with you. You're more fun than Cassalie."

"You don't have to," replied Ariel. "We're sleeping in your house tonight."

"We are?" Zeke said.

Dain turned startled eyes toward Cassalie and Scarl. The two were preparing their supper, and when Scarl bent to retrieve a mussel he'd dropped, Cass tweaked his curls and then smoothed them again. Although Ariel had seen them embrace earlier, even she was amazed by the Finder's good humor about the teasing.

Dain flashed a grin. "Heartthrobs, Cass and Scarl? That's a rich 'un!" Her smile faded. She picked at the dust wedged between flagstones. "I wish I had a heartthrob. There's nobody here who could be it."

Ariel's sympathy rose. "We could use that for our trade! Scarl could find you a heartthrob, I bet—somewhere. And I'll take you there!"

Dain stiffened. "You aren't leaving yet? You said a week."

"No, I mean later. Whenever you want."

Dain shook her head and stared into the fire. "I don't need a heartthrob, anyhow."

Ariel's heart sank. What trade could be better than love? After they ate, Dain showed her and Zeke where she slept. A gap in the stones let in a tendril of wind that, at Dain's coaxing, would spin their lamp flame in an unearthly dance.

Before long, Scarl drew aside the sail that served as Dain's door. "We've used enough of Cassalie's lamp oil tonight," he said. "But there's a mountain of furs in her pantry for you, Zeke, and your blanket's there, too. You'll be as snug as a mouse in a pocket."

Zeke bid the girls sweet dreams and slipped out as Ariel accepted her own blanket from Scarl. She and Dain snuggled in side by side.

"All set? Then sleep well." Scarl turned to leave.

Ariel could not let him go, not just yet. Not knowing he was going back to Cassalie. "Wait. Scarl?"

She winced, but he turned back without a hint of impatience.

"Yes?"

Ariel stammered, too aware of Dain there to hear her. And what did she want to say, anyhow? *I won't peek at you and Cassalie tonight? I'm happy for you, so why do I feel scared? Are you sure there's space in your heart for us both?*

Don't leave me?

"Good night," she managed.

He bent and his hand brushed her hair. "Good night, dear one." After blowing out their lamp, he let the drape close.

"Ariel," whispered Dain, "is your heartthrob Zeke?"

"What?" With her emotions bare, Ariel didn't think before she answered. "I don't think so. I mean... No. I have a heartthrob at home. Nace."

"Say true? What's he like?"

The more Ariel described, the more she missed him. She made herself stop. "Don't mention Nace around Zeke, though, all right?"

"'Cause you're Zeke's heartthrob, huh?" A nod rustled. "Aye, I can tell."

They fell silent. Though the furs made the softest bed she'd ever had, Ariel lay tense, staring into the dark. Pangs for Zeke wracked her heart. It was true that her feelings might have been different if she'd never met Nace... or if illness took him as it'd taken a sweetheart from Scarl.

Appalled, Ariel twisted away from such thoughts. How could she even think them? Terrible things could occur without warning; what if such thoughts made them happen? Losing one love could not increase another. It would only crush half the love out of her heart. The mere idea of Nace harmed made her skin prickle.

Surf swished in the cove without soothing her. The darkness in the house felt too quiet. Restless, Ariel kicked at the furs on her legs.

"Want a lullaby?" Dain whispered.

"Please."

Dain whistled softly. The wind played in its crack in the wall, rising and falling like music. The song swaddled Ariel's troubling thoughts and floated her off into sleep.

Unlike the music, her dreams were unpleasant. She found herself again in the cramped tunnel she'd escaped that afternoon. No sea flooded it, and the exit was near, but some threat waited beyond the arch. A shadow fell over the light there, and fear kept her huddling in the dark.

At last, thinking the danger had gone, she crawled forward. The first thing she saw was the end of a staff. Beside it rose legs that were casting the shadow. Ariel rushed forward, Scarl's name on her lips.

As she rounded the corner, her mistake became clear. A Finder awaited just outside the tunnel, but it wasn't Scarl. Elbert, back from the dead, had collected her staff with his knife still attached. His hand reached to grab her. This time, it took hold. Fingers clenching her hair, he dragged her into the sea.

Ariel started awake, gasping and unsure of where she was in the dark. Struggling to sit up, she recognized the soft weight of the furs warming her. The banging of her heart only gradually easing, she settled closer to Dain, who hadn't stirred. The other girl's steady breathing gave Ariel comfort. Still, she didn't sleep much more that night.

CHAPTER

18

In the daylight, Ariel could evade the grasping hand from her nightmares. Whether it was Dain's doing or not, they enjoyed some fine weather, and Ariel often napped to the surf's soothing beat. When she wasn't dozing, she dived or taught Dain to ride Willow, though they never went far. Sometimes she mounted the horse by herself, going nowhere but thinking of Nace.

Cassalie and Scarl became inseparable. He brushed her hair in the mornings before she plaited it up. She raised creatures from the seabed to show him their beauty before taking them back down below. Together they did chores for the old 'uns. With help from Cassalie's delicate fingers, they even managed to get Scarl's timepiece to work, although not correctly, since the hands counted backward. Laughter filled the house, and he relaxed in a way Ariel had seen only once, in the wood cabin where she'd met his first love.

Dain and Zeke, too, were nearly constant companions, making up riddles and visiting Dain's singing rock whether Ariel joined them or not. Twice she caught Zeke studying

Dain from afar, but when she asked him about it, he blustered about trying to remember a riddle.

She'd heard enough of those lately to last her whole life, but even she was intrigued when, several mornings after their first in the cove, Dain said, "Ho! The Riddlestone! I should show you today!"

After checking the tide, Dain led her and Zeke toward the point and into a narrow fissure called The Devil's Staircase. Slippery steps twisted down into the rock.

Zeke trailed his hands on the barnacled walls. "These stones are surprised to have people between them. They're more used to fish."

"It floods at high tide," Dain explained.

Zeke looked up fast.

"Don't worry," Dain added. "There's no roof. We'd float out."

They reached the end of the passage, a sheer-sided cup carved smooth by waves. A fallen slab rested alone in the center. Creases wrinkled its surface, and a corroded metal ring was affixed near its base.

Zeke halted so abruptly that Ariel bumped into his back. He said, "I don't want to get closer."

Dain turned, her eyes glowing. "You're probably the only strangers to ever see the Riddlestone without wearing chains."

Ariel eyed the thick ring. "Did they chain people here to drown in the tide?"

"Something like that." Grimacing, Zeke closed his eyes, the better to listen.

"In the old days, heaps of smugglers were wreckers," Dain explained. "They lit fires on the point to lure boats to the rocks. When the ships wrecked, they'd steal the cargo."

"That's awful!" Ariel said. "What about the poor sailors?"

"Any crew that washed up, the wreckers brought here."
Dain gestured to the ring. "They gave 'em a chance, though.
They gave 'em this riddle. The sailors who figured the
answer could live. The sailors who didn't..." Her fingers
traced the stone's creases, which looked to Ariel like
trickling tears.

"Don't touch it!" Grabbing Dain's hand, Zeke pulled her
away. "This stone has grown too used to evil. It likes feeling
blood in those cracks. Human blood."

Ariel's mouth dried.

"You really *can* hear stones, can't you?" Dain marveled.
"How else would you know?"

Zeke didn't bother to answer.

At the same instant, they all noticed he was still holding
Dain's hand. Dain gave their linked fingers the same
mystified gaze she might have turned on a talking bird. Zeke
met Ariel's eyes and yanked his hand loose as if burned.

"Let's go." Blushing, he spun back the way they'd come.

"You haven't heard the riddle yet," Dain said.

"Tell us on the way. Your Riddlestone gives me the—"
Zeke stopped.

Ariel followed his gaze. Her walking stick lay at the base
of the wall, tangled in seaweed. Although the leather wraps
on it had swollen and slipped, they still held Elbert's knife.

"—creeps." Zeke hurried past the staff. "Come on."

Ariel glanced quickly in every direction. She half
expected a dead Finder to appear, reaching for her. None
did, of course. Gulls cried and distant waves sloshed as
usual. Apparently the staff had floated here on the tide.

Ariel couldn't walk past it. She nudged it with her foot
and then picked it up, pulling away green and brown slime.
The grip Nace had smoothed for her was salt-roughened and
battered, and the staff's tip had busted. The knife, when
she wiggled it, fell into her hand. Rust—at least, she hoped it
was rust—dulled the blade.

"I wonder if the Riddlestone called it," Dain said. "My
ma used to say 'One wickedness draws another.' Want to tie
it here so it can't float out again?"

"No." Leaving the blade with a stone that liked blood
seemed like feeding evil. Ariel didn't want it, but the sea
had spit it back out. She wondered if it had turned up for a
reason. Even if she could ignore her nightmares, it was hard
not to think the knife had tried to delay her on that day
in the tunnel. It seemed safer to keep a watch on the knife
until she could destroy it completely.

Scarl might be right about using fire. She'd build a
bonfire on the slip at low tide so the waves could bear away
the warped metal and ashes. Waterlogged now, the knife
might resist flame, but she had an idea how to make it burn
anyway.

Flinging away the ruined staff, Ariel gripped the knife's
hilt and hurried after Zeke.

They emerged from the staircase back onto the shore,
where a breeze bathed their faces. Zeke scowled at Ariel's
burden but said, "What's the riddle, then, Dain? I hope it's
good, if people's lives depended on it."

Dain perched on a rock and wrapped her arms around
her knees. "No fair asking the stones for the answer. You
ready?"

When they nodded, she recited:

"Black snakes are poison, but so is the red.
Get bit by the wrong one, and you'll end up dead.
Black snakes are poison, but red's poison, too.
And you've got a red snake a'troubling you.

"No snake-hawk or weapon can fight it—
To kill a red snake, you must bite it.
So quick, now, with courage and speed,
If you want to live, a red snake must bleed."

"Hmm." The sparkle returned to Zeke's eyes. "Snakes, huh?"

"I've never heard of a red snake," Ariel said. "And I sure wouldn't bite one, unless it was already dead and roasted!"

Dain turned a self-satisfied grin to the sky. "Tell me if you need to hear it again. Can't have no hints, though. I've given plenty of those."

Ariel pondered the riddle for maybe two minutes, but her mind had moved on by the time they arrived back at Cassalie's.

Scarl was unhappy to see Elbert's knife. "We can find you another staff, if you want, but you should have walked away from that blade." He insisted she shut it up in the boathouse.

She agreed, but before taking it there, she climbed to the spot on the hillside where he'd chipped out the brimstone. With a few pieces, she could make sure the knife burned.

She pounded the black stone with the knife and a rock. With each strike, the blade shivered, speaking both to her ears and her hand. Cassalie had been right about this being hard work, and Ariel worried she might break the blade.

Resting, she rubbed her cheek, aware her concern was silly. Yet reviled or not, the longer she'd carried the blade, the more it had become not just Elbert's, but hers. Perhaps that was the real reason she hadn't left the knife with her staff. Turning her back on it, letting it go, seemed to deny not just Elbert but her own past and a part of herself. Though not nice, that part felt like something she needed—something that might keep her nightmares at bay. Defiance and survival, that's what Elbert's knife stood for, and she wanted to carry both into her future.

Maybe by burning them out of the blade she could keep their fire, like her memories, warm in her heart.

She managed to break loose three small chunks of brimstone. That should be enough.

Climbing down to the boathouse, she left the knife and the brimstones inside until the evening's low tide. She promised herself the blade would die then.

She stepped toward the door. A clinking sound made her turn. The blade and the brimstones, which rested on a mound of sailcloth, rolled and tumbled together. For an instant, she thought the blade was moving by itself—

No! It wasn't the knife. Like a rat trapped in bedclothes, something was shoving at the sailcloth from beneath. The stones and knife slid away, scattering, as the sailcloth bulged and rose where they'd been.

Ariel leapt backward, sure maggots were squirming from the earth toward the knife—or, more likely, an immense knot of flies. As the lump grew taller, however, like a sail-shrouded corpse, another possibility struck: Elbert was rising from the bowels of the earth to grab her.

CHAPTER 19

Her throat too tight to scream, Ariel lunged for the knife. The shape hidden under the sail beat against it. Dodging, Ariel gripped the hilt with both hands. She'd stab Elbert with his own blade before he got clear of the sail. She'd have to strike hard. But she trembled. He was already dead—what if it didn't work?

The figure rose past her waist. Now or never! She drew back the blade for a thrust.

"Mudbellies! Where's the luff edge?"

Ariel's legs wilted. "Dain!" She sank to the floor.

"Ariel?" With a last effort, the lump under the sail flung it sideways and off. Dain stepped over the folds. "What are you doing here? I thought I saw you on the hill."

Ariel's breath wouldn't come. Seeing Elbert's knife in her hand, she flung it away. "I almost stabbed you!"

Dain tipped her head. "You hated my Riddlestone riddle that much?"

Powered by anger, Ariel bolted back to her feet. "Why'd you sneak up like that?"

"Sneak? I didn't even know you were out here," Dain said. "I hide here from chores I don't want to do. I just didn't expect sail to be fouling the hatch."

Ariel scowled at the floor. The sail had masked a narrow, wooden trap door, shifted now to the side to reveal a hole. "It goes into the house?"

"Just behind it," Dain said. "Next to the cistern. Or out to the point. Or around to the—"

"Never mind." Ariel stared at her hands. Rust smeared her skin. She imagined it blood.

Dain gazed at the knife, which lay where she'd thrown it. "That thing's eating you, huh? Want to drop it down here?"

Ariel looked at the tunnel. "I don't want the tide to take it. Will it stay there?"

"Unless it can walk by itself. This tunnel's dry, if you don't count the drip from the cistern." Dain kicked the knife down the hole and covered the opening with both the wood door and the sail. "There." She picked up the brimstones and set them on top.

Ariel thanked her. "What's the chore you were dodging? I'll do it for you."

"Killing the brown crabs Cass brought up for lunch. Scarl's probably done it by now."

As they walked to the house, Ariel patted Dain, relieved her new friend was alive. Her nightmares now might include running the smaller girl through. Maybe she even deserved dreams like that. She needed to think more about those around her and dwell less on the past.

Yet the past kept intruding. During lunch, Zeke cried, "I've got it!"

"Got what?" Scarl asked.

When Zeke explained, Scarl wanted to hear the Riddlestone's riddle. Dain obliged, also sharing the story behind it.

Scarl pondered a moment before nodding. "Solve it, Zeke."

"The red snake is the shipwrecked sailor's tongue," Zeke declared. "If he didn't bite it and keep quiet about the wreckers, they'd leave him there to drown."

"Aw," Dain said, "I thought it would take you longer! But they only drowned the ones who couldn't solve the riddle. The smart ones had to let 'em cut their tongues on the stone."

"I can't believe you're telling those stories, Dain! Awful." Cassalie rose to take empty bowls. "The wreckers were generations ago. Do you think we're all wild and beastly now, Scarl?"

"I thought you were wild before." He smiled. "Now I might say you were...." He couldn't find the jest he wanted, and the attempt sobered him.

Cassalie laughed. "Come, then, what? Fiendish? Bloodthirsty, mayhap?" She slid her hands onto his shoulders from behind. "If I sneak up too close, do you imagine a blade at your throat? Maybe a stab in the back?"

Scarl's gaze fell away, but he lifted one hand to trace over her fingers. Watching his face, Ariel wanted to warn Cassalie to stop. She didn't know how.

"Tell me true, Scarl," Cass pressed. "A wrecker can take an insult. Do we seem dangerous?"

"Very." Scarl stood and pulled away.

Cassalie's cheer dimmed. She reached after him. "I was only playing."

"I know." He managed a smile and made a show of feeding the fire, but Ariel, at least, was not fooled.

"Perhaps it's *my* tongue that needs cutting," Cass murmured. "It runs away sometimes."

"Don't say so." Scarl returned to her for an awkward embrace. "I'm ill-tempered, that's all. Ask Ariel. She'll tell you."

"It's true," she confirmed, but she wondered what was weighing on Scarl. Perhaps he was remembering blood he'd spilled himself. Ariel would be the first to defend him, but she understood why he might not bring it up with Cassalie, and she couldn't guess what else might have shadowed his heart.

When they went back outside, Zeke taught Dain to skip rocks—or he tried, but the wind kept snatching Dain's stones. Soon she was sharing *her* tricks with Zeke. Growing bored, Ariel wandered to the steep meadow where Willow was hobbled. Her excuse was to make sure the horse was all right, but she mostly wanted to pet him. The animal's calm warmth made her feel closer to Nace.

She was surprised to find Scarl there before her. She thought he'd been helping Cassalie dry fish. Instead he stood at Willow's side, absently scratching beneath the horse's long mane. His other hand gripped his own neck as he stared at the clouds hovering beyond the cove.

He jumped when Ariel greeted him.

"Is Willow all right?" she asked. Scarl's posture was tense.

Scarl patted the horse. "Yes. Getting fat on spring grass. Why aren't you with Zeke and Dain?"

Ariel shrugged and stroked Willow's shoulder. The horse nipped grass and chewed in the silence.

"Missing Nace?" Scarl asked finally.

"Yes. But I'm sure he's all right. Scarl, is something wrong?"

He exhaled and looked away. "Not wrong enough."

She waited, resisting the urge to say, "Want to tell me?" as he would in her place.

"I know I suggested we stay a few weeks," he said at last, without meeting her gaze. "But we need to go soon, Ariel. While I can still bear to leave. And before I do any more damage."

Ariel swallowed hard and plucked at a burr stuck on Willow. Her words snagged, too, in her throat. "Zeke and I could go home by ourselves."

"No."

The speedy denial sent relief surging through her, but she replied, "You don't need to stay with me for the rest of my life, Scarl."

His laugh was flat, without humor. "You haven't had enough life yet to speak of 'the rest.' No. I've met too many ruthless men. Not to mention fires, floods, and lions. I can't let you ply your trade by yourself. Not yet. In a few more years, maybe... but not yet."

Ariel listened to her feet. They hadn't been restless except in the tunnels, and they didn't squirm to walk now, either. "I'm not sure which way we'll go next."

Scarl still stared into the distance, but his eyes closed. "Any way."

She laid her hand on his arm, but he did not respond. Because she knew he would prefer it, she left him alone with the horse.

Ariel returned to the village, intent on finding Dain. She and Zeke were still skipping stones.

"Hey," Zeke called. "Can you do better than six?"

"Probably not," she replied. "But Dain and I need to talk."

Zeke studied her face. "Alone?"

"Please. It's about something I owe her." She'd prefer to have him there in case she needed help, but even more she wanted to save him discomfort—and he'd feel bad if he realized that part of the debt was for saving his life.

His face clouded, but he shuffled down the shore, still tossing rocks.

Wishing he'd gone a bit farther, Ariel kept her voice low. "Listen, Dain. We have to leave—"

Horror lined Dain's face. Ariel shushed her before the outburst could escape.

"Why?" Dain demanded. "You aren't having fun? Or is it that knife?"

"Neither. I'm a Farwalker, so going to new places is how I trade. It's time to move on, that's all."

"But... Cassalie and Scarl!"

Dain's disappointment scratched at Ariel's heart. "I know. But that's..." She felt she'd be breaking a confidence to explain. "We have to, that's all. Tomorrow, I guess." That still gave her time for a bonfire tonight. "So you need to tell me now what you want for our trade."

"Wait. Suppose I wanted you to stay as my trade?"

Ariel could tell Dain was grasping at a new idea, not revealing the old one. "It wouldn't be fair. Like asking a Windmaster to be a Fisher instead."

"Aye." Dain kicked a shell.

"Just tell me what you want. Don't forget that I could take you where you might find a heartthrob. Or a Windmaster to learn from. Or both."

"I want you to take me somewhere, all right."

Relieved the trade would be something she could manage, Ariel sank to a seat on a rock. "Good. We can go now if you want, but it doesn't have to be now. I can—"

"Now. If I don't do it now, I won't never." Dain shot glances toward Cassalie's cottage and Zeke. "But I can't tell you where yet."

"I have to know where. My feet won't feel which way to go otherwise. Scarl will want to know, anyhow."

Alarm twisted Dain's features. "Not him and Zeke! Just you and me."

Ariel shook her head. "Then you'll have to wait till I'm older. Scarl won't let me go by myself yet."

"The wind'll keep him and Zeke here, if I ask."

Ariel's patience broke. She stood. "You know what? I'll get Scarl now, so he can help make the trade. When people can't agree, a Judge helps decide what is fair. Scarl can—"

Dain grabbed her arm. "You owe me," she hissed. "I took you through the tunnel and I put the wind into Zeke. You owe me his life, Farwalker. And you traded on the tide. Tide's come in."

"Dain, I'm not trying to cheat you!" Ariel cried. Beyond, Zeke looked up. Ariel bit down on her voice. "Just tell me where—and why Zeke and Scarl can't come, too!"

"Don't want to put 'em in danger," Dain muttered. "Wouldn't do it to you, but I'm ascairt I might need you."

The words stirred Ariel's interest as well as her frown. "What kind of danger?"

Dain stared off toward the point. "I want you to take me over the bridge. The one that leads out of the world."

A huff of disbelief escaped Ariel.

"It's not far," Dain said quickly. "I don't reckon it'll take more'n a day to go and return. We'll be back again almost before anyone knows it."

"I can't take you there. I don't know where it is," murmured Ariel, glad she hadn't told Dain that she rarely knew her destinations before her feet led her.

Dain's thin lips curled in a humorless grin. "That's all right. 'Cause I do."

Ariel's jaw dropped even as her common sense told her not to believe it. "You've been to the bridge out of the world? How do you know that's what it is?"

Dain toyed with her wind pipe. "Went far enough before to see dead folk on it. I just got the shivers too bad to go farther."

Still staring, Ariel exhaled hard. "What do you need me for, then?"

"For the other side, once we're across. And to find the way back. Those are the parts I'm ascairt of." Dain's eyes burned. "Not too scairt to go, though. Not if you're with me."

"But why do you want to? Because of your family?"

Dain shook her head. "I don't have to say. Nobody tells Fishers why they want a fish, or tells a Finder what they'll do with something that's found." Slyly, she added, "But you should want to go, too. You could lose that knife forever if you took it out of the world."

Ariel's breath caught. She could throw Elbert's knife off the bridge. Fire rose from beneath, or so it was said, and the knife and its past would return to the Essence. Instead of merely destroying the blade, she could *unmake* it—the ultimate victory over evil and fear. Dain's suggestion was daring, but if anyone living could cross that bridge and return, a Farwalker could. After all, she'd stepped out of the world once before. Still...

Dain's eyes narrowed into something just shy of a smirk. "You scairt, Farwalker?"

"Yes," she whispered. What if her nightmares were more than just dreams, and Elbert awaited her on the far side?

"You owe me a trade."

"I know."

"You'll do it, then?"

Her heart thumping, Ariel took a deep breath. The idea was tempting and her curiosity potent. But the bridge out of the world might end both their lives or trap them forever, out of place with the dead—a particular dead man, perhaps.

Her good sense prevailed. "No."

"You have to!"

"No, I don't. Let's talk to Scarl. He'll help us come up with a trade we agree on."

"This or nothing." Her face dark, Dain clambered away up the cliff. "If you won't take me, though, don't expect you'll be leaving."

"What's that supposed to mean?"

Dain didn't answer.

CHAPTER

20

Zeke scrambled along the waterline to Ariel. "What was all that whispering and frowning about?"

After releasing a growl of frustration, she turned to him. "I don't mean to keep secrets from you, Zeke. I owed her a trade, and I thought it'd be best to work it out by ourselves. But I'm going to need help."

"She probably doesn't trade enough to know how it works. What did she want?"

"Something crazy." She told him. "And now look."

Sickly green clouds, the same ones Ariel had seen building a short while ago, were rushing toward the cove. As the sea beneath writhed and turned grey, a boat on the horizon made haste in the other direction.

"She's probably just blowing off anger," Zeke said. "Guess we'd better go inside."

They ran the last stretch as fat balls of rain splattered. Dain ducked into Cassalie's house not long after them. Scarl was already there.

"Are you showing off, Dain?" Cassalie peered out her window.

"It's gotta rain sometimes," Dain replied. "Don't it? Besides, you're always telling me the weather's not all my fault."

"Their poor horse, though." Cassalie turned to Scarl. "Perhaps you should lead him into the boathouse."

"I'll go with you," Ariel said, glad for a chance to talk to Scarl alone.

"You, too, Dain," Cassalie added. "Keep the wind off them."

"Aye." Dain raised her pipe.

Scarl objected that he didn't need help. The wind proved him wrong. Its blasts kept him and Ariel at the door.

Dain squeezed between them to play a single note that was nearly lost in the storm. The pressure eased and all three stepped out together. Dain's piping did not shelter them fully—Ariel's hair tossed and their clothes billowed—but it created an eye in the furor. Ariel merely had to reach her free hand to arm's length for the wind thrust it back at her, hard.

"Don't," Dain yelled at her ear. "The wind's kind enough to heed me and make us a hole. Tease it, and it'll close. Don't none of us want to feel that."

"Call it off, Dain!"

"Can't," she replied. "Once it's going like this, it doesn't much listen again until it's done."

Annoyed, Ariel gave up on talking to Scarl until they escaped the swirling wind and Dain's company.

By the time they'd collected the horse and were hurrying back toward the boathouse, rain drove them, too. Trotting through the downpour was like crossing a river in a leaky glass jar. Water flew past all around but only misted their clothes and skin. Ariel had to admit the effect was impressive.

Willow, just behind them, did not fare so well. Yet when Scarl threw open the door to the boathouse, the drenched horse balked. His large nostrils flared.

"Come on, boy," Ariel coaxed, leading the horse while Scarl fought with the door. "It's drier in here." Dain helped tug on the bridle, and together they managed to lead Willow three paces in—just enough for the wind to bang the door shut behind him. Startled, Willow jumped forward, dragging Ariel with him. She only just kept her feet. Dain let go to leap clear.

Scarl slipped in behind them and dropped the latch on the door. "Forgive me. Wind snatched it. No one stepped on, I hope?"

"We're all right," Ariel said, trying to quiet the horse.

As Scarl came alongside her to help, she caught a whiff of a musky odor she couldn't quite place. She hadn't noticed it until the door stopped the turbulent wind. Her body went rigid.

"Ariel? Did you come back here after lunch?" Dain stood near the hole in the floor. The trap door had been flung aside, and Elbert's knife lay nearby.

With a snort, the horse reared and ripped from Ariel's grip. Willow's terror spoke clearly of some predator, and at once Ariel knew the scent in the air. She yelled, "Lion!"

Willow's heaving shoulder knocked her to the ground. Behind them, Scarl shouted. The lion—where was it? A stomping hoof grazed Ariel's hip, and pain flared. Curling tight, she rolled sideways to avoid being trampled.

A tawny blur shot overhead as the mountain lion leapt toward her from the rafters.

The horse reared again to strike at it and caught the lion mid-leap. Willow knocked it aside. With a pained yowl, the lion whirled for another attack. It looked both starved and insane. Every bone stood out from its dull fur, and foamy slobber dripped from its fangs. Its yellow eyes found Ariel's and bored into them.

Elbert's knife lay just out of reach. She scrabbled toward it, but Willow's stamping hooves got in the way. Scarl grabbed her, dragged her back from the horse, and yanked her to her feet. His own knife drawn, he threw her toward the door. Dain scrambled to meet her. They clutched each other before crashing against the latched door.

The lion leapt again, snarling. Its claws ripped at the throat of the horse, which was still between it and its prey. Willow wrenched his head and neck sideways. Blood splashed. The lion flew off.

The horse backed hard against Ariel and Dain. Crushed against the door, Ariel fought to breathe. Dain raised her pipe and blew. Ariel struggled with the latch, but their tangled bodies pressed against it too tightly to move it.

Willow spun to kick at the lion with his mighty hind legs. The sudden loss of his weight left Ariel flailing for balance.

Scarl rushed up. "Get that door!"

Willow's movement had given Ariel the space she needed. She lifted the latch. The door gave way. She and Dain stumbled into the storm.

"Scarl!" She whirled, reaching for him.

Willow squealed as the lion's fangs sank into flesh. The

horse twisted and bucked. A flying hoof struck Scarl's head with a sick thud. He dropped.

Ariel screamed. Grabbing fistfuls of the Finder's clothing, she yanked him with the force of panic into the rain.

Still blowing her pipe, though the storm stole the sound, Dain slammed the door shut and threw the outer latch. Weight inside crashed against it. The wood shuddered but held. Hooves pounded and stamped. The horse and lion both screamed.

The wind joined them, its shriek rising over them both. With an enormous cracking, the boathouse roof tore away. Slate shingles tumbled into the sky and scattered, followed by sails in great flutters like clouds. The wind sucked and roared. Wailing like a child, the lion was whisked upward, flopping and vanishing into the storm.

"Good 'un!" cried Dain. "Thanks, wind!" She braced against the updraft to throw the door latch again and look in at the horse. Willow, still bucking madly, didn't notice the open way out.

"No, shut it!" Ariel crouched over Scarl, who lay in a heap at her feet. "He'll break legs doing that on these rocks!"

Dain obeyed. "It's good he's so heavy," she yelled over the wind. Its suction had eased, but it still roared around them. "What about Scarl?"

"I don't know!" In the blustery rain, Ariel could tell only that he was unconscious. She gave up trying to rouse him. "Help me!"

She and Dain lifted Scarl by his armpits and dragged him over bruising rocks to the house. His limp weight was almost too much for them.

They kicked Cassalie's door. The Reaper opened it, leaning hard to control it. "What's— oh!"

"A yellow monster!" cried Dain. "With claws, not just teeth! The wind saved us, but Scarl's hurt!"

Zeke rushed to the entry, levered Scarl onto one shoulder, and laid him out near the hearth. Cassalie and Ariel tangled in their efforts to help. Dain slammed the door, pressed her back into it, and blew gently into her wind pipe.

Through the noise of the storm, Cassalie and Zeke had heard nothing. Ariel could barely catch enough breath to explain. Nobody listened to what she said anyhow until they'd confirmed that Scarl's heart was still beating. There wasn't much blood, and his skull was not smashed, but his skin was ashen and his breathing frightfully shallow. When Cassalie lifted his eyelids, Ariel saw mostly white. She looked away with a whimper. When a flame was held near them, his pupils didn't react.

Zeke helped Cassalie strip Scarl of his wet clothes and swaddle him in furs. Ariel scrambled to build up the fire and to mix a wound wash per Cassalie's instructions. Then Zeke wrapped both arms around Ariel while Cass tended the ugly lump on Scarl's head.

"It's my fault," Ariel moaned, clenching her eyelids against flashes of memory. She didn't know if the lion had tracked them or simply followed the knife. It didn't matter. She didn't need more evidence of Elbert's ill will behind it.

"It's *my* fault!" Dain replied viciously. She'd slid miserably down the door to the floor, and her lips quivered as she fought not to cry. "If I hadn't brought in the storm, we wouldn't have been going to the boathouse at all. I just keep killing folk! I ought to—"

"Dain! Stop your mouth! Nobody here is leaving the world!"

Even Dain stared at Cassalie, shocked to hear her voice raised.

Ariel would've liked to blame Dain, but she couldn't. "If we hadn't been bringing in Willow," she said, "the lion would've waited to attack one of us. So the wind saved at least one of our lives. Probably mine."

"I'm surprised it went after Willow," Zeke said. "He's big."

"He stayed between us, that's all." Ariel leaned her forehead on Zeke. "It's rabid, Zeke. Or... or something. Not right. There's no way it should be here this far from the mountains. It came after me because I have that knife."

Zeke took a deep breath, but he didn't deny what she'd said. He just hugged her tight before he released her. "I'll go see how badly Willow's hurt."

"No, I'll go," Ariel said. "He should be calmer, at least."

"Nothing's crossing the cove now without drowning," Dain said. She hadn't stopped piping until seawater crashed all the way to the house. "But we could take the tunnel between here and there."

"Can I cut a sail into bandages? Big ones?" Ariel asked. "Willow's probably got some bad wounds."

"Here." Dain took down the sail that protected the entry.

"I have a good bladderwrack poultice," Cass added. Unwilling to leave Scarl, she told Ariel where to find it.

Ariel sliced a sail into strips, and then they all struggled to open the door. The wind that blasted inside ripped sailcloth from the walls and chased sparks from the hearth. But as Cassalie beat stray embers, the girls and Zeke shoved outside. Only bracing against the stone walls kept them from being blown over.

Getting soaked over the short distance from the door to the cistern, Ariel and Zeke followed Dain into the tunnel. It reeked of the lion, and Ariel wondered how long the crazed creature had prowled there. It was a wonder Dain hadn't encountered it below the boathouse that morning. Ariel put her face in her hands to block the thought and the stink.

As they neared the stone steps they had to climb to the hatch, she shoved to the front. "Let me go first."

Zeke grasped after her. "Why?"

Ariel didn't answer. She just ran up the steps. If by some freakish turn the lion was back, her blood might be the only thing that could save her friends' lives. In that case, she'd throw herself into its teeth. Even if it did mean that Elbert would win.

CHAPTER

21

The thick smell of blood hung in the boathouse. No lion prowled, though. If it hadn't been swallowed forever by the wind, the beast surely lay dead somewhere distant. Having braced herself for pain, Ariel nearly sobbed in relief.

Willow was down—not a good sign—but he rolled his eyes at her touch. He lay in the corner most sheltered from rain. The wind streamed overhead but only rarely dipped to flutter his mane.

Ariel bandaged his gashes as best she could and knelt stroking Willow's head until Zeke tugged at her. She hated to leave the injured horse alone, but there was nothing else they could do, and she was anxious to check back on Scarl.

Zeke had retrieved the Finder's knife from the floor. Dain toed Elbert's blade, which still lay near the hole.

"Should I leave this?" she asked.

Ariel took it sourly. After the surprise with the lion, it seemed wiser to keep dangers in sight.

They returned to the house. Scarl's condition hadn't changed. Cassalie sat clutching one of his hands, and Ariel resisted the urge to take the other. She knew he'd hate so much fuss, and she clung to the idea that he'd open his eyes soon to complain.

Awaiting that moment, she fingered Elbert's knife and considered tossing it into the hearth. The sick flame that had bloomed from the bloodied sponge on their first day in the village convinced her to wait for a bonfire outside. Inhaling evil smoke might hurt Scarl more than she could help by reducing the knife to ashes. Instead, she knotted a spare bootlace around the hilt and tied it below her knee, flat against her calf, so she could tuck the tip of the blade into her boot. That way, she could keep a close watch on it, and it couldn't hurt anyone else.

When night fell, Cassalie made a faint offer of supper, but they all felt too worried to eat. After bathing Scarl's lump with bruise potion again, Ariel sat staring into the fire, listening to the wind's hiss and blow.

Something clattered against a window: *Tap-rattle. Tap-tap.* She leapt from her stool, imagining that the twisted lion had somehow come back.

"It's all right," Zeke murmured, guessing her thoughts. "Listen to it. That can't be anything big."

With the lamps lit and the night black beyond, no one could see what was out there. Whatever it was, the wind did not puff it away. *Tap-tap-tap.*

"I'd better check that's not driftwood." Cassalie rose. "If it broke the window, I'd have to shutter it. We've got no more glass."

"I'll go." Zeke moved fast. Ariel chased him to the door, but he slipped out before she could stop him. As she struggled with the wind on the threshold, he nudged her back through. A bedraggled crow hopped at his heels.

"Grim-golly!" Dain's eyes widened. Cassalie gasped and leaned protectively over Scarl.

"That thing!" Ariel exclaimed, recognizing the crow that had brought her so many bones. "Throw it back to the storm!"

"I tried. But then I noticed it's carrying something." Zeke turned to Dain. "What did you call it?"

Cassalie answered, her voice strained. "A grim-golly. They're said to visit death-beds to coax reluctant souls out of the world."

They all turned horrified expressions toward Scarl.

"You told me the grim-golly was just superstition, Cass!" Dain cried.

"It is. It is! I won't let it be anything else."

"We call it a crow," Ariel said quickly. "It's a pest. Nothing more. Open the door, Zeke." She bent to chase the bird out.

The crow fluttered out of her grasp, and she saw something pale gripped in one of its claws. It wasn't the right shape for a bone.

Not touching the door, Zeke said, "A Kincaller you know might have sent him."

"Oh!" That hadn't occurred to her. The bird didn't take her invitation to perch, but it flapped past her to drop its burden within reach.

It was paper that'd been folded, tied with thread, and dipped in candle wax to protect it. Ariel broke the wax seal and unfolded the page, her hands trembling with the uncertainty of what it might say. Symbols spread before her. Zeke looked over her shoulder.

Butterfly, it began.

"Butterfly?" Zeke raised his eyebrows at her.

Ariel blushed but ignored him and returned to the rest: *Ash says you stopped. He thinks all is well, but my fingers twitch. Shall I follow? Give the crow an answer if you need help. Love, your Nace.*

"His fingers twitch?" Zeke repeated. "Huh. Usually they're making a fist."

Ariel let the snipe pass. She knew what Nace meant. Savoring the love mark at the end, she examined the note. "He must've made more paper. This is smoother than ours—better for marking."

It had merely been an observation, but Zeke turned away, looking wounded. Ariel sighed and tucked the note in her pocket, though she wanted to press it to her heart. All was *not* well, not anymore, but Nace couldn't help Scarl. She would wait to return an answer until she knew what to say—until she could tell him that Scarl was all right. Still, Nace's concern glowed like a beacon of comfort from beyond this terrible day. Grateful, she fed the crow a scrap of dried meat from her pack. It gobbled the tidbit and looked for more.

"You know quite the Kincaller," Cassalie said. "To persuade the bird to do his bidding like that, through a storm. I don't want to be cruel, but I don't think I can bear seeing your messenger here—not with Scarl ill. You needn't turn it out, not in weather like this, but would it stay in the entry?"

"Let me try." With more meat, Ariel lured the crow near the door. It seemed content to perch on the latch like a sentry.

"I'll clean up its droppings," she told Cass on returning.
"That's the least of my worries," Cassalie replied. "We'll
need chamber pots ourselves. In this whale-drowning storm,
we're not likely to make it out to the privy tonight."

She was right. Ariel and Zeke tried to check on the
horse before bedtime. The wind had risen so they couldn't
get out the doorway and needed help from Dain merely to
shut it again. Her piping had worked too well.

"I guess Willow will either be alive in the morning or
not," Zeke said. They returned to the hearth.

They stayed near Scarl all night, sometimes dozing
despite the raging of the wind, rain, and sea. The heat of
the fire became a haze of exhaustion. Ariel started awake
twice to what she thought was Scarl's voice, only to choke
on disappointment when she saw him unchanged. She
imagined Elbert's laugh in the wind. Memories kept
bubbling up to remind her what her Healtouch mother had
done for knocks on the head, but Ariel had seen none of
those healing plants here, and she couldn't get out to collect
them anyhow. Cassalie pleaded with Scarl, teased and
chided him, and once barked an angry command to wake
up. Nothing had any effect.

As dawn turned the windows to grey, the storm was still
strong. Only Scarl had weakened. The spoonfuls of tonic
Cassalie dribbled between his lips leaked back out.

"We've got to do something!" Ariel whispered to keep
tears of frustration from cracking her voice.

"Should I try to bring Tilda?" Dain asked. "She's the
oldest one left, isn't she, Cass? Maybe she's seen a head-
banging like his before?"

"I doubt she can help, and she's too frail to make it here

through the blow, even with three of you propping her up. We just have to watch and hope now." Cassalie bit her lip. "I'm sure those brown eyes will soon open."

By mid-day, though, Cassalie looked nearly as haggard as Scarl, despite the warm soup Dain had made them all swallow. Ariel sat clasping the Finder's limp hand, but she hated how boneless and empty it felt.

"It's been a whole night and day," murmured Zeke at her shoulder. "How can he still be asleep?"

"I don't think it's sleep." Cassalie stroked Scarl's wan cheek. "I think he's standing at the bridge and trying to decide whether to cross it."

Ariel moaned. "Don't say that." She couldn't bear the thought of a future without him.

"All my begging has not swayed him. Perhaps—" Cass's voice broke. "Perhaps he sees his first love on the far side."

Ariel squeezed her eyes shut against what Cass suggested. When she opened them again, they found Dain.

Sympathy shone in Dain's face, but she returned Ariel's gaze. It stretched between them, unspoken. A bridge.

"I think," Dain said slowly, "I'll go take a nap. Not much sleep for me last night." As straight as a fence post, she walked into the room where she slept.

Mumbling agreement, Ariel followed.

As soon as the doorway drape fell to hide them, Ariel whispered, "All right, Dain. You've got a trade." If Scarl stood poised at either end of the bridge, Ariel was ready to cross it.

Whether Elbert awaited her on the far side or not.

CHAPTER 22

"I'm probably the one the crow really came for," Ariel told Dain. "Not just to deliver Nace's message, I mean." The lion had failed, but it had been stalking her. And the bird's eyes had fixed on her each time she'd checked it. "It might have arrived to coax *me* out of the world. To guide you. And save Scarl." The crow had dogged her for weeks, but perhaps it was prescient. This wouldn't be the first time Ariel's path had called to her before she'd been willing to set her boots on it—or indeed, before she'd even understand how.

She refused to acknowledge the nagging suspicion that despite Nace's taming, it might have been Elbert who'd first sent the crow.

Dain nodded. "I got twice as much reason to go now. We can find Scarl and point him back here."

"But how can we sneak out, with the storm?"

Dain nudged aside their bedding. A large flagstone beneath looked suspiciously loose.

Ariel snorted, no longer surprised by a tunnel. "We'll

need a hefty head start or Zeke might catch up. The stones will give us away to him."

Dain smiled grimly. "That shows you don't know the wind. The way isn't all underground. I can't stop the storm once it's started, but I can ask the wind to keep Zeke behind." She pried at the loose stone in the floor.

"Wait. I don't have my pack." Ariel had left it in the entry, where she'd been feeding the crow from her supply of dried meat.

"Don't need it. I told you, it's not very far."

"We've got to take water, though. Maybe some food."

"Here. You got pockets? Smugglers always stay ready." Dain dug through the chest where her spare clothes were stored and thrust cakes of dried fish and seaweed at her. Against her better judgment, Ariel took them, along with a sea mammal bladder that sloshed. The water bag had a strap, so she hung it over her head and one shoulder so it couldn't slip off.

Dain tugged a length of sailcloth from their bedding and slung it around her own neck. "We might need this. We can share it like a blanket, too, if we rest. It's lighter than furs but it'll still keep us warm."

"Let me leave Zeke a note to find later." She didn't want him to worry. If she shared her plans with him now, he'd never let them leave alone, and she hated to place him in danger. Besides, Cass might need help tending Scarl.

She could have reused Nace's paper, still in her pocket, but she found herself unable to part with it. Instead, she tore a strip from one tail of her shirt. Feeling rushed, she scanned Dain's corner for something that might serve as ink. A little spit moistened the patches of rust on Elbert's knife. She transferred the brown juice to its tip to draw with.

The symbols proved more of a struggle. She kept the message short: *Zeke—I'm giving Dain her trade. Back in one or two days. With luck, Scarl will wake up first. Please don't follow. The storm will stop you.*

She hesitated. How should she end it? Since he'd seen Nace's note, her name mark alone felt too curt, and the love mark she would've left for Scarl might pinch Zeke.

Soon, Ariel.

She left the note on their bedding. Dain had lifted the loose flagstone, revealing the tunnel beneath.

"Is there a room here without an escape?" Ariel whispered.

"Not many. This isn't the shortest route, but it'll do."

Dain squirmed, feet first, into the narrow hole. When she vanished, Ariel sat down to follow. She lowered herself and hung by her elbows, feeling no floor or stairs beneath her, only a dark, depthless unknown. Then a light bloomed below, and Dain patted her hip, urging her down.

She dropped. Dain steadied her as she landed and handed her a glowing lamp.

They stood in a narrow tunnel stretching away in both directions. Using hollows hacked out of both walls for a ladder, Dain climbed up to tug the flagstone into place.

"Won't Cassalie guess how we've gone?" Ariel whispered.

"Aye, she'll know." Dain took back the lamp. "That don't mean Zeke can follow. Not far, anyhow. Come." She started down the tunnel. "You can take over once—"

"Wait." Ariel pointed to the kelp-bulb lamps at the base of the wall. "Should we take another for later? Maybe a few?

And some firesticks, too. It might be dark all the time on the other side of the bridge. Plus we'll need one for when we come back, right?"

Dain returned to stuff two lamps and a few firesticks into her pockets. "I suppose that'd be a smart idea, Farwalker girl."

Watching her, Ariel realized Dain still had room in her pockets because she'd taken no food at all. She grabbed Dain's arm. "You *are* coming back, aren't you? I guess you're hoping to see your family, but—"

"No!" Dain jerked free. "My brother, that's all. I hated my pa, and Ma let him thrash us. But Dain—I loved Dain. I aim to tell him I'm sorry." She hurried into the darkness, the flame on her lamp throwing threatening shadows.

Ariel had little choice but to follow. "What makes you think we can find him? Or talk to him there?"

"I've gotta try. Scarl first—he should be easy. And since he's a Finder, maybe he can point us the right way. After that, if we haven't found Dain in two days—"

"We don't even know if they've got days! It might be night there forever."

In the lamplight, Dain's face cramped. "Well, we'll try for a while. You get tired of searching, you come back. With me or without."

Her concession did nothing to soothe Ariel. "You can't trade places with him, Neela, if that's what you're thinking."

"How do you know? And don't call me that."

"Scarl's told me a story about it. The bridge has been blocked so the dead can't get back to this side." The confidence Ariel showed was false, since she'd known a ghost, but she persisted with storycraft of her own. "And you'd better get used to your real name, because you can't take a lie over the bridge. Just like riches or loved ones, those stay on this side. The lamps and our clothes might not even go with us."

Neela increased her pace. "I'd rather be naked than Neela."

Deciding to take it one step at a time, Ariel focused on finding Scarl alive on this side. With luck, he'd make Neela turn around and they'd never have to pass the near end of the bridge.

The tunnel began twisting and branching off on both sides. Neela led her across narrow ledges, through cracks so tight they had to turn sideways, and up steps into storm light, where the wind bullied them before they ducked back underground. They descended a long wooden ladder whose rungs crackled with age. Several snapped under their weight. Scarl would have cuffed Ariel for taking such risks, but her feet were always game to continue. That reassured her the bridge could be reached. She hoped her Farwalker instincts knew the difference between dead and alive.

"You'd better be right about the wind stopping Zeke," she told Neela at the base of the ladder. "He weighs more than we do. If he gets this far, he might fall." It was easy to imagine him chasing, despite the danger, and if the wind didn't stop him, the chilled stone of these sun-forsaken tunnels might bait him on instead of warning him off.

"He won't get this far. Trust me." Neela moved on. "You're gonna have to trust me now, anyhow."

"What's that mean?"

"Come and I'll show you." Neela led her toward a spot of daylight.

A breeze hit Ariel's face. They moved out of the tunnel to emerge midway up a sheer bluff, one face of a deep crack in the land. A long finger of rock thrust from under their feet and pointed crookedly over the chasm toward the opposite wall. The storm had calmed, at least here. Mist rose from the abyss below.

"This is how we get to the bridge." Neela blew out her lamp. "The smugglers called it The Plank."

The stone pier, although wide enough for their feet, jutted out into nothing. Wind or long-ago water had worn at the rock, rounding its edges and nibbling away at its base until what remained seemed too thin to support so much weight. Since time and gravity never gave up, someday The Plank would let go of its hold and crash down to the earth or sea far below. Gingerly Ariel tested the rock and felt no qualms in her feet about going farther. The stone seemed firm today.

"It doesn't go all the way over," she said.

"It doesn't lead to the other side. It leads out of the world."

As Neela spoke, the crow swooped from above to alight on the end of The Plank.

"Ha! Grim-golly knows it," Neela added. "Cass must have shooed it. Which means they know we're gone."

Ariel scowled at the bird. "Are you following us, or am I following you?"

Wishing she'd given it a reply for Nace, just in case, she took a careful step toward the crow. An updraft bore a whiff of sulfur to her nose. She stared over the edge. That wasn't mist below. It was smoke.

"That smell! Flames?"

"Aye. They say brimstone burns down there. The fires of Hell. You sound like you didn't believe me."

"I figured you'd been to *a* bridge. Not *the* bridge! The one the crosses out of the world!"

Neela shot her a quizzical look. "Who said there's only one? There's as many ways out of the world as there are people. Or lots, anyhow."

Ariel had to admit that made sense. "I get confused between what's real and what's only a way to think about things. Which is why I hate riddles. Never mind. You don't mean to jump, do you? I'm not doing that."

"If we were smugglers on the run, mayhap, but we're not." Neela gripped Ariel's hand and lifted her pipe. "The first time I went, it weren't my idea to reach the bridge alive. I reckoned I'd be dead and could go be with Dain. But that's not what happened. Hold tight." She played dissonant notes and pulled Ariel into a trot down The Plank.

"Wait! What are we doing?" Ariel stumbled behind. Her instincts blared: *Drop your weight! Dig in your heels!*

She didn't have time. A shriek caught in her throat as her feet kicked against nothing but air.

CHAPTER
23

Ariel's mind whirled. Her limbs bucked and flailed. Neela fought mightily to keep hold of her hand.

"Stop!" Neela cried. "I don't know what'll happen if you break my grip!"

No rushing air. No sense of speed. Only pain in her fingers. Clinging to each fact like a buoy, Ariel realized she wasn't falling. Neela was the only solid thing she could feel, but they seemed to be safe. She went still and stiff.

"Better." Neela panted.

Ariel opened her eyes, which had clenched shut by themselves. Neela bobbed in midair with her feet treading nothing. Ariel didn't dare look below. She didn't want to see how far above ground they hovered.

"See how the wind lofts me, whether I want it or not?" Neela asked. "You, too. Like we walked through the storm."

"Should have... warned me," Ariel gasped. Her heart banged so loud she barely heard her own voice.

Neela shook her head. "Getting ready makes it worse.

Believe me, I know. And don't mind my feet. They aren't helping. They just won't hold still without trying to swim." She played another note on her pipe. "What you'll feel next is—"

Her instruction came too late. The wind slammed Ariel into Neela, and they tumbled head over heels. Ariel squealed and clutched Neela with both arms and legs. But although they were falling, they weren't falling *down*. They were falling forward, or sideways, perhaps even up—like tumbling in a wave without being slammed to the beach. Earth and sky traded places. Dizzying glimpses of color and shadow whipped past. The sail draped around Neela's neck flapped.

Neela squeezed out a few words. "Ho! This is worse... with someone... banging against you."

"When does it stop?" Ariel cried.

"At the—"

Air sucked at them, a sudden riptide that slowed their motion. They dropped to the earth, knocked about but unharmed, and Neela released Ariel's hand. The ground beneath them was cobbled, but a murky grey fog hovered everywhere else.

"Bridge," Neela whispered.

They untangled and got to their feet. Although the place was cheerless and dim, they could manage without lighting a lamp. Ariel rubbed a bruise while Neela gathered the sail more neatly around her neck. Mist curled around them in tendrils and swirls. Anything could've been lurking just an arm's reach away.

"Scarl?" Ariel called. The fog muffled the sound.

A dark shadow swooped up, far too small to be him. As Ariel shied from it, the crow's shape emerged. It perched on the water skin, which she'd dropped. Shooing the bird, she retrieved the bladder and slung it back over her head.

"I expect if he's here, he'll be farther along," Neela said. "This is only the start of the bridge. I've gone a mite farther." The cobbled way beneath them arched gently upward, leaving no doubt which way it extended.

"We should hurry," she added, starting off. "I've seen frights here."

Ariel did not ask what kind. She remembered what Scarl had said when he'd first told her the bridge's story: *The people put clever barriers on the bridge, hoping to keep the dead and demons where they belonged.* She saw no barriers yet. After just a few paces, they came upon enormous black timbers inset parallel in the stone underfoot like a cart track of wood. Cracked and roughened with age, the dark wood made Ariel shudder. *They say ebony wood forms the bridge,* Scarl had said. *That's why it looks blackened and scorched.*

She avoided the timbers, walking on the cobbles between. She would have preferred a bridge unlike the one in Scarl's story. Then she could've believed they wouldn't meet demons, either.

Wary, she trailed Neela, alert to warnings from her feet. She didn't have many choices for where to place them—the pinched bridge was only a few paces wide. Drops yawned on both sides, and mist boiled up from below. She would have taken it for smoke rising from the bridge's fabled flames, except it was icy. Cold fingers of fog writhed around her, some glowing almost as if lit from within, others more like grey veils over shadows. Twice she thought snarling faces formed alongside her before melting away.

Uneasy, she called Scarl's name. Her voice seemed to drop at her feet, felled by the fog.

"Hush!" Neela said. "You might summon a fright!"

"I don't want to miss him! Will we see his spirit, do you think, like a ghost? His body's not here like ours are."

Neela pursed her lips. "I reckoned I'd recognize Dain in my heart. But I don't see or feel anything like Scarl up there—do you?"

The mist revealed a black gate ahead. Its narrow metal bars stretched over their heads, too close to admit more than a rat between them. Rusty barbed wire, sharp against the fog, tangled around the pointed tips of the bars. Broad snarls spilled over the sides of the bridge to prevent daring trespassers from swinging around the gate at either edge.

A movement flickered on the far side of the gate. Ariel opened her mouth with a hail—and then went stiff. What she'd thought was a person obscured in the mist was only age-darkened bones, held together in places by small knots of wire. The skeleton tottered and hopped, plucking at a length of barbed wire out of reach. The lengths of the skeleton's limbs did not match, and its movements jerked in a way that suggested they hurt. Of course, any motion from a creature without flesh was a wonder. A low keening started in Ariel's throat.

It couldn't be Scarl. And though the next name in her mind froze her heart, Elbert's bones were now nothing but dust. So it wasn't him, either. Still, his bones had been back in the world. Did the dead have a second set once they got here?

The bone-man's skull turned, its empty sockets staring at her through the bars. Ariel clutched Neela.

The smaller girl nodded furiously. "Like I said—frights!"

But the bone-man merely jumped again for the wire. Some bones were missing, including a shoulder blade and most of the ribs. Nothing but mist filled their places. And what Ariel had taken for one thighbone was actually a broken length of the gate's metal bars. She saw the narrow gap where it'd been.

"I don't see Scarl." Ariel fought to control her quivering words. "Maybe he woke up at Cassalie's." They'd been gone for well over an hour.

"I hope so," said Neela. "No help if he chose to cross over, I guess. Just one more that's my fault. We can keep looking, though. You could at least say goodbye."

Ariel winced. Goodbye was not an option she was ready to face. "How do we open the gate to go through?"

Neela slipped the sail from around her neck. "Far as I know, we can't. But I bet we can fling this up, snag one end on the top, and climb it like—"

Something hit Ariel's shin. She jumped, choking on a scream. A length of wire lay at her feet. The skeleton on the far side of the gate clacked its teeth at them and waved its own piece of wire.

Neela and Ariel exchanged an uncertain look. Was the tossed wire a threat?

With a clatter of bones, the skeleton crouched at the gap in the gate to wrap the wire behind the next bar. It pulled the wire back and forth, sawing as if through a sapling. The wire scratched on the metal with a grating that hurt Ariel's teeth.

Her hands flew to cover her ears. She crept closer. Thin fragments of wire littered the ground where the skeleton worked. It must have taken forever, but the bar had already been worn through in one place, an arm's reach above where the bone-ghoul sawed now. When its work there was finished, the length of bar would drop out. Alongside the gap that already existed, the space left would be big enough for bones to squeeze through.

"It's trying to get to our side," whispered Neela.

"And we're trying to get over there," Ariel said. Sawing the bar would take far too long. But someone with more weight than mere bones had might be able to use it.

Rather than getting within reach of the bone-ghoul—which may have been what the macabre thing really wanted—Ariel slipped Elbert's knife from its thong on her leg. She banged the blade on the gate near the skeleton's skull.

"Get away!"

The skeleton's teeth clacked as though it might bite, but it drew back into the mist, taking its wire with it.

Ariel handed the knife to Neela and grabbed the bar near the break to test its stiffness. It gave.

"Help me." She propped one boot on the gate for leverage.

Neela set down the knife to join her, and they pulled hard on the bar. Slowly it bent until they could use their feet, too, stomping it horizontal and finally jumping on it.

The bone-man dashed up. Before Ariel could do more than snatch her knife from the ground, the skeleton thrust its skull through the gap. Ariel and Neela jumped back. The skull dropped with a crack on the cobblestones and rolled a short way by itself as the rest of the bone-ghoul jammed through behind. Its larger bones rattled and jumbled together. Smaller ones split away and slid fast between the bars. As the girls stared, jaws agape, the bone-ghoul reassembled, collected its skull, and galloped away into the mist.

"We've let something horrid into the world," Ariel murmured.

Neela's face pinched. "Best make it worth it, I guess." She thrust one leg through the gap and wiggled through sideways, dragging the sail behind her. Ariel followed, afraid she'd get stuck. The cold bars banged her hipbones and scraped her backside and ears, but she forced herself through.

Soon she and Neela stood on the far side. The cobblestones and timbers of the bridge stretched before them, still arching up.

"Do you know what's ahead?" Ariel's feet were willing to show her.

"I've never got past the gate."

Wings flapped above them, hidden in the mist. Ariel hoped it was only the crow.

She secured Elbert's knife at her leg again and stepped forward. "Let's hurry. I don't like how the mist collects around us when we stop. Did you see the faces back there?"

Neela followed. "Spooky hands, too."

A small cluster of golden sparks, stunningly bright, zipped out of the colorless fog and between them. The girls flinched apart. Both turned to watch as the lights flew through the gate and beyond.

"Baby stars!" Neela said. "Or ball lightning?"

Ariel had been reminded of burning flies, but Neela's

words changed her mind. "Maybe sparks of the Essence. I wondered if— oh! Look."

A shadow slipped toward them through the bars of the gate. Taller than Ariel, it fluttered like a dark flame, one moment squeezed narrow, and the next, broad as a man. A smear of light glowed where a heart might have been.

Neela twitched to flee.

Fear numbing her tongue, Ariel held her in place. "Scarl?"

Giving no sign it heard, the shade passed them and headed on up the bridge. Ariel couldn't justify her relief, but her heart said it hadn't been him.

"I wondered if we'd see the dead crossing," she whispered. She hadn't noticed any on the other side of the gate, but more shades appeared soon, slipping in and out of sight and all gliding in the same direction. None struck Ariel as someone she loved.

"And the sparks?" Neela asked as they trotted forward.

"The Essence of those about to be born? Without the shadows of bodies they haven't got yet?"

"The spirits of babies?" said Neela. "I like that."

As they progressed up the arch, which was gentle but long, Ariel and Neela grew used to both shadows and sparks. Wings beat overhead in both directions, too, sometimes too thickly to be only one crow. Ariel tried to pretend it was the passage of angels, but vultures or demons seemed more likely.

To keep fear from pressing too close on her neck, she fell back on her farwalking song, though she whispered so the sound wouldn't draw attention. New words flowed to her tongue, as they so often did.

"Crossing the bridge with Dain—
She's really Neela—
Hoping to find a friend.
We'll turn him back.

"We'll turn him back, and then
Seek out a brother.
Dain, do you wander here
Lost in the mist?

"Mist-bound, but never lost,
We'll just keep walking
Over the bridge and back,
Thinking of fr— oh!"

Suddenly wracked by a shiver, she stumbled aside from a hunched shade she'd walked into. "Sorry!"

The shadow wavered forward as if she'd never touched it. Its disinterest reassured her, since any demons they met here might also ignore them. Still, passing through the same space as a spirit had stolen her breath. She didn't want to repeat it.

"That's a good song," said Neela, who'd tipped her head close to listen. "Keep singing."

"No. I'd better pay more attention."

Her decision paid off. She noticed immediately when the cobbles finally began to slope downward.

"We've passed the top of the arch," Ariel whispered. "Halfway."

"You going to throw the knife off now?" Neela asked.

Ariel struggled, reluctant without knowing why. "What if we need it?"

"For what? Everything here that might bother us should be already dead. You suppose it would work anyhow?"

"I don't know."

Flames leapt from the fog just a few feet ahead. The girls froze. Heat washed over their faces and shriveled mist all around before the fire receded through a hole in the cobbles.

Scarl's words echoed in Ariel's mind. *The hole couldn't be fixed. Anything near it fell in and was lost. Flames boiled up through the breach, and demons sometimes rode on those flames.... Those who claim to have ventured partway on the bridge always mention a light—the glare of flame through that hole.*

So this part of his story had also been true. Ariel edged closer to the gaping hole. Nothing living was said to be able to cross.

CHAPTER

24

A cobblestone fell away just ahead of Ariel's toes, dropping silently into the void. She scuttled backward.

"Think we could run and jump across?" Neela asked.

Even Ariel's sure feet balked at that. "No." The gap ahead could have swallowed a boat. She scanned the mists beyond for Scarl. The empty fog mocked her. If she knew he'd turned away from the bridge and had awakened again in the world, she could bear being turned back by this hole. But she knew no such thing.

Closing her eyes, she asked her feet to take her to him, berating herself for not trying that sooner. They failed to answer, neither turning her back nor urging her in any direction at all—as if he didn't exist or had moved forever beyond her reach.

"Can the wind help us?" she asked Neela.

"Carry us over? I'll ask." Neela blew on her pipe. No sound came. Her face cramped in disbelief.

"Uh-oh. No wind here?" Ariel gripped the strap of the

water skin she carried. The clammy fog did make even the air feel dead. But they might need the wind to get back to the world.

"There must be! Like fire and stone." Neela blew harder. Her face flushing, she forced a low moan from the pipe.

"It sounds nasty," she said. "The wind might not like it."

"Well, don't make it mad."

Neela inhaled deeply and played on, the groaning notes unlike any she'd played before. The mist near their feet stirred and slipped into holes, draining like water. More fog rushed behind. Creating a current, it rose up their legs. The river of mist pulled Ariel's right boot forward.

She jerked it back. "Stop! This won't lift us over, it'll suck us down."

Neela lowered her pipe, but the pressure around their legs swirled and grew. "Wind? If that's your doing, what do you mean?"

"Oh, it might be a demon!"

Ariel's feet whisked from beneath her. She slammed onto her back. The water bladder slung on her shoulder bounced alongside her.

The river of fog dragged her over the bridge toward the hole. With a cry, she threw her arms wide to grab Neela, the cobblestones, anything. Her fingers found no hold she could keep. Digging in her boots only wrenched her ankles. Feet first, Ariel slid toward the edge of the hole.

The mist sucked her down. Several loose cobbles went with her. She gasped one last breath, expecting to fall.

Instead, the current tugged her forward, stronger than before. She felt only its pull and the space all around her. One heart-stopping breath, two.... The whirling river of mist swept her up in an arc. Her body smacked stone and timbers again. More cobblestones broke away as the current scraped her up and over the far rim.

It dumped her on the bridge where the cobbles held firm. Aching, she opened her eyes and lifted her head.

Nearby, Neela groaned. "Must not be dead. My skin hurts too much to have lost it."

Ariel pushed herself upright. She was surprised to find the water bladder still twisted around her. She and Neela stared back over the huge, jagged hole. They must've looked like flapping fish being reeled in through a stream.

"I guess not even the wind can pass over the hole," Ariel said shakily. "Only below it." She wondered if the crow had gotten this far and if it'd flown underneath, too.

"I sure don't want another go of that." Neela inspected bruises that were already blooming. "Even knowing the wind wouldn't drop us. I hope you can lead us back some other way, Farwalker girl."

Ariel was starting to doubt they'd survive even one crossing, let alone a trip back. But the wind had helped them. Other forces might, too. At least her feet were willing to move forward again.

They sipped their water and moved on. Fog knotted around them again, but the path slanted downward, speeding their legs and encouraging their hearts that the end of the bridge must be near. Ariel kept noticing groups of two or three cobbles, apparently broken loose from the edge of the hole, playing leapfrog—or that's how it seemed. They tumbled along purposefully like empty boots walking. The first time, she stopped to watch. When the rocks changed course toward her, she hurried onward again.

"Rock monsters," said Neela. "Zeke could keep 'em as pets."

"Too creepy." Wistfully Ariel hoped Zeke was still warm and safe.

A few paces later, two oblong stones loomed through the mist. They marked the edge of the bridge like gateposts with no gate. The gap between was just wide enough for the girls to pass shoulder to shoulder.

She and Neela had just slipped between them when Ariel sensed somebody watching. She whirled. Only tendrils of mist trailed behind. The two stones were not blank, though. Complex symbols were etched on them both.

"What do they mean?" Neela asked.

"I don't know. And I'm not sure I want to." There were only five marks, in different combinations and sizes, sometimes upside down or sideways. Ariel didn't recognize any. Perhaps it was only their tangle, compared with the neat rows Scarl had taught her, but they had a sinuous cast that made her uneasy.

"I suppose since they're facing this side of the bridge, they're not speaking to us, anyhow," she said. "The gate at the other end is supposed to keep out the living. This might be some kind of gate for the dead. The marks must be a message or warning for them." She wondered what the stones could have told Zeke, if he'd been there.

She touched one of the marks. It squirmed and flowed onto her finger, losing its shape to twine over her knuckles. The symbol had somehow come loose from the stone. The remaining marks writhed.

"Oh!" Ariel shook her hand, hard.

Neela glanced up from inspecting the cobbles at their feet. "What?"

The creeping thing on Ariel's skin had not been dislodged. Like a rivulet of water or blood, it streamed to the back of her hand. Retaking its original shape there, it gleamed.

"This mark!" Ariel scrubbed it against the leg of her trousers. The symbol doubled. One remained on her hand. Another appeared on the fabric. The same mouse brown as the wool, the second mark had just enough shine to see it. It slid to stop over her pocket and twisted into another symbol shown on the stones.

"Ariel...?" Neela pointed to Ariel's sleeve. Three more marks wiggled up it like caterpillars. They also must have spawned from the one on her hand. Ariel flicked at them, but they would not be knocked off. They settled atop her shoulder and stilled. She'd been infected by the whole set of five.

A moan escaped her.

"Easy, Farwalker girl," Neela said. "Do they hurt?"

"They tickle when they move." Ariel took a shaky breath. "But I can't feel them when they don't."

Before Ariel could stop her, Neela jabbed the one on Ariel's leg. It twitched but remained. She turned and touched a mark on one of the stones. Nothing squirmed onto her.

She shrugged. "They don't want me."

A puzzled curiosity replaced Ariel's fear. "Maybe they know I'm a Farwalker! I carry messages all the time. Not on me, exactly, but... maybe this message wants to be delivered somewhere."

"Where? Or to who?"

Ariel shook her head. "I don't know. But maybe they'll crawl off if I get there." She certainly hoped so. She didn't want to wear the sinister marks for too long.

"They're on the ground here, too." Neela swished one leg to chase off the mist at their ankles. The same symbols lay snarled across the width of the bridge, one lengthy stride ahead of where they stood now. The large marks looked like chunks of the ebony timbers, inlaid in the cobbles to mark the bridge's end. The cobblestones petered out just beyond.

"I stepped on one, that's how I noticed," Neela added. "Something slid under my foot. When I jumped back, I saw it moving. It didn't crawl on me, though."

Ariel bent for a closer view. As she stared, they seemed to writhe into her thoughts.

She looked away quickly. "Let's jump over and get off the bridge. If we can." She leapt.

"Don't go without me!" Neela bounded over, too. "That wasn't so hard."

"If we haven't just jumped through a curse." Ariel moved forward, alert to warnings from her feet. Once the cobbles ended, the ground shifted under her tread like sand.

"The dead's end of the bridge," she murmured.

Neela brightened. "Now to find Dain."

In the fog, finding anything seemed unlikely. The shadow-spirits they'd seen had no faces, made no sound, and had taken no interest in them. Ariel thought of Scarl, but just as before, she felt no inclination to walk anywhere. She hoped that meant he was with the living, not anywhere here among the dead. Her farwalking skills might not be reliable here, though. Certainly Neela's piping hadn't worked as they'd expected.

"I could call to my brother and see if he answers," Neela said. "Except it feels wrong to make noise."

"Let me try something first." Ariel shifted her focus to Dain. The faster they found him, if he could be found, the faster they could return to confirm Scarl was all right.

Ariel summoned every scrap Neela had told her about Dain, closed her eyes, and moved her awareness to her feet. Oddly, they twitched with opposing impulses. The first was a desire to move back onto the bridge. The second, less familiar sensation was like standing in the sea while waves sucked the sand out from under her bare feet.

Alarmed, Ariel looked down to see if the current that'd dragged them across the hole had returned. If anything, the mist seemed to creep toward the bridge, but the slurping under her boots pulled the opposite way. She shook her head, dizzied by the conflicting impressions. Perhaps she'd confused her feet by asking for both Scarl and Dain.

"Do you feel anything in your feet?" she asked Neela. "Like the ground's sliding away a few grains at a time?"

"No." Neela stamped. "Feels solid to me."

"Let's try this way, then." Ariel followed the suction.

The shadowy spirits still accompanied them, some overtaking, some being passed. Faces of mist formed and melted away when Ariel looked directly at them.

Twice the crow fluttered up for a visit. When Ariel offered, the bird perched on her arm before tipping its head and flying off again. Ariel wondered where it went and why it kept coming back. It wasn't with them enough to be coaxing them on.

Uneasy, but trying to attend to her feet, she gave no thought to other senses until Neela said, "You hear that?" Heavy footsteps approached.

CHAPTER 25

Ariel and Neela halted. At their silence, the footsteps paused, too.

"Dain?" Neela called.

Ariel elbowed her. "Shh!"

Clump, clump, clump-clump. The noise moved faster and closer, but the fog masked its direction. Ariel shifted her weight, wanting to run but unsure which way to go.

Clump-clump-clump—whack! Something hard hit her back.

"Ow!" Ariel pitched forward to her hands and knees.

A cobblestone flew up to strike Neela's belly. She doubled over. The sail she carried slipped from her neck. Instead of dropping, it fluttered into the air.

"Yesss!" hissed a thin voice in the mist.

"Is that the wind?" Ariel jumped up.

"No!" Neela grabbed for the sail. It whipped out of reach.

Ariel scooped up the cobble that'd knocked her down, ready to heave it at their attacker. But there *was* no attacker, except for the rocks. The sail had whisked out of sight.

The marks on her shoulder raced down toward her

hand—the one holding the stone. The rock wiggled out of her grip and away. Changing direction in mid-air, it swooped back at her. She flung up her arms, protecting her head. The stone landed and hopped closer for another try.

Not thinking, just reacting, Ariel stomped it. The cobble squirmed under her boot.

"Giiive iit!" wailed a new voice. Ariel searched for its source. A serpent of mist stretched between the two rocks, one at each end like hands on rubbery arms. A misshapen face hovered midway between. Its mouth was a dark, flapping hole. "Giive!"

Neela grabbed the second rock and held it at arm's length while the mist monster tugged it this way and that in her hands. More mist had gathered as if drawn by the fight. Tendrils tugged at Neela's wind pipe, its lanyard stretched to full length and sawing into her neck. A lamp popped out of her pocket and bounded away.

The waterskin bounced at Ariel's side, too, lifting and yanking against its strap. She clamped the bag under her elbow to keep it. A clammy wisp slid up the strap to her cheek. When it branched into fingers, she slapped it. Another misty hand reached over her shoulder. The symbols at her wrist squirmed back up her arm toward it.

"Forrrm, youu haff fforrrrm." The hiss pierced Ariel's thoughts, not just her ears. Goosebumps rose on her skin. "Niice forrm... I waant it!"

The hand at Ariel's shoulder shot to her lips. Two cold fingers thrust in and yanked her mouth wide, plunging in to the back of her throat. Ariel gagged. More clammy tendrils probed around her tongue and cheeks as though an icy octopus writhed inside in her mouth. Something black flashed past Neela, but Ariel had no thought for the crow. It was not cramming itself into her throat. Her hands scraped her face, finding nothing to grab. Yet the thing trying to slide down her throat blocked her breath.

Ariel jerked Elbert's knife from its thong and slashed it through the mist, putting all her defiance into the strokes. Her ferocious motion scattered the mist near her face and sucked cold streams from between her lips. She fought to keep her gorge down, but at last she could breathe.

"Giive!" The rock still under her boot struggled harder. Squirming loose, it jumped to hit Ariel's hand. The knife flew. Its arc halted as a misty hand snatched it. Ariel cringed. Would it fly back to cut them?

"Mmmore!"

"I'll give you more!" Neela flung her cobblestone at the knife, knocking it well away. The second stone tumbled after the first as if chasing. Streams of mist trailed behind. But more mist had wound its way inside Neela's pipe. The shell glowed from within as it yanked at her lanyard, working to jerk the cord over her head. Neela fought to keep it as the crow swooped around her. With mist tendrils lashing, the shell finally burst. Sharp fragments flew.

"Run!" Ariel grabbed Neela and they tore away. Ariel braced for a knife flying into her back. Neither of the voices she'd heard had been Elbert's, and the blade hadn't been the only thing stolen, but oh, how she wished she'd been strong enough to hold it! Now it might strike against them, far more deadly than stones.

"Is it a trick, or is it brighter up there?" Neela asked as they ran. "Like the sun breaking through?"

Something did shine ahead, though a moon seemed

more likely. They'd left the world in the daytime, but hours had passed—and surely the dead needed no sun.

They jogged on with caution. The tug on Ariel's feet had grown reassuringly stronger. Within a few moments, the glow ahead split the fog and a tall shadow took shape beneath.

"Oh, a fire beacon?" Neela said, panting.

"Or a lighthouse." Ariel wondered if it might be the source of the sparks. "I've heard Fishers tell stories about them." She squinted at the round tower under the light. It appeared to be built of brown stones so lumpy that they were more suited for cobbles than walls, but the glow atop soothed her, even if the beacon couldn't be meant for them.

Growing confident that they'd outrun any pursuit, Ariel slowed them to a walk as they approached the lighthouse. "You all right?" she asked Neela, who was holding her ribs.

"Except for my busted pipe. Curse those cold squirmies! None got in you, did they? I saw that one try."

"It nearly choked me!" Ariel said. "But I got it back out."

"Or your message marks stopped it. They ran to your neck."

"They did?" Ariel glanced at her hand when it tickled. The symbols had settled together in her palm, almost as though painted there for her to carry.

"Aye. It looked to me like they kept the mist from getting in farther. Maybe their message is 'No monsters allowed.' Anyway, they helped more than your grim-golly did. It was darting all around us, but I guess it's gone now."

"Maybe it was flapping at the mist with its wings." Ariel doubted it, though. After all, crows were scavengers. It had just been awaiting its chance at her—

Bones. She sucked in a breath. She could see more clearly now. The odd stones of the tower were not stones at all. "It's bones, Neela! Bones!" Pelvic bones by the hundred formed the tower's foundation. Brown with age, they'd been nested and stacked ten feet high. Above those rested the knobby ends of thighbones and shins, stuck out from the center like spokes of a wheel. The next round made Ariel shudder the most—human skulls staring outward, row upon row. Up and up rose the tower, without stairs or a door, until details were lost in the glare at the top.

Ariel pulled her gaze back to the base. Gaps in the rows showed some bones out of place, leaving dark hollows or uneven tangles. No wonder the ghoul at the gate had looked cobbled together. Clearly it'd drawn some of its pieces from here.

"That's the bones of a whole lot of people," breathed Neela.

Ariel shivered. "But whose? Dead things leave their bones in the world."

"Not everyone, maybe," Neela replied. "Smugglers used to say if you're not buried right, your bones get up and walk. They might all come here."

Ariel swallowed. Elbert hadn't been buried at all. But she'd stomped his bones to dust. Maybe these had been here since the days when the bridge had been easier for the living to cross. They looked old enough. If so, though, few who'd come here alive seemed to have found their way back to the world. Her bones and Neela's could end up here, too.

A light hit them from above, so bright it was painful. Shading her face with her hand, Ariel squinted up. The beam fell from the tower like a column of flame. Someone or something had noticed them there.

She took a few steps. The light followed her. But nobody hailed them and nothing else moved.

Then the ray of light folded into a glowing staircase, which rose toward the blaze at the top.

"That looks like an invitation," Ariel whispered. "But to what?"

"Maybe Dain's up there!"

Whatever it was, it already knew they were there. Ariel lifted one boot toward the stairs. Her feet didn't protest. "I guess we'd better find out."

CHAPTER

26

Ariel stood on one foot, prepared for the other to
pass through the staircase and slip back to the
ground, but the glowing stair held her. She mounted with
care. The staircase of light was no wider than she was, steep
and without railings. Ariel's arms helped her balance, but
she didn't dare glance away from her boots.

"Ariel?" Neela called.

Ariel rested her hands on a step so she could look back
without toppling off. Neela remained at the foot of the stair.

"What are you doing?" Ariel called. "Come up!"

"It won't let me." Neela raised one foot. The first step
went dark and vanished, and her boot plunged straight back
to the ground. Once she stood squarely, the light reached
her again. "And I don't want to be in the dark by myself."

Ariel's perch felt more precarious than ever. Reluctant
to leave Neela, she tentatively lowered one foot. The stair
below blinked away, leaving nothing but space. She yanked
her dangling leg back up.

"I get it." Swallowing the quiver in her voice, she told Neela, "I have to keep going. I don't have any choice."

"I saw it," replied Neela. "Just come back quick! If you can."

Ariel resumed climbing. The ascent strained more than her legs and her nerve. It made her heart ache, because memories tumbled through her with each step. She recalled moments with Scarl during the first frightening journey she'd taken with him—especially the short time they'd rested in his village. The woman he'd loved had left the world soon thereafter, so Ariel felt she'd stolen days he could've spent with Mirayna. The tower's shining staircase carried her back to that sorrow as if she were climbing a stair of bright, hard mistakes. Each one brought the pain of regret.

With a final step, she moved into a light too bright to bear. She hid her eyes with her hands, but her palms only seemed to push the brilliance into her head. A flickering shape like a heat wave stirred against the bright background of the Essence.

"Ariel Farwalker. I might've known I'd meet you again." The voice was not human. It sounded more like chimes rippling through water. But Ariel understood, and her heart knew who spoke. The memories on the staircase had warned her.

"Mirayna?"

"Once."

Ariel cracked her eyelids, trying to look through her lashes and fingers to see the Allcraft Scarl had loved. The chime rose in a fiery laughter.

"Don't wound your eyes. Tell me instead why you've

dared to come here. You ought not have. But I know how rarely you heed good advice."

Ariel swallowed hard. "Is Scarl here, too?"

"Scarl Finder turned away from the gate. Which you would know if you'd stayed in the world. Is that why you've come?"

A cry of relief fell from Ariel's lips. "Oh, thank you! Yes. Thank you."

"I suppose I can't chide you, since my presence here isn't so different from yours. Some serve at this beacon to help guide those who follow. We're rewarded with glimpses of those we have loved."

Ariel's breath caught. She tried to focus beyond Mirayna. "My mother—?"

"No. That one moved on when she saw that you wouldn't be left alone. And I have tarried too long. But I wanted to see Scarl love anew, if he could. Now I, too, will proceed."

Ariel said, "I almost wish he were with me to…" *See* wasn't the right word. "…meet you again."

The light rippled. "No. That would only be cruel. Please don't tell him we've spoken. I know you can fib when it's called for."

Ariel didn't understand but did not dare to argue. "All right."

"You don't know how important you are to him. And to me. If he hadn't turned around and come back to you after your trials near the Mouth of the Mountain, when I was newly arrived here, his soul might've been lost a long time."

Not sure she deserved any credit for that, Ariel ducked her head. Scarl still bore the five-fingered mark on his chest that he'd gained on the day Mirayna meant. A ghost had given it to him in a dream. Nonetheless, it showed on his skin. Though she rarely saw it, Ariel hadn't forgotten; it'd played a part in his promise to her. She'd never considered what he'd be otherwise, but she could imagine him callous and bitter.

"It is my gratitude, Ariel, that has built you a stairway and allowed us to meet. My gratitude to you, and your regrets about me."

"The stairs are made of feelings?" Ariel murmured. "No wonder."

"Yes. You are accustomed to form having power, but tangible bodies and physical strength don't matter on this side of the bridge. Emotions have more power here. Love and compassion keep this beacon alight, but those lost in the mist are filled with hatred and greed, and they use them as weapons. The most envious could rip your limbs from you simply by wanting them badly enough. Which is why I insist you and Neela go back as you've come. Right away. You know you don't belong here, and you're in terrible danger."

In her awe, Ariel had nearly forgotten about Neela. She said, "There's another reason we're here. Neela needs to see her brother, Dain."

"Guilt binds the living, not the dead. The dead are bound mainly by anger and fear. If Dain bore any grudge, he'd be lost in the mist. I promise you he is not. Go back."

Ariel wanted to obey, but she doubted Neela would be swayed without proof. "What if we keep going to search?"

"You risk falling prey to those who are lost, and the risk grows every moment. Go back while you can." Mirayna's

Essence receded, melting into the background of fire.

"Wait!" Ariel cried. "You said you could peek at people you loved from here. Can I, too?" When no answer came, she whirled away from the light toward the stairs. Hope and longing opened a window at the backs of her eyes. Staring blindly into the mist, Ariel saw much farther.

A cold tremor went through her. She'd wished, perhaps frivolously, to glimpse Nace. But worry loomed large in the back of her mind, and unpracticed with using the force of desire, she instead saw two others she loved and missed— Scarl and Zeke. A bandage swaddled Scarl's head, and they both kneeled on The Plank. Zeke's lips were moving as he sang to the stone.

Ariel groaned. If the stone told him what she and Neela had done there, Scarl and Zeke might try, too. But they wouldn't have the help of the wind.

Mirayna's voice tinkled in her ear. "You knew they'd pursue you. Go back to them before it's too late, or risk sorrows your soul may not bear. I cannot intervene further."

Nudged from behind, Ariel lurched forward a step. Neela stood at her side, mist curling between them.

"What are you staring at?" Neela asked.

"Oh!" Ariel clutched her friend, dizzy. She wasn't sure when she'd opened her eyes, let alone how she'd descended. Perhaps her body had never moved far and only her spirit had climbed. She'd returned to Neela at the foot of the tower. The beam of light dwindled. The vision of her friends on The Plank melted with it.

"I saw Scarl and Zeke. They're coming behind us!"

Neela turned and squinted.

"Not with my eyes." Ariel moaned. "I should have known they'd find some way."

"Don't fret, though," Neela said. "They can't follow us here without help from the wind, and the wind won't give it to them."

"I'm not worried about that—I'm worried they'll leave the world dead! We've got to stop them before they try something crazy." Ariel grabbed Neela's arm and pulled her in the direction they'd come.

Neela resisted. "I haven't done what I came for."

"We can't stand still and argue!" Ariel glanced for threats in the mist. "Here, walk around the tower with me."

They circled, moving faster than the clinging mist. Ariel tried to explain what she'd understood from Mirayna: that Dain had moved on long ago, and he couldn't have if he'd needed anything from his sister.

"I've got to make sure for myself," Neela said. "Just go back without me then, Farwalker girl. I reckon I can make my own way home. If Dain doesn't want my form like those spooks did, anyhow. If he does want it, I aim to give it."

"Don't be stupid."

"It's not stupid. I killed him. I owe him my life."

"I didn't mean that," Ariel snapped. "Although that's stupid, too. I meant I can't leave you."

"Aye, you can. Go back to Zeke and your Scarl. And... and Cass." After a wistful glance up at the lighthouse, Neela stepped firmly away.

"Neela!" Ariel's whole life seemed shaped by horrible choices she did not want and couldn't possibly make.

Neela didn't look back.

CHAPTER

27

Neela strode into the fog, looking small and alone. But she whistled through her teeth and sang out:

"Wind! I'm your piper, and I'm begging your ear.
Blow me to Dain, or carry him here.
My wind pipe is busted, so now I can't play.
Please, won't you heed me and help anyway?"

She finished the verse with a sickly tweet that was dampened by the oppressive gloom.

No wind swooped to respond, but as Neela continued to whistle, streams of mist coiled around her. They looked like snakes tensing to strike.

Ariel raced after Neela before she vanished into the murk. "Stop. I don't think whistling is helping."

"Something's happening, though, so—"

The ground heaved. Ariel stumbled against Neela. A wave passed under their feet, peaked, and gathered into human shape before them.

"Dain!" Neela crowed. "Thank you, wind!"

The figure grew more distinct, mist filled out by sand and pebbles that whirled up from the ground. Flung to the edges, the sand formed a seething false skin. The face took on sharp features that were grey but not unlike Neela's. The male form rose and rose... too tall, unless Dain had grown into a man here.

Neela's joy flipped to horror.

"Where have you been, you disobedient wretch?" Grit scratched in the man's voice. A big hand made of sand, wrapped around mist and memory, shot forward to grab Neela by the throat.

"Papa?" she squeaked.

"Well, I sure ain't the wind!" He shook her. "Never said you could run off like that, neither. But all that rain leaking in was your doing, weren't it? And you called in this fog, too, I bet! Think you'll show me who's boss, eh?"

"Oh, no," Ariel murmured.

"Where's Dain?" Neela cowered, raising her arms for protection. "Isn't he here?"

"Don't you worry about him! It'll be you who gets beat! Where's my lash?" He began to drag Neela away. She struggled in vain.

"Hey!" Ariel jumped after them and grabbed the sand man's arm. Her hand passed right through him, grit peppering her fingers. He didn't seem to notice. Was he so lost in bitter memories that she was invisible to him? He certainly seemed unaware that he'd left the world.

Ariel tried again. It was like catching hold of a sandstorm. As she swiped at him, the symbols on her hand flared, shining forth like tiny flames. Instead of helping her, though, they pushed the arm of sand and mist out of her reach, just as ashes floated away from the heat of a fire.

Yet the dead man had no trouble grasping Neela. Strengthened, perhaps, by her fear and his anger, his fingers were making red marks on her neck.

Ariel leapt around to face him. He shoved her aside, his push knocking her down even though she hadn't been able to grab him. It was as if she'd been moved not by a hand but by the force of his fury.

"Outta my way, Dain," he muttered. "You argue for her too much. This is for your good as well."

As Ariel scrambled to her feet, he jerked Neela along farther and said, "I suppose you made off with my best lash again?"

"I know where it is, Papa," Ariel said quickly. She avoided Neela's confused look. "I'll show you."

The face of sand turned toward her. "You took it? I'm warning you, boy...."

"No, I just saw it. This way. Over here." Ariel stepped sideways. To her relief, the sand man followed.

"See?" he grumbled to Neela. "Obedience. That's all I ask. A few licks taught your brother. You'll learn, too."

Ariel walked stiffly before him, her steps choppy with fright. She'd acted mostly on instinct to get his attention. But where was she leading? She bent her thoughts to her feet and again found that sense of the ground leaking out from beneath her. Stronger now, it pulled hard. She followed with long strides, though she was certain the current drew them farther from the bridge.

A wide glow rose ahead. Another lighthouse? The first was lost in the gloom behind them.

Neela's father grew restless. "So where's that lash, boy?"

"Almost there," Ariel said.

But the sand man stopped. "Here it is." He bent to snatch something from the ground near his feet. When he raised his fist, it looked empty, but he waggled it as if holding a switch.

"Ready to pay for your impudence, girl?" He spun Neela and jerked her shirt up to bare her back. His other arm snapped—*crack!* Neela yelped through clamped lips. Although Ariel saw nothing to explain the noise, his intent or his anger alone was enough. A welt rose on Neela's skin.

"Stop!" Ariel cried. "Neela, fight!"

"Hush and stay outta this, boy. Or you're next."

As Neela's father cocked his arm for another lick, Ariel's mind raced to come up with an idea or weapon. The cobblestone ghoul had stolen Elbert's knife. She had nothing but the empty thong still tied on her leg, the food in her pockets, and the waterskin dangling from—

Water. Ariel yanked the strap over her head. Fresh water was supposed to stop ghosts. It had ended the blood oozing from Elbert's knife. Maybe it also could wash away sand—or at least distract the man long enough for Neela to jerk free.

Crack! Unable to keep her teeth clenched, Neela wailed.

Desperate, Ariel loosened the thong that held the waterskin closed. Gritting her teeth, she swung the bladder as hard as she could at the man's swirling head.

She also swung the full weight of her anger and outrage, and that made a difference. Instead of passing through him like her hand had, the bladder struck so hard it burst. Water gushed out. The deluge broke the dead man's control of his shape. Sand fell with a *splat* to the ground.

The man roared, and misty hands grasped for Neela. They fell short, the arms anchored in the wet pile of sand. Dry and easily swirled, it had given him form, but now his spirit appeared bound to it.

Ariel grabbed Neela and ran. Her feet took the easiest route, following the current. It increased with each step to speed them.

Neela's father needed only a moment to gather his sand about him again.

"He's c-coming!" Neela panted.

Though the wet sand was misshapen, he surged after them. He caught Ariel's hair and yanked her off her feet.

"I'll show you," he hissed.

"Papa, no!" Neela threw her arms around him. He shrugged her off, flinging her to the ground, too.

A black arrow sped over Ariel. The crow! It darted at the dead man's sandy chest. He bellowed and released Ariel to swipe at the bird. She skittered away.

Dipping and dodging, the crow circled to dive into his back. It emerged out his chest in a shower of sand. Pinched in its beak was a single grain, glowing dully—the Essence from Neela's dead father.

The loss didn't slow him. He shouted, "Thief!" As the bird sped away, also following the current, the man snatched at Neela and dragged her behind. "No! Take this one instead!"

Ariel chased to wrest Neela from her father's grip. Unable to free her, she flung her whole weight on the

struggling girl, wrapping her arms around tight and digging
in her heels. Neela's father slowed, but only a little. The
growing current swept them all along now.

The man skidded to a halt, the clot of sand falling back
on itself. He dropped Neela to backpedal, stumbling over
both girls. They rolled out of the way, not sure what had
happened. He turned to run back the way he'd come, but
his sandy legs churned without much effect.

The crow flew on ahead, where the fog vanished, sucked
down to flow into a great maelstrom. Currents and mist
drained from all sides to the center. The shadows of the
dead stood out against that white carpet, and they were
drawn, too, rushing and eager. They converged at the vortex,
slipping in with the mists.

Yet splashing back up were fountains of light even more
brilliant than in the lighthouse. Ariel could only squint at
the edges. Sparks burst up in flurries, twinkling amid the
incoming shadows. They tumbled and danced before falling
again. A few sparks shot higher and arced away toward the
bridge.

The crow, small and black against the inferno, released
the stolen spark from its beak. The bird soared away while
the dull spark spiraled into the fountain.

"Not yet!" howled Neela's papa. "Give it baaa..."

As his spark joined the blaze, the mists that gave him
shape vanished. Sand flopped to the ground.

Ariel and Neela were still picking up speed with the
current. It pulled hard at their sprawled bodies.

"Get up!" Ariel cried. They scrambled to their feet to
run back the direction they'd come. Straining, they pumped
their legs without gaining ground.

Remembering a lesson she'd learned from the sea, Ariel turned to angle across the current. "This way, crosswise! Don't fight it directly."

"Like rip tides, aye. Good."

They plowed a zig-zag course away from the maelstrom, shadows and mist flowing opposite them, until they could pause to catch much-needed breath.

Neela ran a hand through Ariel's hair and turned up a palm full of sand. She eyed it sadly. "I asked for my brother, but I guess all that's left of him is Papa's warped memories."

"And his anger. Let me look at your back. Does it hurt?"

Neela shrugged. "Aye. But I've had thrashings before. It'll heal." She looked back over her shoulder. "It seems like a good fire, doesn't it? Not brimstone and pitchforks and such. All those sparkles looked to be having fun."

"I won't be afraid to go there someday." Gently, Ariel added, "I'm sure Dain wasn't, either."

"You think his spark's in there, dancing 'round in that pool?"

"Or it might have already flown back over the bridge. His spark could be in someone else now. Someone new."

"I'd like that." Neela poured the sand from one hand to the other. "You don't think he'd remember me if we met?"

"Do you remember anything from before *you* were born, Neela?" Ariel slipped her crooked arm around Neela's, both as a comfort and to encourage her on.

"No," Neela said faintly. After weighing the grains in her palm a last time, she flung the sand into the air, where it drifted into the streaming mists and vanished behind them.

"Bye, Dain," she said softly. "Wherever you are." With new purpose, she matched Ariel's strides.

The crow flapped up to circle their heads.

"Thank you," Ariel told it. "You saved us back there. That makes up for every bone you ever brought me." Perhaps plucking and delivering bones in the world had been practice for snatching sparks here.

Neela lifted her arm, and the bird perched there with a smug tilt of its head.

"I bet I was a bird before I was born—before I became Neela," she said. "And that's why the wind likes me."

Ariel squeezed her arm. "I bet you're right, Neela-bird. But since we can't fly, let's run. We've still got to get home."

She thought, but did not add, "If we can."

CHAPTER

28

Ariel peered at the shadows they met as they ran. She dreaded spotting one she knew, but she couldn't stop searching. What if Scarl and Zeke hadn't given up at The Plank?

"I don't mean to tell you your trade, Farwalker," Neela panted, after they'd loped for a while. "But are you sure we're going the right way?"

Ariel slowed. She'd been running without thinking about a direction. Her feet often worked best that way.

"It seems like we should've passed the lighthouse by now," Neela added.

She had a point. Ariel stopped to search for any glow. The crow had long since taken flight, but as they paused, two sparks passed overhead from behind, and—

BHOOM!

Ariel and Neela clutched one another. A wall of fog surged over and past them.

As the shock faded to silence, the mist began knotting again.

"What was that?" Neela breathed.

"Sounded like the bridge falling down." Ariel's stomach twisted. She wouldn't put it past Zeke to knock the gate flat with a boulder. And if he needed to knock it down, he must still be living. But if the effort had torn down the bridge....

"Prin-cess..."

Ariel whirled. Were her ears playing tricks, or had a whisper come out of the mist?

"Did you hea—"

"Pr-rin-n-cess."

Grabbing Neela's hand, Ariel bolted. Only one person had ever called her princess: Elbert.

"What?" Neela gasped. Ariel didn't waste breath with an answer. They sprinted until their tired legs slowed them. Ariel cried out with relief when the bridge's guard stones loomed ahead, merely indistinct shadows.

"You were right," Neela said. "But we never did pass the beacon."

"It might only shine in the direction it's needed. Never mind. Start begging the wind—" Ariel jerked to a halt at a noise from ahead.

"Shh," she breathed into Neela's ear. They crept toward the bridge, eyes scanning for faces or hands in the mist.

A voice came instead. "There they are!"

Ariel gasped. "Zeke?" She clapped a hand to her mouth, fearing a trick.

He charged from the fog near the guard stones, Scarl right behind him. The Finder's sharp strides quickly put him out front. Both were too robust to be shadows.

"Scarl!" Ariel's voice broke with relief and she hurried toward him. "I'm so glad you're all right!"

He didn't greet her. As they met, he slung a coil of rope off his shoulder, and the look on his face stopped her from throwing her arms around him.

"I told you once before I would leash you again," he said, his voice deadly even. She'd expected a growl, if not barking, but that flat weight told her better how angry he was.

Neela approached, cringing. "Blame me, Scarl, more'n her."

Ariel tried to distract him. "How'd you get here?" She didn't resist as he caught one of her wrists and looped the rope's end around it.

His cold silence scared her. She shot a look of appeal to Zeke.

"Don't expect me to discourage him."

She gazed at Scarl's hands, which were knotting the rope. "I wanted to convince you to stay in the world. I was so scared you were leaving."

His busy fingers paused. "Then you should know how I feel," he replied in a tight voice. "You're not as infallible as you think."

"I know." She forced a small laugh, relieved to get a reply and hoping to ease his anger with humor. "Like I should have hidden your rope! But I was trying to get back before anyone noticed."

It was the wrong thing to say. "Before anyone *noticed*? And what if..." He choked. He held very still, not even breathing and certainly not meeting her gaze.

"That was a joke," she whispered. "Mostly."

He released the breath he'd been holding, flung off his grip, and spun out of reach to vent his fury alone—where he couldn't strike out and do damage, she guessed. Feeling worse than if he had smacked her, she shifted uneasily, wanting to go to him and knowing it was unwise.

Zeke approached with a sour look and helped her untie her wrist. "It's a wonder he doesn't kill you himself," he said quietly. "But I know he doesn't mean this. Let's get back to the world. If we can."

"Good idea." Ariel started to ask how they'd come, but she changed her words when Neela leapt away from a troubling curl of mist. "We shouldn't stand here long, anyway. I thought I heard... something bad." She glanced at Scarl, who was still showing her his back. She took a step toward him. "Scarl? We need to go."

He exhaled at length before turning, though without meeting her eyes. "Yes."

"Begging your pardon," growled a voice behind them. "I think not."

CHAPTER 29

Ariel spun to search the fog. Something skittered and scratched, and her friends edged together.

Through the trailing mists came a dark figure with almost as much form as they had, though no flesh. A tangle of wire, it rose in the shape of a man with broad shoulders. The wire was rusty and barbed, and Ariel could guess it had originally come from the gate. Strands writhed and scraped as the thing scrabbled toward them. It did not walk, exactly. Clumps and lengths reached from the base to pull the rest along, moving as an octopus might. But the thing's head was worse. Where eyes might have been were two holes filled with mist, barbs stabbing out from their centers. Below, the wire knot parted in thin, prickly lips. It needed no teeth.

While they all stood aghast, the mouth spoke once more. "Hello, princess. Remember an old friend?" The head tilted slightly to Scarl. "An old friend, betrayed?"

Swooning, Ariel clutched both Zeke and Neela to keep herself erect.

"Who... who is it?" Neela whispered.

The wire man could never look like anyone or anything but a menace, but Ariel's heart knew, as it had with Mirayna, who owned the voice.

"Elbert Finder," Scarl breathed with more awe than fear in his voice. "Foul luck."

Neela squeaked.

"Oh, no luck, my friend," said the Elbert of wire. "Preparation. I have dreamed of another chance with you, dreamed and prepared. And the more I did, the more you dreamed of me. I could feel it. Your attention increased my strength. But the princess..." Elbert laughed. "She's more frightened of me—and the small ways my hatred could stretch past the bridge. So helpful of her to cling to my knife. And return it. That gift lit a fire in my heart." A loop of wire spooled out from his innards. Elbert's knife dangled from it. "I could use it to finish the job it once started. But I don't need a blade anymore, do I?" He flung it toward the bridge. It flew past them, glanced off one of the guard stones with a clank, and tumbled into the void underneath.

Ariel watched the knife vanish—quickly, without fuss. After so many long days of carrying its weight and pondering what it stood for, like that, it was gone. As it should've been from the moment she and Scarl had found it. A terrible truth sliced into her heart, along with the responsibility for all that might come. If she'd only found the will to walk away from that blade, to put it behind her, none of them would be here!

"You had to arrive sometime, separately or together," Elbert added brightly as if hearing her thoughts. "I didn't expect you'd still be living. That's a feat. But it will make what comes next even more fun than I'd hoped."

"Keep hoping," Ariel spat, mostly to hide her terror. "You're dead. You can't harm us."

"Ah, but you're wrong, princess." Wires scraped and grated. "I'm not like some of these fools, who don't even know which side of the bridge they're stuck on. But I've not wasted time trying to get back across. I've been finding instead. A few friends. A few secrets."

"A few scraps of wire?" Scarl's lips twitched.

His taunt impressed Ariel more than Elbert, who replied, "Laugh while you can, Finder. Because now I will put what I've found to use."

The wire must not have been as tangled as it looked. Loose ends plunged into the ground like eels into a seabed. Loops unfurled to follow behind. With a horrific scratching, Elbert shrank in place and then vanished.

An uneasy glance flashed between Ariel and Scarl. They ran for the bridge, Zeke and Neela behind. Nobody spoke. They were too busy listening for a scrape or a twang.

Their boots struck cobblestones. The guard stones loomed just ahead.

"Watch out for— ow!" Zeke's warning was lost. Four strands of wire—two from the left and two from the right—whipped toward them from under the bridge. The strands curled around their shins and yanked tight. Yelping, Neela fell. Ariel's ankles cracked together. Barbs bit into her flesh, and then she, too, hit the bridge with the others. Her heart in her throat, she kicked against the pain. Blood trickled into her socks, but Elbert's hold only tightened.

Elbert dragged them in pairs toward the sides of the bridge. They clutched vainly at the cobblestones and each other while Scarl sawed at the wire with his knife. It was too thick to be cut without a crimp and a hammer. Ariel clawed at the noose on her legs to unwind it and almost got free before it yanked tight again. Zeke shouted nonsense, no doubt a plea to the stones for their help. A deep, stony grinding seemed to reply, but the pull of the wire never stopped. Relentless, it drew them to the sides of the bridge.

As she went over the brink, Ariel clamped her arms on it. She couldn't hold the smooth surface of stone.

Her stomach clenched as she swooped through space. A choked scream escaped her. She and her friends fell into bottomless fog.

CHAPTER
30

Falling, Ariel hoped the flames below would close her eyes swiftly, without much more pain, so she'd never again have to hear Elbert's voice. Not with her ears, anyhow. Perhaps once she and her friends were only shadows themselves, he'd be less able to hurt them.

The wire jerked her to a halt. She writhed in midair, hung upside down from her agonized shins over a seething orange tumult of fire.

Pain and mist whirled together as Elbert reeled her in.

The first surface she hit was gritty and soft. The sand gave way to stone as she was dragged up a slope—the underside of the bridge abutment, thick with shadow and mist. Her companions all arrived as she had, struggling and bleeding. Elbert squatted at the top of the slope, which slanted to meet the end of the bridge overhead. Drawing his victims in, he piled them together and vaulted over, trapping them in the tight angle between the slope and the underbelly of the bridge.

The pain in Ariel's shins eased as the barbs pulled from her flesh and the wire slid away. She took a shuddering breath, righted herself, and peered through the gloom at her friends. They were gasping, and strain contorted their faces, but they were alive. She ran her hands over each, reassured by the contact. Neela nearly crawled into Ariel's lap. Zeke crowded in on the opposite side. Scarl turned to face Elbert, positioning himself near Ariel's feet. He reached a hand back and rested it on one of her boots. Though she could barely feel his touch through the rage of pain in her lower legs, the gesture brought a lump of gratitude to her throat.

Seeing his knife still in his other hand, she whispered, "Maybe you should cut our throats and get it over with faster."

Zeke groaned softly. "We're not in the world, Ariel. We may not be able to leave it from here. No matter how badly we're hurt."

Ariel blanched at that gruesome thought. Scarl ignored them both.

Elbert didn't. "She may be smarter than you," he told Scarl. "But she's not very sporting." A strand of wire flipped out to snatch the blade. Scarl resisted, but without success. Elbert flung the knife to their right, and it clattered out of sight across the cobbled slope.

Ariel scanned for a way to escape. The stone ramp where they sat met the underside of the bridge right behind them, near enough to bang their heads. Elbert hunkered before them, all of his strands knotting together again. Not far beyond, the ramp dropped into space. Mist boiled over the lip, lit in orange from beneath. Firelight flickered against the bridge's belly and reflected across her friends' faces.

Ariel shot a glance to each side of the abutment. Perhaps if they split up and ran both directions, at least some of them might escape.

A shadow moved in the mist to her right. Cobbles clunked like footsteps. Ariel thought she'd heard those stony feet before.

"Forgive my bare hospitality." Wire grated under Elbert's voice. "But we'll have privacy here. I don't want to share you."

The footsteps to their right drew closer. A wave of cold sweat broke from Ariel's skin when she saw the sailcloth Neela had lost to the cobblestone ghoul. It flapped and jerked in midair above the two stones like a child playing spooks with a blanket. Scarl's knife slashed the air before it, pointed at them. A long strand of barbed wire flailed around it as well, zinging like a whip. Zeke kept an exclamation trapped in his throat.

"Don't mind him," Elbert said. "It seems a few of the dead can't get comfortable without body parts—lucky for me, since spare wire and loose rocks are among the things I can trade here. I've made friends that way. I'm glad this one wanted to see what he could get for my knife, because otherwise, I might've missed your visit."

Ariel rubbed her bleeding ankles and cursed herself again for ever touching that knife.

Elbert noticed her movement. "What's wrong, princess? Don't you like my prickly new clothes?"

"They suit you," Ariel snapped. "Listen, Elbert. You can...." Her voice failed. She'd planned to say he could do anything he wanted to her, if he'd let her friends go. But a fresh look into that wire mask stole the words.

"I can take them off, if you'd rather." With a twang, the knot of wire collapsed to the ground. A jagged shadow oozed out, both darker and more torn than others she'd seen. Moving like liquid, it bled past Scarl to her. But Elbert did not leave the wire completely. It dragged after him, clinging and scratching, like the wet sand had weighted Neela's papa. Elbert's wire seemed to be a burden as well as a tool.

Ariel lost hold of that thought as the shadow wrapped around her. Neela clung tightly to Ariel's right side, but she couldn't stop it from slipping between them. Despite a clear struggle not to, Neela recoiled. Ariel didn't blame her. Elbert's touch froze her, his contempt dripping indecently over her skin. She understood better now how helpless Neela had been in the grip of her papa. Gritting her teeth, Ariel fought to stifle her goosebumps because she knew they'd please Elbert. She failed.

"Elbert." Although Scarl said it amiably, Ariel could tell by the tension in his body that the ease in his voice was false. He hadn't turned, but merely glanced over his shoulder, perhaps daring Elbert to attack his blind side. "I'm the one who knifed you. In the back. A coward's murder by any account. Aren't I the one you really want?"

"Oh, I'll get to you," Elbert hissed from somewhere near the back of Ariel's head. "But there's no need for haste. We've got eternity here."

He slid away. Ariel blinked back tears of relief as Elbert's wire once more rattled and rose around him.

"Uncle Elbert?" Neela gulped to stiffen her warbling voice. "You don't remember me, do you?"

The motion of Elbert's wire stopped.

"Surprise, Elbert," Zeke said. "That's Dain. Or, uh, Neela. Your own kin."

"You weren't bad to me when I was little," Neela said. "You oughtn't be so mean now. And you don't have to be stuck in the fog forever. You could follow the shadows. There's a fountain of light. You'd like it. It's nice."

For a long moment, Elbert stared at Neela. Then his laughter echoed. "Thanks for the advice, pet, but you'll be going without me. Should we start with you first? I bet that'd please the princess." A prong of wire ruffled Neela's hair. She winced at the gouging barbs. "Any friend of hers is no kin of mine."

The wire looped around the back of Neela's neck. She grabbed at it but couldn't resist as it pulled her from the others.

Scarl caught the wire, between barbs, where it passed him. "Before you start on them... As I recall, Elbert, you enjoy a good wager. I'd like to propose one."

Elbert chuckled. "What can you offer me, Scarl? I'd like to know. Any fool can see you're at my mercy."

Scarl coolly met Elbert's gaze—if empty sockets could be said to have one.

"You're bluffing," Elbert added. "You've got nothing. Admit it."

"I see overconfidence is still your greatest weakness."

Elbert stood silent and motionless except for the tips of a few wire strands, which twitched like the tails of irritated cats. Ariel held her breath, feeling a grim satisfaction, yet terrified of any wager Scarl might suggest.

Something tickled her right palm—probably a dribble of

blood from trying to free her legs from the wire. When it persisted, she turned her palm up and glanced.

The symbols she'd picked up from the stone on the bridge all clustered there. They overlapped, shifted, jockeyed for position. Then they stilled, her pulse throbbing beneath them.

Thoughtfully, she turned her palm back out of sight just as Scarl asked Elbert, "Do you want to hear it or not?"

"All right," Elbert growled. "Amuse me with your pitiful hope, then."

"If I win, you let all three of them go, unharmed."

A protest rose into Ariel's throat. As she opened her mouth, a hand clamped on her leg to silence her—Zeke's. He kept his eyes on Elbert, but she decided to trust his advice.

"You'd best lay down the wager before babbling about stakes," Elbert told Scarl.

Scarl turned to look at Ariel, his eyes cool and distant. She knew she was supposed to take some message from them, but she wasn't sure what. He said, "I have a timepiece. If it works here." He drew it out of his pocket to check it. "Hmm. Still backward, but... yes." He raised it toward Elbert. "See how the longest arm swings around the circle? I'll bet I can withstand your... embrace, without a whimper, for a full round of that arm."

"No!" Ariel hissed. "You'll be cut to shreds!"

Elbert snorted and told Scarl, "You couldn't withstand my handshake, let alone my embrace. I'll strip your flesh to the bone in a heartbeat."

"Try me."

Ariel wanted to kick Scarl to shut him up. All she could think was that he hoped to occupy Elbert long enough for the rest of them to escape. But she wasn't leaving without him, and certainly not as Elbert whittled him to bloody rags.

"Nope," Elbert said, to Ariel's relief. "That's not a bet I will take, friend. Not because I think you can possibly win. But you might die too fast and miss the rest of the fun. If that happened, I'd feel like you'd won either way." His empty gaze shifted to Ariel. "But I will make the same bet with her. For a nice, leisurely handshake, that is. No embrace."

"No." Scarl pocketed his timepiece.

"Come now!" Elbert exclaimed. "A wager was all your idea! And a good one, perhaps. Let's keep it."

Scarl shook his head.

Ariel's lips pinched together, but an idea formed through her horror, so she loosened them again. "I'll take your bet," she told Elbert. "If you'll let Zeke and Neela go now, before we begin. No matter who wins."

Scarl whirled to grab her ankle. "Over my corpse, you might. Not a moment before."

"Hmm," Elbert said, sounding pleased by Scarl's reaction. "A hard bargain." He scraped a few wires together in what must have been consideration. They screeched like the wings of an unhappy cricket.

Ariel leaned forward to breathe words at Scarl that Elbert might not hear. "It'll happen anyway! At least let me win freedom for them!"

He groaned.

"And in return, princess?" said Elbert. "Because I don't believe you can shake this hand in silence." He raised a tangle of barbs. She tried not to see it. "I don't believe anyone could, least of all a smart-mouthed, stripling girl. So what do I get that I can't simply take?"

"Well..." Ariel fumbled for an answer until Scarl's face gave it to her. She had to look away from him to say it. "Scarl abides it, instead of trying to fight."

"Ah," Elbert said. "Abides and watches. No turning away. Not even to track that timepiece. My friend with the heavy feet can do that."

Flapping, the ghoul to the right clomped closer.

His eyes already closed, Scarl murmured, "You're killing me, Ariel. Stop."

"Yeah, don't," Zeke added. "Not for us. It's all right."

She had to let them know, somehow, that she had an idea. Ariel made a show of turning clumsily to her hands and knees before rising, giving her the chance to think and to dart meaningful looks at both Zeke and Scarl. "I've been here long enough," she muttered. "Long enough." Would they guess what she meant?

"You can't stop me," she added, louder and mostly for Elbert. She rose to glare at him. "So do we have a bet?"

"Done," Elbert said. "Your apprentice friends mean little to me anyway." Wires reached to prick Zeke and Neela. They flinched. "Go on. Get."

At first Zeke refused, but Neela whispered in his ear and towed him away, giving Elbert wide berth. Seeing them go wrenched Ariel's heart, but once they'd passed out of sight, it felt lighter.

"We can tell which of us has more honor, eh, Scarl?" Elbert said.

"If what you have is honor, I'm not ashamed to have none."

"You *will* honor this wager, however," Elbert replied. "Or she'll pay the price."

Afraid he'd push Scarl to action before she was ready, Ariel said, "One last request, Elbert."

"The bet's already laid, princess. Too late."

She pretended she hadn't heard him and pointed. "If your... sailing friend is going to watch the timepiece, let me hold Scarl's knife in my other hand while you do this. It's like... a touchstone between us, that's all."

Elbert snorted, a grating sound. "It's also a fast way for you to escape by plunging it into your own heart. Forget it. In fact, let's remove the temptation." A wire spooled out toward the cobblestone ghoul. The sail drew back in a crumple, but it gave up Scarl's knife when Elbert's wire fist touched it. The wire flicked toward the end of the slope, and a second blade flew into the chasm below.

Scarl did not suppress a small groan.

Ariel thought fast. "His walking stick, then."

"What stick would that be?"

Ariel turned. Elbert was right. Scarl did not have his staff.

"Left in the tunnels," he said, his voice dead.

Ariel deflated. "Oh."

Elbert laughed. "You should learn to get along without these physical forms! You'll lose your own soon enough... though not too soon, I hope. Ready to hold hands with me, princess?"

CHAPTER 31

Ariel forced her feet toward Elbert. With only her hands and nothing to use as a pry bar, her plan wouldn't work so neatly. Still, she had to take her best chance.

"Left hand or right?" Elbert asked her. "Or shall I choose for you?"

"Left." Her throat was so dry, the word croaked and she had to repeat it. She kept her right fist loose at her side and tried not to imagine how it might shortly feel. The symbols tickled there now. She hoped Neela's observation before had been right and they'd respond to protect her somewhat when she needed. The sand around Neela's papa had shrunk from them. Elbert's wire might, too. If not, they'd be the last message this Farwalker would deliver. And the most meaningless.

Elbert's wires slid and shuffled, a knot growing broader and reaching toward her. He jerked his head toward the ghoul. "Make yourself useful and come take this timepiece. And quit flapping. You'll block his good view."

As the sail went limp and the cobbles thumped forward, Ariel sensed a small movement behind her. Briefly hidden by her body, Scarl was gathering himself, most likely to stop her. To delay him, she blurted to Elbert, "You probably don't know I'm a Farwalker now. I carry messages, and I have one for you."

Elbert growled. "I think the last message you gave me was spittle. I should have wrung your neck then."

"This one's not from me. I'm just carrying it. See?" She flashed her right palm, hoping the symbols might distract him. Then she flattened that hand into a blade and plunged it into his chest. Just as the crow had dived into one dead man, maybe she could reach into another and pluck out a dull light that would shift Elbert's focus and make him easier to fight.

Barbed wire proved more solid and biting than sand. The first pain felt like slamming her hand into ice. The second was worse, a fire that ripped. Ariel's torn fingers couldn't feel anything in Elbert except agony. She didn't know if they'd recognize his spark if they found it, but now she couldn't close her hand upon it even if they did.

Chaos erupted around her. Elbert roared, first in startled laughter and then in outrage. Scarl leapt up. He'd slipped out of his coat and now thrust it, and himself, between Ariel and Elbert. The oilcloth snagged and hindered the wire, and Scarl's body shielded Ariel—except her right arm. That was already trapped.

To her astonishment, Elbert released her. Continued pain blurred her view, but the wire of Elbert's chest sprang away from her fingers like a fanged mouth gaping in shock. Abruptly her right hand was free.

She yanked it to her chest. She expected to find a spark in her palm, delivered by some miracle of fumbling and luck. She saw only blood. But a light flared past Scarl, illuminating them both. There were five sparks in Elbert, and they weren't merely dull points. She'd delivered her message better than she'd hoped, and the symbols had slipped from her palm to the wire. Fiery, they raced along strands, taking shape for a blink before streaming to reform somewhere else. The wires kinked and shook at their passage.

Elbert's shadow sprang from the wire, which collapsed with a twang, Scarl's coat tangled with it. Unable to escape the wire completely, Elbert's shade stomped down the pile of barbs. Reaching up, shadow hands clenched around Scarl's throat.

Although without substance, those hands wielded the full strength of hatred. Scarl dropped hard at Ariel's feet.

Knocked back by his fall, she cried his name and stumbled toward him. Sailcloth battered at her to stop her. The ghoul had rushed in. A cobblestone hit her thigh, numbing her leg so it wouldn't bear weight. Hopping, Ariel fought, trapping both cobblestones under the cloth and sweeping the blood-streaked sail into a mound.

As it shifted and tugged to get free, the sailcloth snagged on the pile of wire. The more the ghoul churned it, the more barbs the sail caught. The five symbols, still racing along strands of the wire, glowed through the cloth. They blazed more brightly, and the whole knot went limp.

Whirling, Ariel clawed with her uninjured hand at the dark grip around Scarl's neck. Her fingers and his pulled in vain at what felt like a collar of ice.

Another voice joined the tumult: "Another bet for you, Uncle!"

Neela and Zeke ran up through the fog, Scarl's rope stretched between them. They faltered when they saw the fight, taking it in.

Neela darted closer. "I'll bet flames can melt you!" With an aim as precise as she'd shown on the seashore, she tossed a noose over the cloth-tangled wire. Zeke yanked the lasso tight, and they both pulled the rope—with the wire and sail—down the steep slope toward the drop-off. Elbert's shadow, bound to the wire, dragged behind.

Unfortunately, so did Scarl. Ariel threw her weight on him. She slowed him, but not enough. Elbert's anchor of wire and sail was heavy, and as Zeke and Neela drew close to the dangerous edge, they stopped pulling and began shoving the useless snarl over. Elbert couldn't break free, but he was taking Scarl with him.

Ariel cried, "Zeke, stop!"

Over the grinding of the wire on stone, Zeke and Neela either didn't hear or didn't heed. But Scarl did, and he must have realized he was nearing the brink. Although the strain on his swollen face said it took his last effort, he stopped fighting Elbert to shove Ariel off him.

"No!" She scrambled back to him, clinging, as the wire mound plunged over the edge. Elbert's shadow slipped after it, feet first, until his whole dark length dangled from his grip on Scarl's neck.

Zeke dropped on Scarl, too. For an instant, they hung balanced, Scarl purple and choking between. Ariel clutched at his shirt, more ready to fall with him than to let Elbert take him alone.

A gleam flashed near her straining right wrist. The marks on Ariel's palm had not crawled off after all, but spawned onto the wire as they had from the guard stone. The original set pulsed on the back of her hand now, glowing pink amid her bloody wounds.

With a cry, she thrust her wounded hand forward and plastered it against Scarl's shadowy noose. The marks zipped between her fingers and down to his neck.

Recoiling as he had from the marks on the wire, Elbert flung his hands wide, letting go. The weighted wire took him.

His fall was silent, but flames leapt high to meet him.

CHAPTER 32

Zeke dragged Ariel and Scarl from the edge as sand beneath them tumbled into the void.

The Finder rolled to one side and lay fighting for breath. His chest convulsed with the effort, but he only managed a raspy wheezing. Under the smeared blood from Ariel's hand, his throat was visibly crushed and bruises already darkened his skin. She crouched at his shoulder, fumbling to get him more air.

Neela rushed to her side. Zeke was already there.

"He can't breathe!" Ariel's heart fluttered. "Neela! Can you put the wind in him?"

"Like you did me," urged Zeke.

"I don't have my pipe!" Neela whistled and huffed, but the meager sounds that resulted brought no wind in response. "It's not working."

"None of our skills are the same here," Zeke murmured. "The stones haven't listened to me much, either."

Ariel said, "Please keep trying!"

Neela cupped her hands and blew breath to Scarl's lips. Nothing she did made a difference. Scarl's gasps weakened.

Ariel raised his limp hand, pleading. "Don't." She choked on tears.

He gave no sign that he was aware of her.

Ariel thought of Mirayna. Would he die and go join her? Or suffer a worse fate? Here outside the world, he might become trapped in a lifeless body that would anchor his spirit like wire or sand. Mirayna's words of warning echoed in Ariel's head.

They stirred not just regret, but also desperate hope. If hatred and anger could cause so much damage here, maybe other emotions could fix it. Mirayna's gratitude had brought them together at the lighthouse, and Neela's papa had delivered a beating with his anger, but neither example told Ariel what to do now. Yet it seemed to her that when it came to love, the most delicate touches contained the most power—fingertips on her face, a butterfly alighting, a breath tickling her ear as it brought her a secret. The caress of a thumb on the back of a hand, or Scarl's palm skimming her hair when he thought she was sleeping.

Ariel's fingers hovered over his chest where his shirt hid the scar that was oddly shaped like a hand. That, too, had come from a touch of unexplained strength, a reminder from a ghost who would not be ignored. The memory brought Ariel inspiration. The ghost's handprint had returned Scarl to her once before. Maybe it could again.

Drawing on past glimpses, she spread her bloody fingers to roughly cover the welt. Scarl's heart skittered beneath her torn hand, almost too weakly for her to feel it. He was warm in the clammy mist, though. She focused on that.

Ariel summoned everything she felt for Scarl. Memories of their best and worst moments together flitted through her mind, each adding to the fire of feelings in her heart. Love tangled with respect and not a little frustration. They all swirled in her chest so she thought she might burst.

Bending close, she set a feather-light kiss on his neck. As she touched him, she exhaled, imagining everything in her heart running out into him—including, if need be, the force of her own life, her own spark of Essence inside. She willed it to flow from her lips to her hand, flooding Scarl with her life so his heart would keep beating, and with love potent enough to heal his damaged throat.

He twitched and then dragged in a hideous gasp. Ariel recoiled, sure she'd made matters worse, but she kept her hand on him. His chest jerked and stilled. She held her own breath, thinking she'd watched his last one. Her kiss had been only a silent good-bye.

Zeke clutched her shoulder. A rush of love and sympathy like a warm, fragrant breeze slid from him into her. She let it flow through her and exhaled that, too, to Scarl.

At the very end of her breath, the Finder inhaled again. Ariel froze, hardly daring to hope. Scarl drew air in as deeply as she had exhaled, as though they shared the same breath and she'd passed it to him. The air hissed through his throat, but it no longer stuck. Ariel rejoiced when he coughed, which no one could do without air to expel. Slowly the rise of his chest grew less labored. His eyes fluttered open to fix on her.

"It's all right, better now, you'll be fine," Ariel babbled. "Right?"

His eyes closed again, but his hand fumbled, found hers on his chest, and pressed it.

Focused on Scarl, Ariel paid little attention to Zeke until he drew her hand from the Finder's chest and began dabbing blood from it with his sleeve.

"How bad is this?" he asked. "The bleeding's stopped, at least."

Pain rushed back into her awareness. Her right hand was afire. "I'm surprised I have fingers left." Her voice wobbled. "Good thing I need my hands less than my feet..." A warm wave swept through her, threatening to pull her into a faint. Slumping against Zeke, she let him tend her.

Not finding the source of the blood, he wiped more firmly. Instead of gouged flesh, he uncovered a mass of fresh scars. On her palm, the scars and symbols were woven together, the difference between them not easy to tell.

"That's it? No cuts?" he asked.

A pained laugh escaped her. Her own gratitude must've been as strong as Mirayna's, or perhaps the love flowing through her had worked from within. "I'm so happy Scarl's alive, they probably healed," she told Zeke. "But then why does it still hurt so bad?"

"I don't know. Can you move it?"

She'd moved it before, as Scarl's bloody shirt showed, but now Ariel was afraid to increase the burning. She twitched one finger, unwilling to try anything as bold as making a fist.

"I don't mean to be rushing, since I'm not the one hurt," Neela said. "But as soon as we can, we should go. Before more nasty spooks come along."

"Good idea," Zeke agreed. "Let's get out from under this bridge. It's not hard, but Scarl will probably need help."

Ariel leaned over the Finder. "Scarl? Can you sit up, do you think?"

He raised one hand in a weak gesture to wait. His other hand rose to his throat, so Ariel guessed pain was still dogging him, too. Shortly he struggled to push himself upright.

Together they got Scarl to his feet, with Zeke supporting most of his weight. When Ariel tried to help, Zeke waved her off.

"It'll be easier if we're not tripping on each other," he said. "I can carry him on my back, if I have to. It wouldn't be the first time today."

Ariel could hardly imagine Scarl agreeing to that. "When was the first?"

"When we stepped onto The Plank to fall out of the world."

"You know The Plank?" Neela asked.

"How else did you think we got here?" said Zeke.

Neela narrowed her eyes. "Don't tell me the wind helped?"

"It didn't." Zeke ducked out from under the abutment with Scarl. Ariel and Neela followed, angling up the mushy embankment toward the cobbled bridge deck.

"I was hoping you'd quit following when you got to the ladder," Ariel told him. "I thought you'd fall if you tried it."

Zeke grimaced. "We might have, without Scarl's rope." He explained in short bursts how they'd reached The Plank.

"The stone told me how you'd gone, as well as what people called it, and I explained why we needed to follow," he said, huffing. "You probably didn't notice how eroded it was, but it was getting ready to fall, and since it had learned the way from the wind, it'd been thinking of leaving the world anyhow. I begged it to help us. It wouldn't have, I don't think, except it liked cheating gravity by falling out of the world."

Having climbed to the top of the slope, Zeke paused to catch his breath. "The hard part was for it to take us with it alive," he added. "If we'd already been standing on it when it broke, it would have dropped from beneath us and left us behind. But if we stepped on it too late, we'd miss it. Either way, we'd have fallen. We had to hop at exactly the right instant, staying close without touching—like jellyfish sucked into the wake of a boat. And since I was the only one who could hear the stone's signal, the feet jumping had to be mine."

Scarl tried to speak. Little more than a hoarse whisper came out. "Or I would've left him. Rather than risk Zeke's death, too."

Ariel winced. "I'm sorry." The words made her feel worse. They were words for spilling somebody's tea, not for endangering their lives. Her friends didn't have to follow her anywhere, truly, and she wasn't sorry she'd helped Neela, but they'd almost lost Scarl, and more dreadful things might yet come. Ariel hugged herself, thinking of both Zeke and Nace. It was hard to do the right thing for everybody. She could only do what seemed to be the right thing for her and hope those she loved understood.

"I wouldn't have let Scarl leave me behind," Zeke said. "We made it, anyway. I rode The Plank, and he rode on me. After I convinced him I could bear him. I took a big leap...

into nothing, a blur. But when my feet landed, the stone lay on the bridge, and we stood on top of it. Come see."

They hurried onto the first cobblestones of the bridge.

"We heard the boom when The Plank hit," Neela said. "Did it hurt to fall without the wind?"

Zeke shook his head. "It was jarring, but not like a fall. More like bumbling off a porch that wasn't as high as you—hey!"

They were near enough to the guard stones to make out their symbols. But now The Plank stood between them on its broken base, reaching twice as high as the stones. Narrow gaps were all that separated them.

"It stood up!" Zeke said. "It was lying flat when we came."

A shadow slipped through the slender space between stones, billowing out to human shape before sidling past. But unless the drifting mist was fooling Ariel's eyes, none of the gaps between the three stones was wide enough for anyone with flesh to pass through.

CHAPTER 33

No amount of shoving could topple The Plank to give them room to climb over. The stone sat so heavily on its base it was a wonder it hadn't knocked the bridge down. After pointing sideways for lifetimes, it would now spend eternity stretching straight up.

"I didn't notice before how close to these others it landed," Zeke said. "It looks like it's blocking the way on purpose."

"Can you ask it to fall back again?" Ariel asked. "It helped once."

He sang under his breath before shaking his head. "It's ignoring me. All three stones are chanting. They started when those marks got on it."

As Ariel had leaned her shoulder into the stone, the symbols on her sore hand had begun moving once more. They'd squirmed up her arm to spawn onto The Plank. She'd delivered the message again, whether she meant to or not. The symbols had spread evenly across the rock.

Scarl, who was standing on his own now, stepped forward to peer at the marks.

"Do you know them?" Ariel asked. She'd been avoiding the matching set on the cobbles, which writhed under her feet every time her boots touched them.

"Not in any way that makes sense." His voice, though still hoarse, had grown stronger. "They're disturbing."

"They've helped, though." While she explained, Zeke edged nearer, cocking his head.

"The stones are repeating the same ideas, over and over: 'Face ever forward. Forward ever fall. Fallward, forward, faceward, ever.' I don't know if it's a song, strange advice, or a warning."

Ariel groaned. "It sounds like a riddle."

"Mayhap they're encouraging us to go forward." Neela dropped to her belly near the base of the stones, where the gap between was the largest. She wiggled her head and shoulders into that space.

"I might can get through here," she called, her voice muffled. "But I don't know about anyone else." Her legs and feet slid away, too.

"Wait! Don't get separated from us." Zeke knelt to reach through, steadying himself with one hand on The Plank.

He jerked it away. "Ugh, I didn't just hear 'fall' that time. I felt it. Like a threat to knock us off the bridge. If I didn't know better, I'd say this wasn't the same stone that brought us."

"Perhaps the symbols have altered it," Scarl said. "The pattern that keeps catching my eye means madness."

"We might try climbing the short stones to get over." Zeke shuddered. "But I don't think they'll let us."

"Can we sneak around them?" Ariel crept toward the misty edge of the bridge, unsure where safe footing ended. "If there's room, we— oh!" She jumped back. Her toe had stubbed something moving.

"Ho, it's me." A hand flapped on the cobbles. Neela's arm stretched from the far side of the guard stone. Ariel dropped to her knees and eased forward. There was room at the stone's base for Neela's arm, but no more. Beyond lay a dizzying drop into fog, which was lit in ghostly streamers by flickering flames.

Ariel backed away quickly. "Not that way."

When she rose, the mist around them seemed thicker and more purposeful. Zeke kept brushing the same persistent wisp from his face. Neela shimmied back through her hole with mist coiled up one leg. It slithered off when her knee bumped the guard stone.

Scarl reached toward a familiar pocket that was no longer there. "My glass. In my coat...?"

"Gone," Ariel said. "Sorry."

With a sigh, he dropped to one knee and concentrated on his fist. Ariel tried not to watch, aware it might hinder his finding, but she saw him frown and look over the edge of the bridge. Fear gnawed inside her.

Rising, Scarl kneaded his forehead. "Do your feet tell you anything, Ariel? Can we walk back to the world in any direction at all?"

She took a calming breath, closed her eyes, and summoned memories of the cove. She imagined them draining, like water, from her head to her feet, but the usual itch to move didn't come. Instead she felt the weak current that flowed off the bridge toward the maelstrom. She recognized that, and she didn't want to follow.

Bracing against it, she whispered, "Home."

Cramps twisted her feet as though they were trying to turn inside out. Thrown off balance, she wavered. Her eyelids flew open.

"I don't understand what that means," she said to herself as Zeke raised a steadying hand.

"Stop thinking," Scarl said. "You know better. Respond."

"Nothing works the same here as it does in the world," she protested.

"Your instincts are still our best chance to get back."

So as best she knew how, Ariel obeyed the warp in her feet. She took her weight off her heels, tiptoed back a few steps, and pivoted on the balls of her feet. That left her facing the end of the bridge and the shadowy realm that belonged to the dead. The pain in her arches eased, but her feet didn't tickle to move forward, either. She hoped that didn't mean home no longer existed.

A few notes of her farwalking song trilled in her head, and their rhythm throbbed in her palm. She glanced at the marks among the scars there—a message that gripped her instead of her holding it. The words Zeke had relayed from the stones echoed through her, and the message she'd delivered more than once finally sank in to her, too.

She sucked in a breath. She knew what to do. *Face ever forward.* It was no riddle.

Her feet were already poised, but her friends' expectant looks made her queasy.

"This is going to sound odd," she told them. "Can you trust me? Despite the mess I've gotten us into?"

Zeke's scowl made it clear he found the question insulting.

"Would we be here if we didn't?" Scarl asked.

"Good," she said. "Then listen. Get closer to me. Turn around and face away from the stones like I am. And I think we'd better hold hands."

With Neela and Zeke each at one side of Ariel and Scarl on the end next to Zeke, they crowded shoulder to shoulder. Ariel tried not to flinch when Zeke took her right hand, which still hurt. She strained for a glimpse of the beacon that she knew glowed ahead. Her eyes couldn't find it, so she imagined the lighthouse instead.

"Close your eyes," she instructed. "Think of the sun hidden out in that mist. So bright you can't bear it, and that's why your eyelids are shut. But you can feel it light up your face." As they imagined that brilliance, she let her feet do what they wanted. Her heels lifted to draw her boots backward in a small reverse step. Her motion tugged gently on the hands that she held.

Her voice softer, she added, "Now hold tight and back up with me. Slowly. We'll come back here some day. We're always facing that light, and our feet should always be pointed here, too." The ghouls in the fog had demonstrated that nothing good came of facing away. She added, "We've just gotten ahead of ourselves. We need to slip back to where we're supposed to be."

Tense, Neela and Zeke shuffled alongside her. Ariel squeezed their hands, despite the pain, and kept talking to keep their minds from the looming stones just behind them.

"Face ever forward." She took a baby step backward, and then another. A symbol squirmed under one sole. "We're ahead of ours—"

Ariel's next step slipped backward as though on slick rock. Her boot plunged into space. She fell, dragging her friends along with her.

Neela squealed, and Zeke hollered, too. Then a heart-stopping emptiness swallowed all.

A wail of regret rose in Ariel's throat. She'd been wrong! Her feet had failed, and she'd pulled her friends off the bridge into flames. Her hands clenched tighter, but she couldn't feel anything in them.

Water, not fire, engulfed her. Her body slammed against it and rocked in the wake. Seawater quelled Ariel's scream, and she choked. Her head whirled. Then her plunge slowed, and her sense of direction returned. She kicked upward. Her head broke the water, which was icy but flat. She spit brine from her mouth.

Neela splashed alongside her, still clutching Ariel's left hand. The weak right one was empty.

"Zeke!" The word gurgled through the water clogging her throat. Ariel kicked herself higher. Twilight lay on the sea, but the evening sky was clear, and even dim light was welcome after so much endless fog. Splashing echoed around them as a silhouette flailed toward her.

"I'm here," Zeke gasped, stroking so hard he bumped her. "The splash broke my grip."

"Scarl?" A pain gripped her heart. Scarl had never lived near the sea. She didn't know if he could swim, and his recent strangling couldn't help. Frantically she scanned the surface.

"I held onto him!" Zeke twisted to search. "Until we hit the water..."

Ariel gulped air for a dive as Cassalie had taught her, though the light was so thin she knew she'd find nothing beneath the surface unless she bumbled into the Finder by chance.

As she kicked her upper half higher out of the water before folding into her downward plunge, her ears caught the wheeze of a still-damaged throat. Hearing it too late to stop her momentum, she somersaulted underwater, popped back up, and spun. There! Scarl was bobbing behind them, gasping and spitting. His awkward dog-paddle strokes didn't always keep his face clear of the sea.

She swam toward him, veered wide, and grabbed his collar from behind. "I've got you. Zeke and I used to play lifesaver games. Try to go limp and lean back."

She turned her attention to land. Shadowed slopes rose on all sides, but she was pleased when her feet chose a direction to kick. "This way."

A few freezing moments later, they all hauled themselves onto rocks. At first they only shivered and struggled for breath. Then Zeke smacked a kiss on Ariel's uninjured hand.

"You did it!" he crowed. "I can hardly believe it."

"I didn't know we were going to fall." Her voice shook. "I thought I'd killed us all."

"Oh, I'm still planning to beat you to death," Scarl told her. "As soon as I'm warm and dry."

"Any idea where we are?" Ariel asked Neela. It was not Dead Man's Cove.

Although the light was melting fast and no moon had yet risen, Neela inspected the land's shape around them. "I think I know, Farwalker girl. You want to lead us home, or should I?"

CHAPTER

34

Ariel and her friends had splashed into a potboiler hole in the cliff. Neela led them to a wall where they had to dive down and swim through a flooded arch to surface in the cove. Fortunately, the sea was quiet and the tide not too high. Using skills she'd learned from Cassalie, Ariel made the trip twice, first with Neela to learn the way and then back to help Scarl, who swam underwater even more awkwardly than he did on the surface. Neela returned, too, to accompany Zeke.

They emerged onto the shore and clambered over rocks toward the houses. Ariel was surprised to spot the horse near a cottage. Neck outstretched, he nibbled blades of grass that had sprouted from the edge of a roof. In the still evening, with no hint of the storm that had raged when they left, she could hear his teeth grind.

"Look! Willow's all right!"

"Huh. I didn't think he'd live," said Zeke, who again propped up Scarl. "His wounds must be healing, and fast. Cassalie's poultice is magic."

"No, it isn't," said Neela. "She's used it on me. Mayhap that's a ghost." She shivered.

As they drew nearer, the horse nickered to them.

"He doesn't sound like a ghost," Ariel said. "Cassalie must have turned him out. Did you find my note at suppertime, Zeke?"

"We never made it to supper," he said. "Scarl woke up just before, when the storm calmed."

"I could feel your absence from the world like the socket of a missing tooth," the Finder told Ariel. "That might have been what called me back from... the darkness."

"And with both of you missing, Cassalie guessed where you went," Zeke said. "She said Neela—Dain—had once talked about the bridge, and the stones of the tunnel confirmed which way you'd gone. The hard part was waiting until Scarl's dizziness passed."

"It still hasn't," Scarl muttered, rubbing his head.

"The storm was supposed to stop you," said Neela. "I can't believe it quit blowing so soon after we left."

Ariel wondered if the wind knew they'd need Scarl's help or if the crow had warned it about dangerous spirits. Many things in the world seemed more aware than people.

Zeke offered a simpler explanation. "Maybe your trade skills aren't as strong as you think."

Though meant for Neela, his words struck Ariel, too. Contrite, she murmured, "Can you ever forgive me for sneaking away?"

"Not likely," Zeke said.

Scarl didn't reply.

Ariel accepted his silence, which was still tinted with

anger. But if her departure from the world *had* turned him
back from the gate, right now it seemed worth it.

They picked carefully through the deepening dark to
Cassalie's house. The lingering twilight surprised Ariel;
she'd expected the hour to be closer to midnight. It felt as
though they'd been gone long enough, but perhaps that was
due to her fatigue and an assortment of aches. The thought
of a bed sped her feet.

The glow in Cassalie's window was weaker than it had
been on previous nights. Neela reached for the door latch.
She found the door bolted. Her knock was followed by a
puzzling silence.

At last the door slowly opened. Cassalie stood behind it,
her cheekbones more gaunt than Ariel remembered. One
hand was clutching something small to her heart.

"Cassalie." Scarl sighed her name.

Her face worked. "Begone!" With a jerk of her arm, she
threw the thing she held at him. It bounced off his chest,
struck the flagstone, and shattered. Ariel recognized shards
of the fossil he'd found.

He stumbled back, one hand to his chest, while the
others looked on in shock.

"Cass! What'd you do that for?" asked Neela.

"Oh!" Cassalie's gaze darted across their faces, a storm
of emotions crossing her own. "Oh, stars and starfish...
you're real? Not haunts?" She stepped unsteadily forward.
"Scarl? Forgive me, I'm sorry, I... No, no, I'm not! I should
hit you again! You don't know how I've cursed your name!"
Bursting into tears, she whirled and groped blindly. "Dain?
Dain! Where are you—?"

Looking daunted, Neela moved in to hug her.

Scarl stepped closer, too, but Cass slapped at him feebly. "You! Stay away! Not a haunt, but a monster! To come here to me only so I could lose you, and me stranded here, more alone than before! I knew you would leave, but not that way! Not that! And not taking Dain with you!" She clamped Neela tight and buried her face in the girl's hair.

"It's all right, Cass," murmured Neela. "We're back."

Taking a ragged breath, Cass said faintly, "You can't be. How can I believe it? Not after a fortnight. You've been gone so long."

"Two weeks!" exclaimed Zeke. Ariel gasped, too.

"I despaired after the first," said Cassalie. "You weren't coming back. And then Nace came, poor Nace, like the grim-golly's shadow—"

"Nace!" Ariel cried. "Nace is here? How?"

"—and his silent sorrow is even harder to bear. He knew you were gone, your tree-singing friends told him, but he refuses to rest until he's found your bones. I can't stop him. I've tried. And now..." Her brow furrowed. "And now..." She released Neela to sink to the ground, her trembling hands reaching for the shards of the fossil. "And now look. I've broken my memory stone, too."

Scarl dropped to his knees and gathered her into his arms. "I'll find you another."

"No, you won't. You're not here." She clung listlessly to him. "I've gone mad at last, that's all."

"I guess time works differently across the bridge," marveled Zeke. "Oh! I grabbed this from the ground, and then I forgot." He fished in his pocket and pulled out Scarl's timepiece. Seawater dripped from it. He rubbed it on his shirt, which wasn't much drier, and studied its face. "Aw, maybe it's ruined. It doesn't count back any more. It won't go at all."

But the Finder ignored him, and Ariel didn't care, either. She didn't need a timepiece to tell her what to do now. She edged past Scarl and Cassalie into the house, where she searched every room. Nace was not there. She jiggled until Cassalie had been soothed enough to tell her that Nace was in the tunnels that moment.

She explained that he'd arrived four days ago, stumbling with exhaustion. He'd followed their tracks and his bond with Willow, but he'd come only to return Ariel's bones to the abbey. Despite hours of creeping through the tunnels, following the instructions the Reaper could give him, he'd naturally found little sign of their passage.

The thought of him wandering that treacherous maze made Ariel shudder.

She didn't even put on dry clothes. She went straight to the tunnel entrance in Neela's corner, intending to climb down and find him. The others chased after and tried to dissuade her. Cassalie assured her that Nace had come back every night, if later and later. She thought he'd appear soon. But Ariel's heart would not leave her throat. She feared that today, now that they'd returned safely, Nace would run afoul of some hazard. Fate could be cruel. Perhaps she'd even earned it for not considering the pain he would feel if she'd been unable to get back to the world. Too blithely certain she'd see him again, she'd left no message for him, as she had for Zeke, nor answered the one he'd sent her. She ached with the grief he must have felt.

"Wait just a piece," Neela told Ariel. "If he isn't here soon, I'll go down with you to find him. The tunnels are tricky, and mayhap he only got turned around. I don't want you getting turned around, too. Or caught by the tide."

The reminder of their close escape days ago doubled Ariel's worry. "Would you really come with me?" she asked. Neela had to be as sore and exhausted as she was.

Neela reached for a lamp. "If you've got to ask that, we'd best go right now."

Scarl beat Neela to the lamp. "No, you won't."

A muddy hand reached from the hole in the floor and rested a guttering lamp near Neela's foot. A haggard face followed.

"Nace!" Ariel cried.

He froze except for a small, confused frown. His eyes flicked from her to the others, ending on Cassalie's sympathetic nod.

"We're alive." Ariel gripped his arm to prove it. "I'm so sorry you thought anything else."

With a small, voiceless sob, he scrambled the rest of the way out of the tunnel and crashed into her, clumsy with haste. He smelled dank and his skin held a chill. Heedless, Ariel threw her arms around him in an embrace so tight it was probably painful.

"It's all right now," she said.

His cold hands roamed her shoulders, arms, and back as if testing how solid she was. She caught them. How good it felt to grip his fingers and have them respond! She needed those hands more than she needed her own. She clutched them to her heart to warm them, wanting to never let go.

He scanned her face desperately and tried to extract one hand, most likely to gesture. He must be bursting with questions he couldn't ask.

She kept his fingers trapped tight. "I'll tell you everything as soon as I believe you're truly here. Just come sit at the hearth with me. Please?" Leaning closer, she whispered, "I'm done fluttering. Let me fold my wings and be still for a while."

He crushed her in his arms, a welcome cocoon.

Watching, Neela murmured wistfully, "I wish I had someone to hug me like that."

Zeke looked at her.

Neela blushed and turned away. "Someday, I mean."

"I might hug somebody who climbs stones and talks to the wind," Zeke said.

Stiffening, Neela darted him a glance. Even Scarl's eyebrows rose.

"But I don't think I'd hug someone called Dain," added Zeke. "I like girls."

Neela's hands writhed together. "What about someone called Neela?"

"I might." Zeke drew one of her hands from the other. "Someday." His gaze rose toward Ariel. "After I forgave her for taking my best friend somewhere awful."

Neela nodded, her eyes round, and she clutched his hand tightly.

"Does that mean you might forgive the best friend after all?" Ariel asked.

"Someday," Zeke said. "It might take a few weeks."

Conscious of Nace against her, Ariel felt sandwiched between the two boys, but for the first time, instead of tearing her in half, it made her feel supported and safe. It wasn't that Zeke didn't have a place in her heart. He was just in a different corner than Nace was, that's all. And his fingers holding Neela's seemed to show he understood.

She gave him a small, hopeful smile. He returned it.

"Neela." The name sighed from Cassalie, who gave it a musical lilt. "I've often imagined this old wound being healed. Thank you, Ariel. Truly." She wrinkled her nose at Neela. "But forgive me if my mouth calls you Dain—or Daineela. I don't know how fast I can break that habit."

Neela giggled. "Me neither." Her smile fell to a frown. "But Dain Windmaster sounds better than Neela Windmaster, don't it?"

"No," Ariel said. "You're just not used to it yet. When you make a new wind pipe, make this one for Neela."

Neela brightened. "I never had a pipe that was all just for me."

Cassalie insisted on tending their wounds, and they circled and pitched in to bandage each other. Scarl's livid bruises took the longest to treat. As she heated water to use in a poultice, Ariel stared into Cassalie's hearth. The flames murmured to her about Elbert's knife. She hadn't needed her brimstone; a more potent fire had unmade the knife, along with the steely defiance it stood for. Now it existed nowhere but in memory, and any strengths it once had remained only in her.

She smiled. A Farwalker could carry memories and strengths without hauling the weight of an enemy with her. She'd had to walk out of the world to do it, but finally that burden had been left behind.

Later, after their bellies were full and their shivers had been chased away by the fire, Ariel and Neela shared the trials they'd faced before their friends met them at the bridge. Scarl had suggested they wait until daylight, when the horror might not seem so close, but Ariel wanted those memories out of her head so they couldn't loom so large in her dreams. In the time since they'd returned to the world, the message symbols on her hand had faded, leaving only a patchwork of throbbing scars. The cuts on her ankles and shins would soon scab. But the things she'd seen still clanged loud in her thoughts, so the story spilled. When she faltered, Neela chimed in.

It wasn't until Ariel described how the crow had plucked the spark out of Neela's papa that she realized the bird had played no part with Elbert. She hadn't seen it at all once Zeke and Scarl had appeared.

Neela described their escape from the maelstrom's current while Ariel's thoughts stayed on the crow. It may have known all along that Elbert had thwarted the natural order of things, and sought her help by bringing the bones. She could no longer remember if her nightmares had started before or after the first bone appeared, but there was no doubt her attention had fed Elbert's strength. He'd said so himself. Perhaps once that cycle had started, only she could set things right because she'd become part of the problem.

"I guess the crow is still there," she told Nace during a pause in Neela's retelling. She hadn't dragged the bird with her, but she still felt its loss. "I didn't mean to leave it behind. I'm sorry."

"I bet a grim-golly can fly back by itself, anyway," Neela said. Nace agreed.

That eased Ariel's mind. Maybe they'd see it again. "Well, if it likes to take sparks from reluctant souls in the mist, there was definitely still work it could do first."

Scarl whistled. "I'd call that a good day's farwalking work—leading a grim-golly to Hell."

"Hell?" Ariel blinked.

"What would *you* call the waste between the world and the pool?"

She considered. "A place to get lost."

"For a Farwalker," said Zeke, "isn't that the same thing?"

Ariel stared into the fire. "You're right, Zeke. It is."

Scarl took over as the story reached the moment of his arrival with Zeke. He shared only enough with Cassalie and Nace to explain their wounds and account for their escape. Since neither knew much of Elbert, he spared them pointless horror. Still, Ariel mused about what he left out.

She'd hedged only in relating what she'd seen at the beacon, omitting most of her conversation with a flaming spirit, whom she hadn't named. She hadn't promised, exactly, but she felt she should honor Mirayna's last wish not to mention the encounter to Scarl. She fell asleep that night wondering if that decision was right.

It didn't take long to find out. The next morning over breakfast, Scarl cleared his throat, which still sounded hoarse from his choking.

"I want to speak with you about something, Cassalie," he said. "I know you're still reeling from our arrival last night, but I'd rather not wait." His gaze flitted to both Ariel and Neela before returning to Cass.

She set down her teacup and slid into his lap. "Only if I can bite your ear if you keep sounding so serious."

His smile faded quickly. "You know I'm bound to Ariel for a while yet."

"Of course." Cassalie smoothed his shirt. "I can still be glad you're alive, can't I? While you're here?"

"While we're here—that's my point."

Drooping, she started to slip from his lap.

He stopped her, pulling her close. "Don't. Forgive me. I'm bungling this." He paused to choose better words. "I can't ask you to leave your home, Cassalie. But I hope there's some way I can—"

"Who said you can't?" At his startled look, she continued, "If you want to ask it, Scarl, ask. What's left for me here? The boats rarely sail in anymore. A few more years, and the old 'uns will all be gone, too, and Da— Neela and I will be alone."

He tucked a loose strand of her hair into her braid. "I've thought of that, believe me. I want nothing more than to bring you back to the abbey, or near it, so coming home with Ariel would mean returning to you. But don't try to tell me you wouldn't pine for the sea."

A sad twinge crossed Cassalie's face, but she firmly dismissed it. "I *will* pine for the sea." She wrapped her arms around his neck. "But not as much as I'd pine for Scarl Finder. I can reap from the land, too. And couldn't Ariel bring me back, once or twice, for a swim?"

"Every year, if you want." Ariel grinned. "I have to come back anyhow. For my apprentice!"

Scarl didn't seem to know what to say. At last he asked Cassalie softly, "You would do that for me? Leave all you know?"

Ariel shot a sidelong glance at Nace, who sat next to her. He dipped his head and traced his fingers along her arm.

Cassalie turned from Scarl to the others. "Shall I bite his ear now?"

"Yes," Ariel said.

Neela asked, "What about me?"

"I haven't forgotten," Scarl told her. "Can you bear to come with us?"

Relief brightened her face. "I don't care where I go. The wind'll come with me."

"You'll like what it does in the mountains." Zeke took Neela's hand.

They shared a self-conscious smile before Neela turned to Cassalie. "But who'll help the old 'uns if we go, Cass? While they're still in the world? Can they fend for themselves the whole year?"

"I can help with that," Scarl said. "If provisions and chores twice a year would keep them."

"It would." Cassalie snuggled against him. "They're too independent to accept more help than that, anyway."

"I know someone like that." Scarl raised an eyebrow at Ariel. "Too independent for her own good. Or anyone else's. Please, Ariel. I suppose I can't cage you, but I'm not too proud to beg. Would you please keep your farwalking in the world from now on? I don't know how many more trips like this last I can take. And I can't keep my promise if I'm not alive to do it."

"You wouldn't find your way back to accompany me as a ghost?" She meant it as a joke, but she found herself hoping for a positive answer.

One of his hands flapped helplessly. "Oh, I probably would. Having seen a little of what's over the bridge, I'll be in no rush to return."

Ariel knew one thing he'd missed, though: Mirayna. She longed to share that secret with him.

Watching Scarl with Cassalie, though, she decided the time was not right. In a few years, perhaps, when looking back warmed his heart without poking old wounds. Not today.

So she told him, "I'll promise to stay in the world if you will." She thought again of an apprentice who'd been raised on a boat. "We haven't been over the sea yet."

Or under it, either. There was supposed to be a city lost under the sea.

Her feet tingled, and Ariel smiled. The guard stones were right. Today was best spent walking forward.

EPILOGUE

A few summers later, Ariel loaded Willow, scribed a host of messages onto paper so nervousness could not make her forget them, and went farwalking alone. She wanted to prove to herself she could do it. Both Scarl and Nace swallowed protests. Zeke merely kissed her cheek and wished her a good trip, as did Neela, Cassalie, and their Tree-Singer friends. Ariel returned exhilarated, ready both for companions and more solo work.

Not very much later, Cassalie bore Scarl a son. Ariel thought Scarl might burst. Between bouts of joy, he showered her with assurances, no longer needed, that she was not being abandoned.

They called the boy Reyn. The name was Cassalie's idea, and to Ariel, both of its inspirations seemed clear. Gazing into the baby's startling blue eyes, which resembled neither his father's brown ones nor his mother's sea-grey, she often imagined a spark of Essence flowing into the maelstrom and bursting back up. She had no idea what went on in that pool or prompted a spark to fly back over the bridge. Yet Reyn sometimes flashed her a small, private smile that made his Auntie Ariel wonder.

ABOUT THE AUTHOR

Joni Sensel is the author of several novels for young readers, including *The Humming of Numbers* and *Reality Leak* as well as the three books of the Farwalker Trilogy: *The Farwalker's Quest*, *The Timekeeper's Moon*, and *The Skeleton's Knife*. When she's not imagining fantastic journeys or traveling to walk in exotic locations, she keeps her boots on the ground near her home in the Pacific Northwest.

Visit her at www.jonisensel.com.

Made in the USA
San Bernardino, CA
13 November 2013